IF I COULD, WOULD I?
Revised October, 2024

Written by Michale Mohr

DEDICATION

This book is dedicated to a wonderful woman named Jane Yearwood. She's long past, but remains in my heart and mind to this day. She was a brilliant therapist who put me back together after my bout with agoraphobia. After using my writing as a catalyst to help me take my first steps outside, someone recommended her to me. I was out of the house, but not fully functioning. She took the puzzle pieces that were me, and helped me form a new picture of who I was, and who I could become.

She thought the world was a magical place if we let it be. She said that all us dreamers out there are the foundation of everything that is good in the world. Her gentle way allowed me to grow and experience life in an entirely new way. I'm so grateful she was part of my journey in my time on this earth. Everyone should get to have a Jane in their life.

Chapter 1

"Oh my," Emma exclaimed, looking at her reflection in the brightly lit makeup mirror. The harsh glare from the bulbs made her squint. Running her fingers through her hair, she sighed deeply as she noticed how the brown locks were losing the battle with the grey intruders.

"I'm sure glad I don't have this kind of mirror at home," she remarked, trying to joke, but the sadness of that true statement still showed through.

"Don't you worry, Ms. Corbell," the perky makeup girl offered. "By the time you walk in front of those cameras, you'll be absolutely glam," the makeup girl smiled as she readied her sponges and brushes.

"Call me Emma, please." Her sweet smile made her deep green eyes sparkle and dance, belying the sadness that walked with her daily. "Unless you have a magic wand, I don't think *glam* would ever describe me," she added.

"So, is this the first time you've been on national television?" the young woman inquired as she spread the base makeup over Emma's cheeks.

"Yes. First time. I'm really nervous. I hope I don't say anything stupid," she said meekly.

"You'll be fine."

Another woman walked into the room holding a clipboard. A set of headphones hung around her neck.

"Hi, Ms. Corbell. I'm Felicia, the stage manager. Let's get you to the green room, where you can have some coffee while you wait for your segment. You'll be on in about five minutes."

"Thank you so much," Emma replied simply.

Unseen by anyone in the room, a lucent figure suddenly appeared, standing next to Emma. The woman was bathed in a white light that sparkled brilliantly. She stroked Emma's hair gently, smiling at her, then whispered something into her ear. Emma shuddered and looked around for the source of the sound. Seeing nothing, she placed her attention back on the stage manager. As quickly as she came, the apparition disappeared in a bath of golden light.

Within moments, Emma stood in the wings, trembling from head to toe. The stage manager patted her on the arm reassuringly and smiled.

"Ladies and gentlemen, it gives me great pleasure to introduce my next guest, Emma Corbell," the statuesque black woman said as she stood up and applauded when Emma entered. They hugged briefly, and then the hostess offered Emma a seat on the couch.

"Thank you so much for being here, Emma, and welcome to Morning Coffee with Della. I've been very excited to meet you since I heard your story on the news. If anyone belongs on our 'Everyday Heroes' segment, it's you. Is this your first trip to New York?"

"Yes. It's truly a magnificent city," Emma answered shyly, almost in a whisper.

"That it is."

Della turned to the audience. "As you know, every week we profile those that go that extra step. People who, without looking for any praise or recognition, go out and make a difference in other's lives. Emma Corbell is truly the definition of an everyday hero. This amazing woman saved a deaf dog from being hit by a car. She literally leapt in front of a speeding vehicle to whisk the pup out of harm's way."

The audience broke into a long, loud, appreciative round of applause.

"So, Emma. Tell us exactly how it happened and what gave you the courage to leap in front of a car like that."

"Well, it all happened pretty fast. I had locked my front door and was getting ready to start my morning walk when I saw this dog in the middle of the street. He was just sitting there, licking one of his paws, seemingly without a care in the world."

"And was this a big dog, small dog?"

"He was sort of a medium-sized black Labrador."

"So, what happened after you saw him?"

"I was zipping up my jacket when I heard the sound of a car approaching. I could tell it was going very fast. I looked up the street, and it wasn't slowing down at all; it was getting dangerously close. So, I ran as fast as possible and scooped up the dog. The car never slowed down or stopped after almost hitting both of us.

"You must have been terrified," Della exclaimed.

"Actually, not until afterward. I didn't even realize I was moving until I got to the other side."

"That's amazing. I guess it's that instinct that kicks in when we don't even have time to think."

"And I understand the dog did something adorable when you fell."

"Yes, he did," Emma smiled sweetly, remembering the event. "He came over to me and licked my face, then kept using his nose to try and lift my arm, like he wanted to help me up. I think he was thanking me."

"I'm sure he was, Emma. We all thank you. Okay, we're going to cut away for a quick break. We'll be right back. On the other side we have a big surprise for our hero."

Chapter 2

During the quick break, Della sat next to Emma on the couch. She put her arm around her and quietly said, "Honey, you don't have to be so nervous. We're all friends here. The audience loves you. You're doing a great job."

"Thank you," Emma whispered, looking at the floor. "I've just sort of always been a nervous person. I'm not sure exactly why."

The red light came back on the camera, and Della turned and smiled.

"Welcome back. Now, I told you we have a surprise for Emma, but let me set the stage a little bit first," she said, taking Emma's hand.

"In addition to her dog-saving skills, Emma is an advocate and volunteer for disabled children and those with life-threatening diseases. She has worked tirelessly to raise money and awareness for their plight. So, you might say, she is the embodiment of *lifelong* heroism. Emma, tell us about how this began and the tragedy in your life that catapulted you onto this mission."

Emma's cheeks turned red with embarrassment. She didn't like being singled out, and it was difficult for her to talk about herself.

"Well...um...when I was twenty-five years old, I fell into a pond and got some pond water into my nose. It caused a brain infection with a long chemical name, but is very similar to bacterial meningitis, which is initially what they thought I had. I got very sick."

"I understand you got more than sick. You almost died," Della stated.

"Yes. That's true," Emma said quietly.

"It took many, many years, but you did indeed recover. However, in the process, you had to give up one of your most fervent dreams. As they say, *life* got in the way," Della said sadly.

"Yes," was Emma's reply.

"Well, Emma, you give to so many others. We want to give something to you. We want to help you with that dream you've always longed for."

Emma cocked her head to the side, not sure what was coming next. Her hands were clasped in front of her so tightly they were turning white from lack of blood flow.

"Emma, a little bird told me that your dream when you were young was to be a novelist. Is that right?"

"Oh, well, yeah, but that was stupid teenage stuff, like wanting to be an astronaut or something

"I see. Well, this same little bird also told me you had started a novel before you got sick, but with your illness, raising your son, and getting involved in fundraising, you gave up on that idea."

Della pulled a couple of typed pages from the back of the clipboard she was holding.

"This very good friend of yours gave us these," Della said, holding up the pages. "These are a few paragraphs of a book you started to write before your illness. It's called 'Did You Remember to Lock the Door? A Dumb-Ass Criminal Murder Mystery.' I love that title!" The audience laughed. Della took a couple of minutes to read the first page aloud. The audience applauded when she'd finished.

"This is very, very good. I think I speak for everyone here when I say I'd like to read the whole novel." The audience applauded excitedly.

"So, here's what we've arranged for you. After reading these pages and hearing your story, the largest book publisher in the United States has offered you a contract for this book when it's finished. Or for any other book you'd like to write. They'll promote your talent. You'll appear on every television show in the country. You'll be treated like the star you truly are. How does that sound?"

Horrific, Emma wanted to say. Being trotted around like a show pony did not appeal to her. Those dreams were old, dusty, and forgotten. Her life had taken a different turn. You can't rewind the clock. The past was the past. Her life had been her life. It was fine. No one gets everything they want. She was content now, sort of.

"Um...I don't know what to say," Emma managed to utter. "That's just...well, that's just wonderful." She was trying to sound enthusiastic but failing miserably.

"I think she's in shock," Della laughed, observing Emma's obvious discomfort. "It'll sink in soon enough."

The audience was applauding wildly, and Emma's eyes filled with tears.

Della went over and hugged her tightly.

"You're on your way, Emma. Now, everyone will get to see the beauty of your soul. Congratulations!"

Turning to the audience, with one arm still around Emma, Della said, "That's it for today. Thank you so much for joining us, and remember to appreciate the everyday heroes in your life."

The director yelled, "Okay, we're out."

Emma said goodbye to her host as quickly as possible and dashed to the elevator to make her escape as fast as she could.

Chapter 3

Emma stopped and stared at the limousine waiting outside for her.

"You know, I think I'd like to walk back to the hotel," she said to the limo driver as he opened the back door for her. "I need to get some fresh air. You can pick me up at two o'clock to take me to the airport."

"Are you sure, ma'am? After all it is November and pretty brisk out here. It might even rain."

"I'll be fine," Emma said with a shy smile. "We have cold days in Oregon as well."

"Okay. If you say so. Here, take my card. If the walk is too far for you, or you get cold, just call me, and I'll come pick you right up."

"Thank you. You're very kind," Emma said walking away.

Emma's gait accelerated with each thought that ran through her head, her anger and fear propelling her faster and faster.

See my beautiful soul. Ha! What beautiful soul? Scared soul, that's what I am. A meek, whimpering little child who is afraid of her own shadow. Big deal. So I saved a dog. Anyone would have done that. I haven't written in over thirty-five years. I can't do it. I've got not one idea in my head. Then I'll be humiliated when the publishers regret getting roped into printing anything I wrote. I've gotta get out of this. I'll look like an old fool, which is precisely what I am, a sixty-year-old waste of skin, that's what I am.

Now walking so fast she was practically jogging, Emma rounded the corner and ran headlong into an older woman coming the other way, nearly knocking her to the ground.

"Oh my gosh!" Emma cried out, reaching out to steady the older female. "I'm so sorry. I wasn't looking where I was going."

"It's fine, Emma," the woman said in a calm, melodic voice. "No harm done."

"You know my name?"

"Yes, I knew your parents very well. I was hoping I'd run into you."

"What? I mean...did you see me on the show?

"No. Unfortunately I missed it."

"But, then how...I mean...how were you hoping you'd run into me? I don't live in New York you know.

"Yes. I know that." The older woman cocked her head and studied Emma for a moment. "Your eyes are so sad, dear one. Where is that spark of adventure you had as a teenager? How did the curtain fall so deftly over that brilliant spirit?" The tall, stately woman smiled gently, waiting for Emma to work through her confusion.

"I'm not sad. I'm upset. I was on this show, and they got me a publisher, and I can't...wait, wait, wait. This is not making sense. How do you know anything at all about me? We've never met. If you were a friend of my parents I would remember you."

"My name is Willow," the old woman said, eyes twinkling. She reached into her pocket and pulled out a beautiful dolphin necklace. "I believe you lost this. Your parents think it's time it was returned to you."

Emma gasped. "What?" Emma took it from the woman's hand. "This looks just like the one I lost when I was 17...but...."

"One in the same."

"But, what did you mean my parents think I should have it? If you knew them so well, you must know they're long ago deceased."

"We still speak," Willow answered simply, with a glint of humor in her eyes.

"This is crazy? Are you one of those people who talks to spirits?"

"I'm just here to give you your necklace and let you know that with a blink of an eye and a snap of your fingers you have the power to change anything you want to about your life."

"Well, that's very cryptic," Emma said, raising one eyebrow.

"But, true," the old woman laughed delightedly. "Just remember where your true power lies."

Emma looked down at the necklace, caressing it tenderly. When she looked up, the woman had vanished. Turning around a full 360 degrees, she couldn't spot her anywhere.

"Did you see the woman I was talking to?" she asked the man sitting on the bench across the street.

"Nope."

"Are you sure?"

"Yep."

"But, you had to see her. You're only a few feet away. I certainly wasn't talking to myself. Look," she said holding up the necklace. "She gave me this. So, I was definitely not talking to a ghost."

"What ghosts? I didn't see no ghost or anyone. Listen lady, I'm just sittin' here reading my paper and drinkin' my coffee. Today wasn't my day to keep my eye on you and your acquaintances," he said sarcastically. With that he put the paper back in front of his face, signaling the conversation was over.

Emma walked on for a couple more blocks, peering inside store windows to see if Willow had ducked into one of the shops on the street. Passing a coffee shop, she decided to get out of the chill and think this through.

Sitting at the long bar at the front window, she watched the people walking by, some with briefcases, others holding a child's hand, and almost everyone on their cell phones. It was a life not so different from Oregon, just on a grander scale with majorly taller buildings. She pulled her cell out of her pocket.

"Hey, Andrea, it's me." She held the phone away from her ear when Andrea started loudly raving about how she saw her on the show and how 'effing great' she looked.

"You don't have to shout. I haven't lost my hearing in the last twenty-four hours...and thank you. I'm sure you're just being a good friend, but it's nice to hear."

"Good friend my ass," Andrea laughed that bawdy laugh of hers. "You looked great! At least ten years younger. I wouldn't lie to you. And a publishing contract! Girl, you're a frickin star now."

Andrea was the complete opposite of Emma. That's probably why they were such good friends. It allowed them to view life and everything in it through different lenses. Andrea was brutally honest, brave, outspoken, and the kindest person Emma had ever known. She enjoyed her life the way the timid Emma only wished she could.

Andrea wore her feelings on her sleeve and let them be known verbally. 'I love you' was said often, but she would also let you know if she disliked you.

Emma could never see herself doing the kind of things Andrea did. One time, Andrea even did the 'polar bear plunge,' afterward stating it was one event she would never repeat. But the following week, she promptly decided to parachute out of a plane. Her best quality was, however, when she was your friend, she was your biggest champion.

Emma laughed. "Yeah, yeah, yeah, I'm a beauty queen. But I called you for two reasons. The first one being, I know that you had to be the *little bird* Della was talking about that gave her my old writings. How did you even have them? And why would you do that?"

"Because, my dearest friend, they asked me a lot of questions about you. They wanted to know what your dreams were, and asked me if I knew something that you really, really wanted. I could have said a big house or a million dollars, but that would have been stupid. However, the reason I showed them your pages was, selfishly, for me."

"For you? And how does that make any sense at all?" Emma exclaimed loudly.

"I was there, remember? I was there after you got sick and couldn't think straight for a long, long time. I was there when you cried because you had to give up your dreams as a writer. As hard as I tried in the years after, I could never get you to write a word. The studio calling me was a sign. You were good, Em. It's time. You're never too old to write. It's a profession from which you never have to retire. Besides, it checks off a box on my bucket list. I always wanted to pal around with a famous person," Andrea laughed.

"But, Andie, I just can't do it. I have no words in my head. I've got to get out of it."

"No, you won't! It's still there. That dream is still there. Just try. I think you'll surprise yourself."

Emma went silent considering Andrea's words. She had to admit that a tiny piece of excitement was beginning to peek its head out of the darkness where it had been buried.

"Okay, I'll *think* about it. But, let me call you back in a couple of minutes. I want to buy a scone and get out of here—too many people. Then I can walk while we talk. I have something really weird to tell you about."

"Oooh, I love weird," Andrea chuckled.

Chapter 4

"After the show, I decided to walk back to the hotel. Well, I literally almost ran this woman down. She was very old, with long grey hair, but it was silky and beautiful. Now that I think about it, she didn't have a line on her face, so maybe she wasn't that old, just greying early or something. But, that's not important. Anyway, she had this soft, lyrical voice and talked in riddles. Her name was Willow."

"Riddles? What does that mean?"

"Riddles. Like she didn't make any sense. She said she knew my parents back in the day. Said she still talks to them! My dead parents—she still talks to them? What the heck does that mean? She called me Emma before I even told her my name."

"Okay. That's really weird. So, what did she want?" Andrea asked.

"Let me finish before I get to that. So then, get this, she reaches into her pocket and pulls out this dolphin necklace. I was gobsmacked. It looked exactly like the one my folks gave me for my sixteenth birthday. You remember the one, right?"

"Yeah, and I also remember when you lost it. You were absolutely beside yourself. You kept crying that you no longer had your spiritual animal protection or something like that."

"I know. But she said it was for sure the one I lost. Then she said that my parents thought it was time I had it back!" Emma said in astonishment.

"What? What the hell does that mean? What kind of scam was she pulling? Did she ask you for money?"

"No. Nothing like that. She just said I could change my life in the blink of an eye and the snap of a finger. And, oh yeah, to remember where my true power lies. I have no idea what that even means. Do you think it could really be *my* necklace? The one from my folks?"

"Geez. You know I don't give much credence to all that woo-woo stuff. Maybe she found it at a pawn shop or something."

"I thought of that. But how would she know that I had one to begin with? Also, and this is really big...she said she didn't see the show. So, she didn't know I was in New York. How in the world did we run into each other at all? Hold on a sec." Emma stopped and stared through the glass of a store she was passing. She was still looking for Willow and thought she'd caught a glimpse of her. It wasn't her.

"Okay. Back. It's all so strange."

"The only thing I can think of is that she did know your parents at some point and knew about the necklace, then found one somewhere that looked like it...then..." Her voice trailed off.

"I know, right? There are always holes, no matter how I try to fit it together. Mainly, how she managed to run into me at all. Also, was she carrying the necklace with her just in case we ever met?" Emma mused, taking a bite of her scone.

"I personally think she's some nut job who lied about not seeing the show, then watched where you went afterward and deliberately ran into you. That's what I think."

"Maybe. But she didn't want anything. Nothing. She was soft. I know that sounds weird, but that's what she was...soft. Pardon me for using the word weird in every sentence, but that's what it was. The whole thing. I don't know any other way to describe her."

"Well, no matter how it happened, you have your necklace, or a very good replica of it, back. That's a happy accident. Enjoy it. Listen, hon, I gotta get dressed and head to the gym. I may be old and haven't gained one bit of muscle since I've been going there, but I just love looking at all those handsome guys." Bawdy laugh.

"Andrea, you're incorrigible," Emma giggled. "I'll call you when I get home tonight."

Chapter 5

When Emma woke the next morning, she rolled over and stared out the window. She was so happy to be back in her own home where she felt safe and secure. Pulling the fluffy, soft, flowery comforter over her tighter, she tried to go back to sleep. However, that wasn't going to happen due to the pounding migraine growing ever stronger.

Probably jet lag. Okay, no writing for me today. Who could expect me to write when I'm sick, right? I'm going to spend the day in bed. Well, after I take some aspirin, go downstairs, make some coffee, and find something for breakfast. Then I'll stay in bed and watch old movies.

When she sat up, she spotted the necklace on her nightstand. Gently picking up her treasure, she placed it around her neck. Her cell phone rang. Immediately recognizing the number, she smiled.

"Hey there, handsome son of mine."

"Hi, Mom. I wanted to call before the day got crazy. I saw you on the show. You did great! And, a writing contract? You must be over the moon excited."

"I'm over something, but I don't think it's the moon. It would be more apt to say I'm over writing," she laughed.

"Come on, Mom. This is a great opportunity. I remember those bedtime stories you used to write for me when I was a kid. Most kids got 'The Three Bears,' I got 'The Monkey Had Muscles and Drove Race Cars.' Please don't brush this off. You're good and it's time the world knew it."

"Brian, please. I just don't think I have it anymore. I'll look like a fool."

"No, you won't. Listen, I've got to get to a meeting. I'll come over tonight and we'll talk more. Don't give up or do anything stupid like call them and turn down their offer. Okay? Wait until we talk."

"Okay, sweetheart. I'll at least wait until then. Love you."

"Love you too, Mom. Ciao."

Okay, little dolphin, she thought as she headed for the bathroom. *Let's see if you still have your stuff. Help me make this a good day.*

She felt a little silly talking to it that way, but that's what she'd done at sixteen. Back in the day, she'd believed wholeheartedly that her dolphin was magic.

As the lore goes, dolphins were messengers to Poseidon, the God of the sea. Even the Greek God Apollo turned himself into a dolphin so he could direct a ship of merchants safely to their destination. They were sacred animals known to help all mankind. Their mystical powers could calm any raging sea, produce positive outcomes, and were known as altruistic savior figures. She'd lost it before she'd fallen ill. For all the following years, she'd been convinced that losing her necklace was what allowed her to get sick in the first place.

Viewing her haggard, lined face in the bathroom mirror did nothing to lighten her mood. She looked older than her sixty years and tried to avoid her reflection as much as possible. "Worry lines" her mother would have called them. She figured that must be true as she worried about absolutely everything.

Popping a couple of aspirin in her mouth, she continued to stare at her reflection. Willow's words ran through her head. "With the blink of an eye and the snap of a finger you can change anything in your life," she'd said.

Really? What the hell am I going to change in my life at sixty years old, huh? Now if I was seventeen and knew what I know now, wow, there'd be no stopping me. I'd skip the whole sickness thing. I'd be a famous writer. I'd...heck, I'd change about everything, she laughed.

She stood there for a few minutes, scanning her tired-looking self, poking at the extra twenty pounds around her middle.

Heck, I'd be happy if I just 'looked' seventeen again. She started to chuckle. *Now, that would be a sight, a sixty-year-old with a seventeen-year-old face. Ha!* She peered into the mirror, blinked her eyes, and snapped her finger. Quickly, she closed her eyes tightly, making her wish. When she opened them and peered back into the mirror nothing had changed. She was the same pudgy, tired-looking old woman she'd been two minutes ago.

She shook her head and laughed at her momentary belief that it might work. Just for the minutest part of a millisecond she'd found herself wondering if it could be possible. There was the tiniest hope that magic resided in the world.

Silly old woman was all she thought. Within seconds she abruptly fainted, falling to the floor. Moments later when she regained consciousness, she was confused and disoriented. Sitting up straight, she tried trying to focus.

Oh my God. Did I have a stroke?

Standing slowly, she noted that nothing was numb or limp. Patting her arms and legs and flexing her fingers, she opined that she must have fainted due to exhaustion, little food, and jet lag. She was a bit shaky but appeared absolutely fine.

Stepping back in front of the mirror, she turned on the water to splash some on her face. When she saw her reflection she froze like a deer in the headlights. Her seventeen-year-old self was staring back at her. She was clad in tight jeans, a T-shirt, and a short denim jacket. The prized dolphin hung around her neck.

Oh my God! What the hell? Am I hallucinating? What is this? She began pinching herself. *Ouch. I'm apparently not dreaming. Can you feel pain in a dream? Do people pinch themselves in dreams and then feel it? No, of course not; then what would be the purpose of pinching yourself to see if you're dreaming? I seem to be solid and very, very real.*

Emma stared at herself in the mirror for a long time. *Look at me. All of me is seventeen! Look at my figure! How did this happen? Oh my gosh. How will I explain this to Andrea and everyone who knows me? Plastic surgery? Liposuction? Oh, boy, this is bad, Emma, very, very bad.*

Still trying to discern if this was real or a dream, Emma jumped up and down wildly, then ran in place, doing a couple of squats for good measure. *Well, I'm obviously not sixty. I certainly couldn't do that in my...what do I call it, 'my old body'?*

Emma stopped dead in her tracks, looking at the room around her. Slowly, objects started to glow with a bluish-white aura, bouncing and undulating around them. It made her dizzy for a moment. Investigating further, she realized she was not in the bathroom in her condo. The rug was different. It wasn't *her* towel hanging on the rack. The tub had a shower curtain instead of her glassed-in shower/tub. Her makeup wasn't scattered on the counter. The wall colors were different.

Uh-oh. What's happening here? Where exactly am I? Okay, this is scary.

Glancing over at the door, she saw the same haze of soft colors in which the rest of the room was enveloped. She wanted to open it but was a little afraid to. She half expected that her hand would pass right through it, much like a hologram, when she tried to grasp the physical object—but it didn't. Slowly, she twisted it and peeked out into the hallway outside. Nope. It was definitely not her condo.

Tiptoeing down the hall, she reached a bedroom. Stepping inside she gasped, then squealed. Holding her hands over her mouth she told herself to shush. She peeked back out into the hallway to make sure no one was coming, then softly closed the door, staying inside the room.

It was her old bedroom when she was seventeen. Her bed, her dresser, the pictures on the wall, the snapshot photos all over the mirror of her dresser. They were all there.

It's my frickin room. It's absolutely my old bedroom! How is this possible? I don't just look seventeen. I am seventeen, and I'm in my old house.

Finding a picture of her and Andrea at their graduation, she pulled it off the mirror and hugged it to her. She'd graduated at sixteen because they'd skipped her over ninth grade as the material was too easy for her. Andrea was one year older, seventeen at the time. They'd become best friends in high school. The two had stayed friends all her life, even moving to Oregon from California at the same time.

In the picture, the taller Andrea was making a goofy face, as was Emma who was sticking out her tongue. In another, they were standing very sedately with their parents, everyone with their arms around each other, with big happy smiles.

The photo she held in her hand was warm to the touch. The colors danced around and through it as well. But it was as solid as she was. Her confusion morphed into escalating delight and excitement. *Could this really be possible?*

The hallway leading to the living room was filled with family photos. She peered at each one as she passed. They were all of family—happier times before her parents divorced. She'd opted to live with her father, while her older brother, Don, decided to stay with his mom in the family home they'd both grown up in. But, at 18, he'd joined the Marines and was now stationed overseas. She kissed her fingers and then tapped them on the picture of her brother in his uniform, so handsome, smiling for the camera.

She walked around touching everything. The old red couch that her dad had bought, which she hated, had the white pillows stacked neatly across the back. She'd done that, telling her father it took away the anger of the horrible shade he'd chosen.

The coffee table was filled with newspapers, as usual. Old cups of coffee were still waiting for their turn to be taken to the kitchen and washed. Neither she nor her father were the best housekeepers that ever lived.

Picking up the paper on the top, she read the date. It was September 15, 1981. According to that date, she was seventeen and had just started her second year at junior college a couple of weeks ago. Everything she touched had the mist and was warm. She wondered what that meant.

Running to the large window, she opened the curtains, squealing again. Opening the sliding glass doors she stepped out onto the deck. Inhaling deeply, she took in the sea air. The ocean, only steps away, was magnificent in its glory. The sound of the waves playing with each other as they hit the shore was music to her ears.

Stepping back into the room she sighed happily. She grabbed the dolphin figurine hanging from the chain around her neck. "You know, little guy, I always knew you had mystical powers like all the folklore said," she mused aloud. "Number one, I will never, ever lose you again. I will guard you with my life. Secondly, apparently, we have a whole new life to plan. Things will be different this time around. I see great success as an author in my future. I foresee *not* falling into the pond that gave me that horrible illness. My new life will be as magic as you are."

Just then she heard keys in the front door. In walked her father. She stood there stunned momentarily, then ran to him and leaped into his arms.

"Dad...Dad...Dad," she exclaimed, hugging him tightly and kissing him multiple times on the cheek. I love you so much! I've missed you so much!"

"What missed me? I've only been gone fifteen minutes. I wanted to fill up the Olds for you to take to school today. I'm going to take your VW down to be serviced."

"Right. Right. And thank you for that. You're the best dad in the world," she enthused. "How did I ever get so lucky?"

Her father removed the hat he always wore to cover his thinning hair, and threw it on the chair by the door. He crossed his arms and stared at her for a minute.

"Okay. What's going on here? You're not doing drugs or anything are you? We talked about that. You know better, and you also know what would happen if I ever caught you doing something stupid like that."

Emma laughed, thrilled to be actually standing there being scolded.

"Now you're laughing? What's gotten into you?"

"Nothing, Dad," Emma said in a sing-song tone. "Can't a girl just appreciate her father and tell him so?"

"Um, probably, I guess," he mumbled. "This is just over-the-top, even for you.

"Over the top? Right, I used to be over the top. I forgot," she said, grinning from ear to ear.

"What does that even mean?" Her dad grumbled good-naturedly. "Well, I don't have time to figure it out, so rather than try to decipher your incoherent teenage mumblings, I'd better get to work. Do you have plans tonight or do you want to come to the restaurant to eat?"

"Restaurant...definitely! Can I ask Andrea to come?"

"Sure, sure. Andrea is welcome." He kissed her on the cheek, shook his head, smiled, and walked out the door.

Once the door closed, Emma squealed with delight, stretched her arms to the side, tilted her head back, and turned around and around, relishing the moment.

"I'm here," she said out loud to room. "I'm here, and I'm going to stay here. Thank you, thank you, thank you, Willow. This time I'll do it all better. This time I won't screw up. I know where the potholes are and I'll leap them with a single bound.

Running back to her bedroom she found her purse on the bed. She rummaged through it for a second. Inside was her wallet and driver's license, with her young, beautiful teenage face looking back at her. There was forty dollars in her billfold. A pack of gum and some lipstick completed the contents. She couldn't stop laughing happily. Grabbing the keys to the Oldsmobile off the key rack on the wall, she opened the door and then dashed back inside to dig out her pink bikini and stuff it in her oversized bag. Snatching a towel off the bathroom rack, she stuffed it inside as well.

As she was leaving, she saw a milkman pull up. *Oh my gosh! I forgot about milkmen! I love it! We have a milkman!* She waited for him to make the delivery and then put the glass bottles in the fridge.

As she opened the door again to leave, she shouted, "Hello world! Here I come. Or should I say, here I come again?"

Chapter 6

Emma fairly skipped down the steps and around to the driveway where the Oldsmobile sat. It was ten years old, but her dad kept it in tip-top condition. It shined brilliantly as if it had just been driven off the lot.

She'd just put the keys into the driver's side door when she heard a voice behind her. She recognized it before even turning around. It was Willow.

Hello, Emma," Willow said in a soft, gentle tone. Like everything else in Emma's new world, there was an aura around her, but hers wasn't blue and white. Her emanation was completely white with bright gold flecks that shimmered. The rays from the illumination seemed to dance up and down, then jump off and dash towards the sky. She was absolutely brilliant.

"Willow!" Emma exclaimed happily. "I'm so glad to see you. Thank you so much. Here I am, all seventeen years old of me. I did just what you said." Emma rushed to hug the older woman, but by the time she got to her, Willow had vanished and was standing behind her.

"What the...?" Emma said, almost falling over. "Neat trick," she laughed.

"We need to talk. You need to understand some things," Willow said seriously. "You're not supposed to be here. This is a mistake."

"What mistake? You said a blink and a snap, and I could change whatever I wanted in my life."

"Yes...change your sixty-year-old life, the human way, through better thinking and moving forward. Not this, not travel back in time. I'm not even sure how you accomplished this at all." Willow's aura was deepening in color...now it was a midnight blue."

Emma held up her dolphin. "My magic dolphin. How come *you* don't know its magic? After I lost it the first time, my life went steadily downhill. Now, my lucky friend here has brought me back, thanks in no small part to you returning it to me. So, mistake or not," Emma said defiantly, "I'm here. I get to do my life over. End of story."

"Yes, I knew the necklace held magic; I just didn't know you had developed the power to utilize it. But, now you have to go back."

"Not on your life, sister. And you can't make me," Emma said, stamping her foot. She sounded like the defiant teenager that she was. Bravado or not, she wasn't entirely sure that if Willow wanted to, she could send her back instantly. It was not a comforting thought.

Willow simply stared at her for a long time, not speaking. Her eyes bore holes into Emma's soul, making her squirm from the intensity.

"You are correct. I cannot. But not for the reasons you believe. Free will is the nature of human existence. Anyone, even me, who interrupts another's free will runs the risk of disastrous results. Destinies will change—lives will be altered. So, although I have the power to do so, I will not."

"Sounds perfect! I've got it all figured out. I'll just blink and snap to various points in time I want to fix. I'll take care of that, then leap forward to the next thing. Basically, I'll just play around and pick and choose. Or, gee, maybe I'll do the things I liked over again just for fun! This is so bitchin! Ha! Bitchin. I forgot we used to say that." Emma said, flushed with excitement.

Willow sighed heavily, then said slowly, "The *blink and snap thing*, as you put it, doesn't work like that, as I just said. However, it would seem that you believe you have everything figured out and under control then."

"That's right, missy," Emma popped off. "I'm good to go."

"You are certain that you don't want to know how to go back?"

"Have you lost every one of your brain cells? I absolutely do not want to go back to that simpering, whimpering shell of a woman I used to be. Never, ever!"

Willow simply nodded.

"I do have one question, though. Why does everything here have this blue-and-white mist around it? Is there something wrong with my eyesight?" Emma asked.

"There's nothing wrong with your eyesight. You see everything that way because you are a visitor here in this time. The colors may change but will eventually fade the longer you stay."

"Cool. It's kinda rad, though," Emma said, slipping further into her seventeen-year-old persona and language. "I just wanted to make sure I was healthy."

"That you are. And, since it seems you have *everything figured out*, as you said, there's no need for me to intervene any further. I wish you well, dear Emma." With that, she took two steps towards the street and vanished into thin air.

"Wow. That is sooo cool," Emma said, looking at where Willow last stood. "I wish I could do that. Oh, hey...I *can* do that...all with the blink of an eye and a snap of a finger."

Popping happily into the car, she started the engine, giggling at the giant steering wheel and the size of the car—so different from her little 2024 Toyota. All the way to Andrea's house, Emma thought about Willow. She was concerned, but only a bit, about her seeming to be angry with her. Finally brushing it off, maneuvering down the highway, she blasted the radio and sang loudly to her favorite Rolling Stones song.

She took in the beauty of the area she'd lived in all those years ago. It seemed so new, exceptional, and absolutely perfect.

Trotting up to Andrea's door, she could barely contain her excitement. Andrea still lived with her parents while she was finishing junior college. When her best friend opened the door, Emma flew into her arms, embracing her tightly.

"Andrea, it's me. Don't I look great? Can you believe how skinny I am?"

"What the hell are you talking about? You're not any skinnier than you were yesterday," Andrea said, tilting her head in confusion, looking at her friend like she'd just turned green.

Emma had totally forgotten that this Andrea didn't know the older, later, decrepit Emma. She was the only one who had traveled back in time.

"Oh, right, right. Sorry," she said, a little embarrassed. "I just, uh, woke up and, um, thought I looked really good today in these jeans."

"Sure. Great. You're a frikkin model," Andrea laughed. "So, what are you doing here anyway? Don't you have a class this morning?"

"I don't feel like it at all," she whined, "Gag me with a spoon. I just can't face being indoors and listening to the professor's drone on and on. It's totally awesome outside today. Let's ditch classes and go to the beach."

"You wanting to ditch class? That's a first. What happened to 'Miss, I'm perfect and need to get straight A's?"

"I'll still get straight A's. And I am perfect," Emma giggled. "I just feel so alive today. I feel so good, so healthy. I want to do something fun. Please, please, please, please," Emma begged, comically dropping to her knees.

"Oh, good God. Get up."

"Oh yeah, I also want to call my mom real quick. Can I use your cell?

"My what?" Andrea asked, baffled by the question."

"Your cellphone."

"Are you talking about those four-thousand-dollar big block things that rich people use driving around in their Cadillacs? Those things?"

Emma again had forgotten what time she was in. Of course, they didn't have tiny personal cellphones in 1981. It was a new burgeoning industry, and only those with means could afford the luxury.

"Oh, right. I was just kidding. I got confused. You know me, ole hair-brained Emma," she laughed.

"Have you been drinking bleach or something? Your head isn't right. You've been all crazy since you walked through the door.

"No. Don't talk stupid. I'm just having a really good day. I simply want to have some fun, that's all."

"Uh-huh," Andrea answered skeptically. "Okay, let's go up to my room. You can call your mom from there. I was typing out some notes for my philosophy class. Let me finish those, and then we'll go, even though I still think you're a little on the nuts side today.

"Cool," Emma answered, grinning broadly.

While Andrea typed, Emma called her mom. After the first few words were exchanged, she vividly remembered why she had moved in with her dad. She and her mom had never gotten along. Nothing Emma did was ever good enough for her mother. Vowing then and there that this was something she was going to fix this time around, she stayed calm and tried to engage her mother differently.

"So, Mom, is there anything I can help you with at the house? Would you like me to come over in a few days and help you clean? I could do your shopping if you want me to. Or maybe we could just go out to lunch."

"Um...well, sure, Em, that would be nice," her mother said, stunned by the offer. "Are you okay? Is your dad okay?"

Emma laughed. She really wished people would quit asking her that, but then she had been acting sort of weird since she plopped back down in 1981. It might be a good thing for her to do some research on the eighties. She remembered highlights of her experiences but needed specifics, like no cell phones yet. This might just be a little more difficult than she first thought.

"We're both okay, Mom. I just want to spend some time with you, that's all. Just you and me. We could talk. I'll tell you all about school. You can tell me all about...whatever you're doing these days."

There was a long pause on the other end of the phone. "Well, honey, I think I would like that very much," her mother answered.

"Perfect. I'll call you next week, and we'll set something up. I love you," Emma said happily.

"I love you too, sweetheart."

Chapter 7

Emma turned over on her back and closed her eyes to the bright sun. The sand was so warm; it was like lying on an electric blanket with the temperature setting just right.

"I wish I hadn't forgotten my sunglasses," she lamented. "But, I probably wouldn't have worn them anyway, cuz then I would have big white circles around my hopefully soon-to-be tanned skin," she giggled.

"I don't get it. We've spent so much time here this summer, but you're still white as a ghost like you'd never seen the light of day. Why is that?" Andrea laughed.

"Dunno. It's frustrating, though. You and everyone else on the planet spend a day at the beach and go home golden brown. I just look like a lobster, but I don't care. I don't care about anything today."

"So, what's got you in such a good mood? You've been over-the-top cheerful since you showed up at my house. How did you suddenly stop pining over Joshua? Remember him? Your boyfriend who broke up with you? I thought I was going to have to put you on suicide watch. I thought I'd never see you smile again. Now it's like he never existed."

"Oh, right...him. Oh, blah. He was such a dork. I don't know what I ever saw in him."

Andrea raised herself up on one elbow and stared at Emma. "What?" You were already picking out wedding dresses. Blah? Really?"

"I've got bigger plans. So much to look forward to. He'd just be a drag on my whole life."

Andrea shook her head like she was trying to unscramble Emma's words and make them make sense.

"What big plans? We've got this last year at junior college, then state college, during which, if we're lucky, we get internships at some big

27

advertising agency. After all this hard work, we start our first two-woman advertising agency, Morris and Corbell. What's bigger than that?

Emma sat up and ran her hands through the sand, watching the shimmering colors dance as she allowed the granules to slip through her fingers.

"First of all, it's Corbell and Morris," she laughed. "It sounds better; C comes before M. Second, I'm quitting school. I just have to figure out how to tell my dad."

"You're what?" Andrea exclaimed loudly. "Why? Why? Why do you want to quit?"

"Because I want to write. I'm going to be a famous novelist. I know I can do it, Andrea," she said excitedly. "I'm good. I've already gotten started on a mystery novel. Oh, Andrea, it's so much fun. That's what I'm meant to be...a writer," she stated firmly. "Then you can handle all my advertising and book promotion," she added with a smile.

Andrea fell back on her towel with a thud. She was speechless.

"A writer. You want to quit school to be a writer...a writer." She kept saying the word writer over and over again like it was something foreign to her. "Do you have any idea how hard that is?" she said, sitting up again. "Everybody here in southern California is either an actor or a writer. And what are those people doing? Working as waiters and busboys, that's what."

"Not me. You'll see. I can't explain it. I just know it will happen."

"What makes you so sure. Do you have a crystal ball or something?"

"Something like that," Emma said, fingering the dolphin necklace around her neck. "Now I have to just tell my dad. He's going to explode like a pinata at a birthday party. I want to live with him until I publish my first book. Then I'll get my own place with the proceeds."

"Oh, until you're forty, then?"

"Ha. Ha. Very funny. I'm going to have my first book out by the time I'm twenty-two or twenty-three. Wanna make a small bet on that?" Emma laughed.

"No, because when you tell your dad you're going to quit school, he's going to kill you, and then who would I collect from?"

Emma just laughed.

"I'm serious, Em. Getting a book published is tough. Do you know the odds of you becoming a published author?"

"I do not...why don't you look it up on Goog...," Emma stopped herself in the nick of time from saying Google, which was not in existence then.

"What was that? Goog? What's that?"

"I meant good, not goo. Look it up in a good encyclopedia, and then tell me what the odds are," she said, trying lamely to cover her mistake. Looking down at her arms, she noticed they were already getting pink.

"Oh my God, look at me. We've gotta go. Right now. If I come home all red, my dad will know I ditched school and came to the beach. I need him in a good, receptive mood tonight when I tell him. Oh, oh, yeah...my dad and I are going to eat at the restaurant tonight, and he said you could come. Please come. It will be much easier to talk to him with you there. You, plus being in a public place, will keep him from screaming at me, at least."

"Geez, Em. What are you getting me into?"

"Nothing. I need you there to keep the waters calm, that's all. Just back me up if he asks your opinion. Tell him you think I'm a great writer and will do well. He's always thought you were the more stable one of the two of us. He'll listen to you."

"He's not wrong. I am the more stable one of the two of us, but geez, Em, I don't want to lie to him. I don't want you to quit either."

"You're not lying. You're just suspending judgment until you see if I can do it."

Andrea rolled her eyes, after which she became aware of a group of three young men walking up the beach towards where they were sitting.

"Oooh, yummy," she laughed. "I'll take the one in the middle."

Emma turned around to see who she was looking at. She gasped. There, walking straight towards them were three young men, all three of whom she recognized. The redhead on the left was Gary, the dark-haired Italian on the right was Danny, and the tall, handsome man in the middle who had taken Andrea's breath away was none other than her ex-husband, Adam Armstrong, the man who had hit her almost every day of their marriage.

She never told anyone what had happened to her. After finding out she was pregnant, just eight months into the marriage, she'd managed to get out. No way her child would be raised in that environment. Telling her family, 'it just didn't work out,' she'd run to the other end of the state to have her son. It was a terribly confusing time. It was the beginning of the shell of fear she wore for the rest of her life.

Every nerve ending in her body was alive and painful. She felt overheated and about ready to faint. If she'd had a gun in her hand, she wasn't so sure she wouldn't have used it. As they approached, she noticed something. The aura around them was different from the blue/white mist she'd seen everywhere else. All three of them had vapors with blue, red, and black colors. No white was seen anywhere. At first, she thought it was possibly because they were all dressed similarly in jeans and T-shirts. Adam was the best looking of the three. Tall, thick brown slicked back hair, dark brown eyes, and a smile that flashed beautifully white straight teeth.

In an instant, a flood of memories filled her head. His teeth. They were his pride and joy. He had a thing about them. When they were married, and he had gotten into fights, of which he had many, he never allowed anyone to hit him in the face. How badly she wanted to do just that right at this minute.

However, this wasn't where they'd first met in her other life. Obviously, she'd changed something in the timeline by coming here today. Back then, she'd only dreamed of writing, but never quit school to write a novel, so there wasn't a beach day where she and Andrea ditched school.

Watching him intently as they got closer, she felt her muscles tighten. The three walked up to them like somehow they'd been invited to do so. They were cocky, confident, and sure of themselves, like they owned the world. Adam, obviously was the spokesman of the group.

"Good afternoon, ladies. Enjoying your day?" Adam asked in that sweet tone he could use. He spoke with the slightest hint of a Southern accent. Nothing significant or distinctive, but it was there. It gave him the outward appearance of a charm he did not possess.

"Yes, we are," Andrea said enthusiastically.

Emma stood up and motioned to Andrea. "Come on, let's go. I gotta get home," she said, trying her best to restrain the venomous anger just below the surface.

When Andrea stood up, she grabbed Emma by the arm and walked her away a few steps so the guys couldn't hear.

"What the hell are you doing? Did you see that guy? I, for one, would like to get to know him better."

"No, you don't. He's trouble. We've gotta leave...right now," Emma said, stomping back and picking up their towel.

Adam took hold of one of her arms to stop her motion. At six foot one, he towered above her five foot two frame.

"And who might you be, little one?" he asked with an innocent smile.

"Jailbait. I'm only seventeen, so I'll thank you to take your grubby hands off me." She jerked away and continued packing up her belongings.

Walking up and standing beside Emma, Andrea introduced herself. "I'm Andrea, please forgive Emma. She has some problems she's trying to work through right now. Say you're sorry to the nice man," Andrea instructed her.

Emma shot her a look but gritted her teeth and mumbled that she was sorry. She didn't want to embarrass Andrea or anger Adam.

"That's better. Now, would you like to sit with us for a while?"

"We would," Adam said, sitting cross-legged in the sand. "This redheaded mop of hair is Gary, and this is our mighty Italian friend, Danny," he said, introducing his friends.

Chapter 8

After about thirty minutes of conversation, Emma couldn't stand to sit there any longer.

"I'm going to take a walk," she said abruptly, turning away from the group. She grabbed her towel, draping it over her shoulders, not wanting to get any more burnt than she already was.

Within minutes, Adam caught up to her.

"Hey, hey. Did I say something to upset you?"

"No. I'm just upset in general," she said, looking straight ahead, not slowing down.

"Are you okay? Is there anything I can help with?" Adam asked earnestly.

Don't do this. Please don't do this, she thought. *Don't be nice.*

"I'm told I'm a pretty good listener," he smiled. There was no guile there. No tough guy.

This is precisely what she didn't want to see. This was the sweetness of Adam. This was the man she fell in love with. Before they were married, he'd sucked her in with this side of him—the side that had hopes and dreams. The side that could be gentle.

If this was 2024, Emma thought, *this is the guy you'd see on Dateline where every neighbor said, "But he was such a sweet guy. I can't believe he killed his wife."* He'd never even raised his voice to her before they were married. She'd had no idea of the depths of his dysfunction. Sucked in was an apt term.

"Look. Let's start over. Hi, I'm Adam. I'm twenty-one years old, I work as a mechanic, and I hope to one day have my own shop. I have six brothers and sisters. Um, let's see, what else. Oh yeah, I make a mean chocolate cake."

Emma smiled despite herself. Underneath, she felt the slightest rumbling of the attraction she'd experienced the first time they'd met. The other thing she noticed was that the red and black colors surrounding him earlier had now changed to blue and white. *Fascinating,* she thought.

"Okay, Adam. I'm Emma. I'm seventeen years old. I live with my dad, and I'm in my second year of college."

"College. Wow. That's really big. At seventeen? What...you some kind of genius or something?"

"No, just started school early, and they skipped me a grade."

"So, college-girl, whadaya want to do when you grow up?" Adam said with a chuckle. "I'll bet you want to be a model... you're sure pretty enough to do that."

Emma smiled. As they continued walking and talking, his sweetness melted away her reserve. She was struggling to resist him. The side that hated him was warring with the side that loved this part of him.

He talked of his simple dreams, family, business of his own, and a big house. It all sounded so normal. She even found herself talking about her own dreams of being a famous writer.

"I've already got the title of my first book. I'm going to write murder mysteries, kind of like the old Agatha Christie, Miss Marple series, but sort of funny. I don't like all that blood and guts stuff, so my first book is titled, 'Did You Remember to Lock the Door.' It will be the first in my Dumb-Ass Criminal Murder Mystery Series.'"

Adam laughed long and hard. "I like it. I'd read it. You should definitely do that...write, I mean. I never read any of that lady's books, that Agatha lady, but I'm sure yours will be better."

At that moment, Emma was completely torn. But she knew what she knew and couldn't let herself get sucked into this man's life again.

"Oh my God. My son!" Emma exclaimed out loud.

"Your what? You have a son?"

"Oh...no...I mean, I was talking about my sun...my sun...burn, my sunburn. My sunburn will let my dad know I ditched school today."

Her heart sank. Her brows furrowed as she tried to find a way out of what she now knew she had to do. No way would she give up her son. No way. But that meant she'd have to become an abused wife again. How in the world could she even think about doing that? Actually, there was no real thought involved. Without marrying Adam, she wouldn't have Brian.

Okay, Em. Maybe I can make it different. I know what to expect this time around. I can duck and dodge. I could outrun him. It's only for eight months. If I could get pregnant fast enough, perhaps I could even shorten that time frame. But no way I'm giving up my son.

"Okay then, jailbait, we'd better get you home. But first, I want to ask you a question. When is your birthday?"

"November seventeenth," Emma replied with a smile.

"That's great!" Adam enthused, then felt a little embarrassed by his own excitement. "Look, I really like talking to you. Maybe until you turn eighteen, we could meet in a park somewhere and have picnics or something and just talk. No funny business. Then, if we like each other, we could go on a real date when you turn eighteen." Adam stopped talking and waited for her answer.

"Yes, Adam, I'd like that very much," Emma answered softly.

"Whoo hoo!" Adam shouted. "You've made me a very happy man."

Emma sighed deeply, letting out the air slowly. She knew that at least the months before they got married would be really nice ones.

Why couldn't you stay like this? Emma thought as she watched his happy face.

Emma allowed Adam to gently take her hand and lead her back to the group. The three were laughing, and Andrea seemed to be having a great time.

"Oh, hey, you're back. These two should be on the stage," Andrea giggled delightfully. "They're real comedians." She glanced down and noticed Emma and Adam were holding hands.

"Oh, I see a connection has been made," she said with a smile. She was happy for her friend. Yes, she thought the guy was handsome, but Andrea had always gone for the quiet, nerdy type anyway.

Before the guys left, everyone exchanged phone numbers and promised they would all get together soon. Once they had joined the others, Emma noticed that Adam's aura had returned to the black and red mist.

That's all gotta mean something, Emma thought. *Good versus evil? Something like that?*

Adam held Emma back when the others started towards the car. He smiled down at her and tucked an errant hair behind her ear.

"I can't wait until we see each other again. Can I call you tonight?"

"Um, actually, Andrea and I are having dinner with my dad. How late do you stay up?"

"As late as you need me to," was his answer.

"Okay. We should be home before ten. My dad goes to bed early. So, I'll call you around then."

"Sounds good." He leaned over, gave her the gentlest kiss on the cheek, then took her hand and led her back to the car.

And the saga begins, Emma thought sadly. *God help me.*

Chapter 9

The talk with her dad went surprisingly well. He didn't like her dropping out of school, but they finally agreed on a one-year timetable. She was young and had graduated early, so waiting a bit to finish couldn't hurt anything in his estimation.

Jumping up and running around the table, Emma hugged her dad around the neck, kissing him multiple times on the cheek. "You are the best dad ever!"

"It would seem so since that seems to be your mantra today," her father laughed.

"True words need to be repeated," Emma giggled.

Emma agreed to the year but knew that wouldn't come to pass. Especially since she knew she would marry Adam in six months and would be pregnant soon after. It was odd. There were tiny gaps in her memory now that she was back here. She couldn't quite remember her wedding. Didn't they elope? Her memories of that time were becoming like pictures in an old photo album that had faded to the point where the faces were no longer discernable. She could see some things clearly but not others. It was troubling to her. How could she possibly avoid or bypass some of the beatings if she didn't know when they were coming?

As Emma sat back listening to Andrea's conversation with her father about advertising for his three restaurants, she watched the people in the room. The waiters scurried between tables, smiling and tending to their patrons. Then, something odd began to happen. The blue and white mist she'd been seeing seemed to change. Some people and items now had multicolored auras that utilized all the colors of the rainbow. Some were green and white, others yellow and blue, and so on. Some people had solid colors, while others emanated a combination. She closed her eyes tightly, then opened them. Nothing changed, except for the fact that as people interacted with each other, their colors varied. What the hell did that mean? She felt like it was important, but she was not sure exactly why.

"Dad, you should let Andrea draw up some plans for you. Let her show you what she can do to enhance your patronage," Emma said, rejoining the conversation. She's wicked smart, and once she graduates, you'll definitely want to hire her."

Emma's dad ran his hand over his rapidly balding head and smiled. "All right. Do your deal there, Andrea. I wish you two were doing it together, but let's see what you've got."

It was Andrea's turn to run over and hug Mr. Corbell. "Emma's right. You're the best!" she enthused. She turned around quickly and accidentally walked right into a waiter holding a tray over his head, causing him to drop it all over the floor.

"Oh my gosh! I'm so sorry," Andrea said, bending down to help him pick up the spilled plates. Emma jumped up as well. When she did, she noticed the young man's aura was pure yellow.

"No. No. It's fine. I wouldn't want you to cut yourselves," he said, pushing them back. "It's okay, really it is."

As the young man said those words, his aura turned pink and white. Emma just stared at him. *Hm. Maybe yellow means caution?* she thought. *"Kinda of like a yellow flashing light on a detour sign maybe. Why does this feel so important to me?*

Once the crisis was handled, the three left. Emma was anxious to get back home so she could call Adam. She wanted to get this whole thing over with. She had books to write and fame to achieve.

She hadn't told her father about Adam yet. She knew he would immediately object to his age, and even though he wasn't judgmental at all, he might not like that he was just a mechanic. Like all dads, he wanted his daughter to marry a professional man, a doctor or a lawyer. It was better to wait a little bit before she had that conversation.

She gave him a kiss goodnight, then headed down the hallway.

"Oh, Dad, did you..." she said, turning around just in time to see him stub his toe on the couch leg as he juggled the coffee cups in his hand that he was taking into the kitchen. His aura had turned yellow.

"Dammit," her dad exclaimed.

Got it. Yellow means caution. Something is about to happen to that person. Apparently, not anything too earth-shattering, she thought.

"Are you okay," she said, running over to him. "You didn't break anything, did you? Are you bleeding?"

"No. I'm fine. Just tripped over my own big feet." His aura had turned back to blue and white. "What did you want to ask me?"

"Oh, right. I wanted to know if you remembered to pick up your suit at the cleaners? You said you needed it for some meeting."

"Completely forgot. Would you mind picking it up for me tomorrow?"

"Sure thing, Dad. Nite."

"Nite, pumpkin."

Once back in her room, she kept her conversation with Adam light and as short as possible. He was sweet when he talked humbly about just squeaking through high school. His family had no money, so college was never in his future. But, on the other side of the coin, he was proud of his work as a mechanic. He'd already become well known as the guy to see for all your automotive woes. He worked on everything from fancy sports cars to old beaters.

Emma cut the conversation short, stating she was tired, but they made plans to meet the next day at the park during his lunch hour. She would bring a picnic. He was happy and seemed excited. She was not. All she was thinking of was getting off the phone so she could start her book.

Hanging up, she sat at her desk and put a piece of paper into the old bulky machine. *Boy, do I miss computers,* she chuckled. She began typing: "Did You Remember to Lock the Door? A Dumb-Ass Criminal Murder Mystery." The title she'd come up with made her smile.

She moved on to Chapter 1 and began reading aloud. "Criminals come in all shapes and sizes. Some look like the guy next door and wear suits and ties, while others often have missing teeth and uncombed hair. They seem to always have a disgruntled sneer, practically advertising their evil intentions.

Some could aptly be defined as mentalists. They woo, cajole, and maneuver their prey into doing their bidding. These are the white-collar guys who fleece unsuspecting men and women or, at times, large corporations out of their millions.

Then there are the killers. Scary word, killer. The word itself immediately evokes mental scenes of stabbings, shootings, and the like. Some of those, as well, are educated people of wealth and means that no one would ever suspect could do such a dastardly deed. These can be hard to apprehend. They have brains, take time to plan, and often manage to frame others for their actions. The missing-teeth guys aren't generally so well-versed in the art of deception and concealment. They often act first, then try to cover up later.

Then there's David. You might say he's a hybrid of the educated killer and the missing-teeth guy. He has all his teeth, boasts a minimal education, with a couple of years of college before he dropped out, but is as dumb as a rock."

She leaned back in her chair and stared at the page. "Good start," she thought.

Chapter 10

When Emma arose the next morning, she was full of excitement. She'd slept in, and her father had already left for work. She had the whole day to write, save for making a lunch and meeting her soon-to-be husband. The only thing troubling her was her fading memories. She really needed to have a roadmap for her upcoming marriage to help her survive it.

She walked into the bathroom, staring at herself in the mirror. *Why can't I see colors around myself, I wonder? Maybe it's because I'm a visitor in this time like Willow said. Geez, I really was a little snotty to her. Perhaps I should have asked a few more questions before she went poof.*

She tied her hair back in a bun, brushed her teeth, and stared at her face in the mirror again.

"I really, really don't want to do this again. There has to be a way out where I still get to have Brian," she said aloud to her reflection. "Why did I ask to look seventeen? If I'd been smart, I'd have asked to be twenty-one. I was free of him by then."

She put on some mascara, started to leave, then stopped abruptly, returning to the mirror.

"Yeah, but I didn't know then how it worked. I was just playing around. What if I can blink and snap myself to twenty-one right now? I'll still be here, or *there* rather."

She raced into the bedroom, got dressed, and took the paper out of the typewriter. Folding it up, she tucked it into her back pocket. Taking the dolphin necklace from the nightstand, she hung it around her neck. "Not going anywhere without you."

Walking back into the bathroom, she again stood in front of the mirror. She took a deep breath and let it out slowly.

"Okay, Em, this is for all the marbles."

She stopped and laughed. "This is beginning to sound a lot like 'mirror, mirror on the wall, who's the fairest of them all,' from Cinderella.

Rubbing her hands together, she said, "Okay, I want to be twenty-one and in my own apartment with my son Brian. And...I don't even care about the date. Just make sure we're far away from Adam. She blinked her eyes and snapped her finger. Just as before, she crumbled to the floor.

When she came back to consciousness, it took her a few minutes to gather her thoughts and remember what had happened. Once she did, she jumped up and looked around her. She ran to the mirror. Her heart sank. She was in the same clothes, in the same bathroom, and nothing had changed.

Just to be sure, she ran out to the living room. With tears in her eyes, she picked up the newspaper. It was still 1981. She hadn't gone anywhere. Falling to her knees, she held her head in her hands and wept.

Once there were no more tears, she stood up and shouted at the top of her lungs to the room around her. "Dammit! What do I do now?" She stormed over to the coffee table and swept her hand across it, knocking everything loudly onto the floor.

Her anger spent, she sat down on the sofa and stared off into space, trying to feel absolutely nothing.

She blew out a long breath of air. "Okay, Em. Get it together. You have a sixty-year-old brain that lives inside this seventeen-year-old body. Use it. Once you stepped back into your teenage life, you stopped listening. You didn't want to hear anything Willow had to say that day by the car. You were sure you knew it all. Well, guess what? You don't. She wasn't kidding about the snap/blink thing not working. Now you have a big, big problem. You have no way to get back and stop this madness. But then, would you want to go back if you could?" she asked herself, getting up and pacing around the room.

"You came here to change your life, become a writer, be famous, and rid yourself of that horrible, weak, woman-living-in-a-shell life. Okay, tell the truth. However, you got here, accidentally or not; your initial desire was just to look *pretty*," she said sarcastically. "You were vain and absorbed by your looks. It wasn't until *after* you got here that you thought about your writing."

She walked over, poured herself the last of the coffee her dad had left in the pot, and sat down at the counter, twirling the cup around and around in her hands.

"So, Miss Know-it-all, what have we figured out so far? As I did with my mom, I can change things as they're happening. Also, my first meeting with Adam was different. I didn't meet him on the beach originally. I changed that meeting by skipping school and announcing to Andrea that I was going to be a writer, none of which I did the first time. So, everything has to be done at the time it is happening. That's a good thing to know."

Looking in the fridge, she pulled out a couple of eggs and popped some bread into the toaster while continuing the dialogue with herself.

"So, if I have to go through all this again, apparently, I can change it while it's happening. Also a good thing. Although, I would suppose that would carry with it the possibility that I could die because one day I decide to cross a different street or something and get hit by a car," Emma shuddered. "Don't think like that. There must be more to all of this than I understand right now. There just has to be. I guess it's a learn-as-you-go sort of thing. Just like the yellow auras, I'll figure it out. I can do that. I still have my sixty-year-old wisdom; I'll use that."

Emma threw her eggs on a plate and buttered her toast. She started to laugh.

"My sixty-year-old wisdom. That's a joke. I absolutely possessed no wisdom in my time. But...but, but, but, I *was* more thoughtful," she argued in her own defense. "I reasoned things through more, but I wasn't so impulsive. At least I have that much. So, here's the plan. I'm sure the red aura has to mean rage. So, when I see it, I'll find a way to leave the house. Whenever I see it, I'll figure out a way to avoid him. I can do this. Who knows? Maybe I can get through the whole deal unscathed. Then, once I'm pregnant, I run, and I'm home free. What's eight months? Nothing. I'll have my whole life ahead of me again."

By the time she'd eaten and cleaned up the dishes and mess she'd made in the living room, she felt a lot better. She had a plan of sorts.

"I have a great plan. It'll work. "Time will tell," she laughed as she sat down at her typewriter. "Pardon the pun."

Chapter 11

The months prior to her wedding went just as before, save for changes in some meeting places and such. There were lots of quiet talks, snuggling, cooing, and sweetness between them. She'd finally told her dad about Adam when she invited him to her eighteenth birthday party, which was held at one of his restaurants. Watching in amusement, she could barely stifle her laughter as she watched the two circle each other like two alpha dogs, trying to discern who was indeed the dominant male. As she suspected, her dad was unhappy about her latest choice of suitors. He would have been positively apoplectic if he'd known then that she would marry him in a few months. But, all in all, they were civil and even shared a couple of laughs.

For Adam, he never introduced her to any of his family before the wedding. As before, he kept saying, 'later' or 'soon.' Of course, she now knew why, but she'd had no idea back then. Her initial meeting with his parents the first time they were married was *after* they'd said their vows.

It was a horrible scene. They'd walked in on them in the middle of a fight. It was not just a verbal fight; it was an actual fistfight. His mother poured coffee over his dad's head, and his father responded by slapping her in the face. It was frightening. It was then she'd realized where his own rage came from. This was his model for marriage.

As before, they married at the courthouse on May 5th, 1982, with Andrea standing up for her and Danny standing up for Adam. She wore a simple floor-length white sheath dress, with her hair worn up, adored with tiny, shiny silver combs inserted carefully throughout. She was a vision. Adam wore the only suit he owned. Missing, however, were her parents. They'd exploded when she said she was going to marry Adam and refused to be a part of it. It hurt her, even though she knew from the past that they would reconcile shortly thereafter, but it still stung in this present reality.

As they received congratulatory hugs and kisses from Andrea and Danny after the ceremony, Emma felt like she would faint. The reality of what was coming next was almost too much for her. She considered becoming a runaway bride, but the visions of her son kept her by Adam's side. She couldn't quite remember, but she knew that the first time he'd hit her was a couple of weeks later, perhaps as long as a month. Now, if she could only recall the exact circumstances. The closer they'd gotten to the wedding, the further the memories receded. How was she going to protect herself?

Adam brought her home to the tiny house he'd rented for them as a surprise for her. It was right across the street from his parent's home. Gag. It was old, small, and not in the best shape, or very clean, for that matter.

Right after he carried her over the threshold, he dragged her over to meet his folks, which didn't go well, They entered just in time to see a physical fight between his parents. This is why he hadn't introduced her to him before. What he didn't want her to see. The entire day was entirely too much for her. It was not the ideal beginning for her supposed wedded bliss.

She made the bed with the clean sheets that were already in the cupboard, changed her clothes, and went to bed. Adam, to his credit, let her sleep.

The first four weeks passed without incident. She was beginning to believe that perhaps everything had changed since she'd intervened in this timeline, meeting him at a slightly different point. Could it be possible that he loved her so much that he just couldn't hit her, ever?

That dream was short-lived, however. It was one month and two days after they'd taken their vows. Adam was in the bathroom, shaving and getting ready for work. Just as she was about to walk in and tell him his breakfast was ready, she had a flash. This was the day. This was the first time he'd hit her. It came vividly and with such force that she had to stop and catch her breath. It was in there, in the bathroom, where they'd gotten into an argument over her wanting them to go that night and visit her father. He didn't want to go, said he "didn't like her old man," and both of them needed to stay away from "that old crackpot."

Stopping where she was, she silently turned around, quietly returning to the kitchen. *No argument, no hitting,* she thought to herself.

"Hey, sweet husband of mine, breakfast is ready," she hollered from the kitchen, trying to sound happy and loving.

"In a minute, hon. Be right out," he answered.

Whew! Just get him out the door.

Smiling brightly, she gave him a big kiss when he sat down at the table, then busied herself washing the dishes.

"So, what are you going to do today?" Adam asked between mouthfuls.

"Oh, not much. Just write, of course, and maybe do some grocery shopping. You know, lady of leisure stuff because I'm married to the sweetest man on the planet and don't have to work," she smiled.

"Okay, sounds good. Could you pick me up some shaving cream at the store when you're there?"

"Sure, hon. I might drop by Andrea's on the way home. I haven't even had two seconds to talk to her since the wedding. She's going to think I abandoned her as a friend," she laughed, sitting in the chair next to him at the table.

Adam's face turned cold. "So, you guys can trot off to the beach and show off your bodies, like the day I met you? You're married now. You shouldn't be hanging around with your single girlfriends anymore."

"What? That's just silly. And, no, we aren't going to the beach. I'll be at her house, and we'll chat, and I'll come home. It will be short and sweet. And I'm not giving up Andrea for you or anyone else. Absolutely not. Adam, honey, you can trust me. I'm not going to be looking at other guys."

"So, what I say doesn't matter?" Adam exploded. "My feelings aren't important? I'm just the guy who keeps a roof over your head and pays the bills, right? You have your life, and I have mine. Is that what you want?"

"Adam, you're talking crazy," she attempted to say with as much gentleness as possible. "I love *you*. I married *you*. I don't want to lead a single life. Please. Come on. Think about what you're saying," Emma tried to reason. She knew already she'd made a massive mistake by even mentioning Andrea. Her hope had been that if she didn't mention her father, all would be fine. Plus, she had always believed that he liked Andrea. Then in her mind she heard Willow's words to her, "certain destinies will remain the same."

In the blink of an eye, almost before she could detect the movement, he'd raised her hand to hit her. That's when something magical happened.

She didn't feel herself make any motion, but suddenly, there was a flash of blinding white light that burst into the room, then dispersed as quickly as it came. As soon as it dissipated, she realized that she had a hold of Adam's wrist and had slammed it onto the table, having stopped his momentum and keeping him from connecting with her face. Time literally had stood still.

"You don't want to do that," Emma said softly, with a steely glare that caused Adam to freeze momentarily. He felt like her green eyes looked into his very soul. As she sat there, she watched as his aura turned from red to muddy red, which she felt indicated fear.

Adam jumped out of the chair, stunned and unnerved.

"How did you do that?" he asked, totally confused.

"Magic," she smiled. In her head, thoughts were shooting by so fast that she almost couldn't decipher her own inner dialogue. *Of course! This is a different time. I've changed this present just by being here. But how in the world did I do that? Hell if I know, but I don't care. This is bitchin'!*

"Now I have a question for you?" Emma said softly, walking over and taking his hand. "Why did you want to hit me just now? What was that about?"

"I...I... don't know," Adam stuttered. "Well, you were defying me. You shouldn't do that. You're my wife."

"That's right. I'm your wife. Your partner. I'm not your possession. We're equals. I realize that may be a foreign concept to you. But that's what we are. We love each other. We're supposed to talk things out and compromise. No hitting."

Adam scratched his head and got a funny, awkward little smile on his face. He was in shock and more than a little in awe of her at that moment. Her words touched him in a way he'd never felt before. It intrigued him. He didn't quite understand all of it, but it felt nice when she said it. He'd not seen the flash, only the effects of the power it emanated.

"Well, jailbait, you are really something."

"That I am," Emma smiled. "No, go earn some money so I can work on my book and become a famous author. Would you like me to drop by today and bring you lunch?"

"Yeah. Yeah. Sure," he said, still baffled and unsettled by the events. "That would be good. Yeah, good...nice."

He couldn't quite regain his equilibrium. His eyes were question marks as he looked at her. Shaking his head, still in disbelief, he smiled, kissed her on the cheek, and walked to the door. With his hand on the knob, he turned around. "Oh, say hi to Andrea for me." Then he was gone.

Emma waited until she heard the sound of his car disappear, then began jumping up and down wildly, laughing and shouting, "Yes, yes, yes. Now, *that's* what I'm talking about. I can fix this!" She turned on some music and danced around the house as she happily cleaned up before sitting down at her typewriter. She looked down at her right hand, the one she'd caught his wrist with.

"How *did* I do that? That could come in very handy. Geez, I really wish there was a manual for this stuff."

Over the next two months, they had other little dustups, but with each event, she was able to talk him down. When his aura turned red, it was her signal that he was becoming angry, but he never again physically lashed out at her. Like the bell in a firehouse, the red became her guidepost. But he was changing day by day. They had more heart-to-heart talks. He opened up about his fears, self-doubts, and regrets. The magic continued.

"I think I came out of the womb swinging," Adam said during one of their long conversations about his need to hit. "My mom used me as a shield against my dad."

"That must have been awful," Emma said, taking his hand. "You were just a kid. Your parents were supposed to be protecting you, not the other way around."

Adam looked down sadly, and she could physically feel his pain. She also noticed that his aura was turning a more pinkish-white color.

"Yeah, well, that didn't happen. Then I just started hitting everybody for a while, classmates who looked at me sideways, old girlfriends. It was like I couldn't control it. I just felt this rage build up inside me, then...well, you know, you've seen it." He shook his head like he was trying to oust the memory. "I'm so sorry, Em. I'm so sorry."

"I know you are, hon. But, and this is a big but, you didn't hit me that night, and you've not even attempted to since. So, doesn't that tell you something?

"Yeah. I'm afraid of you. I think you could kick my ass," Adam laughed. "I think you have a hidden black belt or at least black magic or something, and you could lay me out."

"You just might be right," Emma laughed. "But seriously, you've changed so much already. There is another you buried deep inside that is sweet, gentle, and kind. Let him lead. I see him all the time. Even my dad said that you seem different lately."

"You really think so?"

"I really think so."

Adam smiled, gently pulled her to him, and snuggled her in his arms.

"I love you, jailbait."

The other side effect of Adam's changing rage was what was happening to his parents. As he was calmer, they seemed to be as well. She really didn't know them, as they hadn't exactly been the *drop-in and bring you a lasagna because we love you* type of family, but when she'd seen them, they'd been nicer to her *and* to each other. It was baffling. The air around her seemed fresher, cleaner. She was grateful for the peace she was experiencing without the threat of violence. Still, she hadn't gotten pregnant. The first time around, she'd been pregnant by month two. Had she inadvertently screwed things up?

Chapter 12

Month three came and went without Emma becoming pregnant. She wondered if this do-over had taken her precious son out of the equation. She'd already changed so much in her time here. Her relationship with her mother was improving, Adam didn't hit her, and her book writing was going well, but there was no Brian on the way. Had she changed everything to the point that she never had Brian? That was totally unacceptable to her. Sure, she came back accidentally, but now that she was here, she was determined to fulfill her dream of becoming a famous author *and* to be a renowned author with her beautiful son. Even with the happiness she was experiencing in her marriage, it all meant nothing without Brian. That was never the plan.

Her only alternative would be to go back, but she'd blown that option and wasn't sure she was ready to give up, but she would have preferred to have had the choice. Willow asked if she wanted to know how to return, but did she stop and listen? Nope. She was too enthralled with herself and her youth. She lamented everything now as her fear grew incrementally with each passing day.

Sitting at her typewriter, she stared dully at the paper. It mocked her. The blank page said, "I'll just take a snooze. Wake me when you have anything close to a great idea." No words would come to her. She was only half done with her novel and hadn't written a word in the past two weeks. Angrily leaping up from the chair, she decided to take a walk. Her eyes were bothering her and felt dry like sandpaper. The auras she typically saw daily were beginning to fade.

Willow had said they would fade the longer I was here, but I wonder if there is any particular significance to that. Will it turn off the magic of my dolphin? I couldn't stand that.

Walking slowly through the neighborhood, it was as if she was a roamer with no home. She meandered, head down, lost in thoughts of her dilemma.

The beauty of the trees and gardens blurred, like scenery speeding by when riding in a fast moving car. There was no definition; it was simply one long blast of color. She felt the tears stinging her eyes. She couldn't settle. It was like a coin spinning on its side, then wobbling wildly just before falling flat again. Everything was off-center.

She stopped at the park a couple of blocks up and sat on one of the benches. Moments later, an old woman walked up and sat at the other end of the bench. Looking over at Emma through her sunglasses, she smiled, pulled out her knitting, and began her task.

"Lovely afternoon," the old woman said, never taking her eyes from her stitches.

"Yes. Yes, it is," Emma replied distractedly.

"I see some tears there in those beautiful eyes. What troubles you dear?"

"Oh...nothing really," Emma said, using her sleeve to wipe away a tear off her cheek.

The woman nodded and continued her knitting. Emma sneaked a sideways glance at the older woman, concentrating on her task. With great speed, she maneuvered the needles with incredible ease. Emma envied her apparent peace.

"My mother knits," Emma stated, breaking the silence. "I could never get the hang of it. Not enough patience, I guess."

"Yes, it does take that, indeed. So does life," she said cryptically.

"Um, yes. I guess it does, but sometimes...sometimes patience isn't enough. I mean, there are times a person needs guidance."

"True. The trick is knowing when you are given it."

"What does that mean?" Emma asked, intrigued.

"Guidance doesn't always come in words. There are all forms of delivery systems."

"Like what?" Emma scooted closer to the woman.

"For example. Take those toddlers over there playing on the grass with their mothers. That could be a sign that you need to be more playful and carefree. Perhaps your life has gotten too tunnel-visioned."

"I suppose. But then, how do you know which signs are meant for you? You could make up stuff about the ordinary things you see; perhaps they weren't meant for you."

"Ah. A thinker, I see. You believe absolute logic, and your eyes. You want it all written down nice and neat."

Emma laughed at that. She had been pretty methodical once upon a time. In her old life, she was so controlled, worrying about everything that could possibly happen because of her fears. She liked *neatness, tidiness, and routine.*

"I guess I'm sort of like that," Emma crossed her legs Indian style and turned to sit facing the woman. "I think I've gotten a lot better this time around. I mean, recently, I've gotten a lot better," she said, catching herself.

"May I ask you a question?"

"Of course," Emma answered.

"What color am I?"

"Black."

"Not my skin, dear. My aura. What color is my aura?"

"How would I...I mean...your aura? What would I know about auras or such things?" Emma sputtered.

"Because you can see them, just like I do. Would you like to know what I see?"

"Very much," Emma answered, taken aback

Still, without looking directly at Emma, she continued knitting and said, "Yours is multicolored. You're in turmoil at the moment. You can't pick a side or find a direction. Life is jumbled. Nothing sounds palatable or right. All doors seemed closed, while at the time standing wide open. How am I doing?"

"I'm... I'm amazed. I have so many questions. Are you...I mean...how do I ask this?"

"A traveler? Yes, dear, I am. But not like you."

"I travel through time, yes, but for a very different reason. I travel for others, never for me. I assist others in finding their way out of their confusion. Now, what color am I?"

Emma was gobsmacked. This woman knew she traveled through time. How did she know so much about her? Could Willow have sent her?

Stopping her runaway thoughts, she took a moment to answer the woman's question.

"You're pure white, like Willow. Do you know Willow? Do you work together or something?"

The old woman laughed delightedly. "We don't have an organization with monthly meetings if that's what you want to know. There are millions of us all over the world. And, yes, I know Willow. I have watched you every day since you've come to this time, seen all your interactions."

"What's your name," Emma asked.

"I'm Florence. Nice to meet you, Emma."

Emma hadn't introduced herself but was not surprised the older woman knew her name. The longer she sat there, the calmer she felt. As she looked around the park, the pastel colors again became vibrant and alive, causing her to get a rush of excitement.

"So, are you like my guardian or something? Could you help me get back to my old life if I decided I wanted to do that?"

"Is that what you want?"

"No. At least, I don't think so. I just want my son to be born. That isn't happening. Nothing is happening right now. There's just a sort of normal, boring, day-to-day thing going on. But I don't want to live in this time for years and years without my son."

"I see. Quite the dilemma. Let's walk," Florence said, standing and placing her knitting back in her bag. She adjusted her sunglasses, straightened her clothes, and smiled. A ball that some kids had misdirected landed at her feet. She picked it up and threw it back to them.

"Let's walk for a bit in silence, if that's all right with you. We need to listen for a while."

Chapter 13

The two walked quietly, Emma's mind bursting with questions. As they moved through the residential streets, Emma was suddenly struck by the beauty she saw everywhere. Did Florence make the colors so vibrant? Was it her energy that caused the incredible peace and serenity? Could her simple presence elevate the mundane to the magnificent?

They silently walked well over a mile until Florence guided them to another park. She picked a tree in the back where they could view the entire expanse. She plopped herself down on the grass with a smile, sighing happily.

"I love parks. Everything is so alive here," Florence remarked simply.

"Yes, there's lots of activity with the kids playing and people sunbathing and the like," Emma answered, sitting beside Florence.

"I'm not talking about the people. I'm talking about the trees, the grass, the flowers. They give of their beauty completely with no guile or pretense."

"Yes, I guess that's true," Emma said quietly, hanging on every word.

"Ask your questions, dear, before your mind explodes," Florence laughed.

Emma felt her face flush with excitement. She was convinced that Florence had been sent to tell her what to do and how to get pregnant.

"Okay, before we talk about Brian, I want to know something else first. What was that flash that happened when I was able to miraculously stop Adam from hitting me? In fact, how was I able to do that at all?"

"Ah," Florence nodded with a gentle smile. "Your powers."

"My powers?"

"Yes, dear. Thoughts, deep desires, and fervent wishes all carry with them a certain magic if you will. Thoughts have great power and give you the ability to manifest concrete events into your life. They were so deep and profound that they propelled you to grab his arm to protect yourself."

"But, I don't even remember doing it, and then there was that bright light or flash or whatever it was."

"That, unfortunately, is something you didn't want to happen. Not to scold, but had you taken the time to listen to Willow, you could have avoided the results you've now created."

"Wait. Wait. Wait. So, I should have let him hit me?"

"That's not what I said. Had you listened to Willow, there would have been alternative ways to prevent him from hitting you without taking away his free will. You two now have attained a peaceful existence, but by interrupting his choices by force in the manner you did, destinies have changed, and they are not just for you and Adam."

"What do you mean, change our destinies?"

"When you throw a rock into the lake, the energy created causes a ripple effect throughout the entire body of water."

"So, that's a change of destiny?"

"No. That's an example. It illustrates how one action can change a sequence of events, like a twenty-car pileup. The first person suddenly slams on their brakes—the car following rear-ends them, and the energy carries backward, affecting all those behind it. When you remove another's free will, it changes their fate. Had Adam made the *choice* not to harm you, all would have stayed intact. He would have changed his own fate. As it is with you. You are here with your entire lifetime of memories intact. Every time you alter an action, word, or thought, you create a new future for yourself. These current actions could change whether you even have a child, and if you do, when that might be."

Emma was quiet for a long time. Florence's words made her afraid. Had she done something terrible to Adam? Would this cause him harm down the road? And no Brian? It was unthinkable.

"Did I hurt him?" Emma asked emotionally. "Will something bad happen to him in the future? I would never want to do anything to make him suffer, particularly not the way he is now."

"I don't have an answer to your question. No one can see the future. It is written in probabilities and actions."

Emma's head was spinning. She felt like the sand was shifting beneath her feet. She didn't understand anything. The more Florence spoke, the more confused she became. At that moment, she wanted desperately to be back in her sixty-year-old self, safe in her cozy townhouse. She seemed to be screwing up everywhere here, and they still had no child. Her book writing had become almost a drudge. But, when she had those thoughts, she also realized that now, the way Adam was presently, she didn't want to leave him. She was totally, completely in love with her husband. As her thoughts intensified, she yanked up blades of grass from their quiet existence in the soil.

"Don't overthink it, Emma. The ability to let go is the greatest asset one can possess. Ruminating about past mistakes only keeps them present and continues to push them into the future."

Just then, a beautiful Irish Setter dog suddenly appeared out of nowhere, wagging its tail and panting happily. Florence reached out to it. The dog immediately laid down, placing its head on the older woman's lap. The owner, a middle-aged, athletic-looking gentleman, appeared within moments.

Panting from the chase, he stopped at their feet and bent over to catch his breath, sweat dripping from his brow.

"I'm so sorry. She got away from me. Normally, she stays right by my side, and I don't even need a leash, but she just stopped, perked up her ears, and took off running right for you guys."

He walked over and began petting his furry companion, who was very content where she was. She didn't even look up at him.

"Come on, Ruby, let's go. It's time to go home," he said, patting his leg for her to come to him. The dog didn't move. She just closed her eyes peacefully, enjoying Florence's lap.

"I've never seen her take to anyone like this. Usually, she's pretty skeptical of new people."

Florence smiled, then took Ruby's face in her hands, looking intently into the dog's eyes. "You're such a beautiful girl. Thank you for the visit. Go enjoy your day now."

With that, the dog sat up and stood beside her master, never taking her eyes off Florence. As they walked away, the Setter kept sneaking a look behind her until they were out of sight.

Emma was dumbfounded. That animal saw something in Florence. It was drawn to her. It understood. She came here and immediately was at peace. Emma so badly wanted that.

"So, tell me, please. How do I quit screwing up? I don't want to change anyone else's destiny that way. What should I have done? What should I do now?"

"That will be a longer explanation," Florence smiled. "First, I think I would like some ice cream." Just as she spoke, from around the corner, a man pushing a frozen treats cart appeared in the distance.

Chapter 14

Florence seemed in no hurry to continue the conversation they'd been having. She seemed to revel in the children, delighted by their antics. She smiled broadly while watching a tiny one lose the battle with a melting cone. Licking faster and faster, the toddler couldn't keep the now almost liquid mess from falling away and landing on the ground at her feet.

Emma's excitement at their conversation quickly turned to frustration. Why couldn't this woman just tell her what she wanted to know? Why all the stalling?

"It's not stalling, darling," Florence answered Emma's thoughts. "It's called learning patience."

Emma literally jumped. "Don't do that! Stop reading my mind." She immediately regretted her outburst. "I'm sorry. But, I feel like there are cracks in my life...I don't mean cracks; I mean unsteadiness or fragility of everything like it could all just crumble at any moment."

"A bird sitting on a tree is never afraid of the branch breaking because its trust isn't on the branch, but on its own wings," Florence answered sagely.

"God! I must be the dumbest person on the planet. I don't understand anything you say. It's like someone has jumbled up the words. How do I stop doing bad and start doing good, or whatever it is I should be doing? That's all I want to know. Tell me exactly how to behave," Emma whined.

Florence laughed. "My darling, child. No one can do that. Those are *your* *choices*. All I can impart to you are the rhythms of life. These apply to all people, not just travelers. Do good, and good will be manifest in your life. It's as simple as that."

"See? I don't get that. I thought I *was* doing good. I'm making friends with my mom. Adam doesn't hit anymore. Aren't those good things?"

"Indeed. But who are those things good for? You didn't marry Adam out of a deep, abiding love. You married only because you wanted your son. You didn't make friends with your mother because you thought she might have made some good points about your behavior or choices, and you wanted to atone for some of the bad times you'd given her. It was all for you. Playing at being nice would keep her off your back. No thought to the consequences for others."

"Okay, so I get your point. I'm scum, but I don't want to hurt them in any way."

Florence laughed heartily. "Scum? My, my, you are very hard on yourself. You are not scum; you're just making your choices from your ego and desire for your own personal comfort. I'm simply stating that what becomes manifest from those choices may not be to your liking."

Florence's words frightened Emma. "But if I didn't stop him, he would have hit me," she screamed in frustration.

"Perhaps. Although, had you listened to Willow, there might have been an alternative that would have caused him to change course by his own choice."

"And what would that I have been?" Emma spouted sarcastically.

"Say, pretty please don't hit me?"

Florence looked at her for a long time before answering. "The time has passed. There is nothing to be done now. The best option is to let it go and learn from it. That is what our histories are supposed to be, tools of education. Mistakes made can be approached differently if they come around again."

Emma hung her head, feeling ashamed and humiliated. Florence was right. The whole time she'd been back, it had been, 'me, me, me. ' All she thought about was how to get what she wanted. She was stubborn and didn't listen to Willow, now finding herself with an entirely new possible future, which might include Brian not being born at all.

"I'm so, so, sorry. You're right. Please forgive the way I spoke to you just now."

"There's nothing to forgive," Florence answered simply.

Emma sat there, tears running down her face. She could never remember feeling so ashamed of herself.

"So, before I leave you, let me explain one thing. Pay attention to the auras around you. They can give you information and guidance. Most don't see them at all, but you are fortunate that you do."

"Can you tell me what each one means?"

"I cannot. That is for you to figure out. You've already unraveled the meaning of the yellow and red ones. These are what they mean in your life only—not universally. You see red as rage and possible violence. I may see it as deep, heartfelt love. Understand?"

"I think so," Emma mused quietly.

"And Emma, step outside yourself and remove the tendency towards self-absorption. If you become other-involved and self-directed, rather than self-involved and other-directed, you will see every bit of magic you could ever wish for."

Emma nodded, hesitant to ask anything else, but the Brian issue still crawled under her skin. Would she get pregnant? If not, she might consider going back. But, before she could even speak the words, Florence answered them in her own cryptic way.

"A child will come into being only as a direct result of your growth," the old woman smiled.

"And if I want to go back. What about that?"

Florence got up and then bent down to retrieve her bag. As she did, her sunglasses fell onto the grass. Emma grabbed them, got up, and handed them to the older woman. She gasped. Florence's eyes were completely clouded over.

"You're blind," Emma exclaimed. "How did you...the dog...the ball you threw back to the kids...how..?"

"Many have eyes but cannot see. My vision is clear."

"But,..."

"Take care, dear Emma. Just remember where your true power lies."

With a gentle gush of air through the trees, causing them to rustle melodically, Florence disappeared.

Chapter 15

E mma jogged quickly back to her house. She didn't realize how much time she'd spent with Florence. All the way back, her mind was trying to assimilate all Florence had said. It was all so big, so massive, yet the older woman made it sound like it should be simple. She hadn't realized how selfish she'd become, wanting everything her way for her benefit and tunnel-visioned goals. That's one thing she believed she could change.

Dashing in the door, she ran to the kitchen and quickly put together a pot of spaghetti. She was just starting to put the garlic bread into the toaster oven when Adam walked in. Running up to him, she leaped into his arms, kissing him continually on the cheeks, ending with a long kiss on the mouth.

"Whoa. I'm not complaining," Adam laughed, "but what's got into you?"

"I'm just married to the sweetest, kindest person on the planet, that's all. And so very handsome. I wonder if I should be worried. How many pretty women come to get their cars fixed every day?" she laughed, her green eyes twinkling with delight.

"Oh, too many to count," Adam chuckled, "but then I just show them my ring and tell them I am extremely happily married."

"Perfect answer," Emma said, taking his hand and leading him to the table. "Sit. Dinner is ready. Just gotta heat up the garlic bread."

"Well, I have some exciting news," Adam exclaimed with the happiest of grins she'd ever seen on his face.

"Oh, I love exciting news. Wait one sec. Let me get the sodas and sit down." She did so, then said, "Okay. The stage is yours."

"Let me set it up a little bit cuz you'll be surprised at what I did."

Emma was immediately intrigued. As she looked at all the happiness he was exuding, his aura all pink and shimmery, she didn't really care how it came about. Florence's warnings moved quickly to the back of her mind. If she'd changed his destiny, so be it. She would protect him and make sure that no harm came to him. That was her vow.

"All right. We've been married a little over a year, and I decided it was about time that I..." Adam began.

"Um...excuse me, but we've only been married three months. Are you getting senile in your old *older-than-me* age," Emma giggled. "It's August 15th, and we got married in May, three months ago."

Adam made a funny face. "Okay, very funny. Stop interrupting. I'm trying to tell you what happened today. It'll blow your mind."

"I'm not joking; it's you who's pulling *my* leg. Today is August 15th, 1982," Emma said, furrowing her brow.

Adam rose, picked up the newspaper off the coffee table, and handed it to her. She looked at it in shock. The date read clearly, August 15th, 1983. Her hands began to shake. She went into fight-or-flight, feeling like she needed to run. Dropping the newspaper, she stood up and immediately fainted.

A green mist enveloped her. She looked around, and Adam and her entire apartment had disappeared.

"Emma, Emma, Emma," someone called from far off. She couldn't see through the mist. "Dad? Dad, is that you?" she cried out, confused and disoriented.

"Emma...Emma," another voice called. It was high-pitched and sounded female. She didn't recognize it at all.

She found she was lying flat on some kind of floor, but it wasn't her living room. It felt velvety and soft, like pillows, yet still sturdy. Getting to her knees, she crawled a few inches and then felt a hard object. She used it to stand up. More voices. They got louder and louder, joining together, increasing in volume. Then, it became a sound similar to monks chanting. Her name was no longer discernable. The hum increased in volume. She covered her eyes, letting out a long scream.

Stumbling, she fell to her knees. With lightning speed, images flashed before her eyes. They were bright, almost blinding. Like a slide show, the still pictures were reminiscent of a family photo album. They showed her and Adam at a baseball game, and she and her father at one of his restaurants. There were some of her and Andrea, with Andrea having graduated from junior college. She closed her eyes tightly, then opened them again. What was that? Andrea hadn't graduated yet. She and Adam had never attended a baseball game. There was even one of her at her doctor's office. The feeling from it was somber and sad.

The images came around again in the same order, but she was *in* the pictures this time, not simply viewing them. She was feeling them, talking to the people, smiling for the photos. She could see Adam dragging her to her first baseball game, which she thoroughly enjoyed. There were romantic dinners where she and Adam talked into the early morning. As things slowed down, it was as if she was living this time period at a breakneck pace. The last photo was the saddest. The doctor was telling her that she still was not pregnant yet, even though she appeared healthy and able to conceive.

Emma covered her eyes and wept for a long time. The mist seemed to gather close around her in a protective fashion, almost like a big hug. In the distance, a white spot appeared, growing slowly in size. First, it was like a front door peephole, then enlarged to about the dimensions of a television set. There, she could see herself on the floor of her house, Adam kneeling beside her, frantically calling her name. He put his ear to her chest to see if he could hear a heartbeat. He patted her hand and rubbed her cheek. His face was a portrait of terror. Jumping up, he ran to the phone to call an ambulance.

Emma reached her hand out from the green mist and called Adam's name. He, of course, could not hear her. Struggling to free herself from her ethereal captor, she squirmed around, attempting to crawl to the Adam in the distance.

Am I dead? What is happening? "Willow! Florence," she called out. "Help me." She kept struggling.

As if time itself stood still, the mist let her go. It was still around her but not animated as it had been. A glow of brilliant white light appeared before her, causing her to close her eyes against the glare.

"Open your eyes, Emma," a male voice said.

Standing before her was a huge, muscled man—at least, she thought it was a man. She could only see his head and shoulders. The rest of him tapered down into the mist and was indistinguishable. He not only had a blue aura, but his skin seemed to be blue, sort of like a genie in a fairy tale. He smiled gently, then laughed loudly.

"Did I scare you?"

"What? Scare me? What the..." Emma stuttered.

"Sorry, just my little joke. If I was human, I'd be a film director. I'd do lavish, colorful productions for kids. There'd be lots of heroes and defending of the innocent...stuff like that. Just showing off a little bit."

Emma shook her head as if the shaking would make the vision disappear. She couldn't even find words to speak. *I must be dead. That's gotta be it. This must be the transition people talk about, but where's the white light? Where are the dead family members coming to greet me?*

"No, you're not dead or anything close," the man said, reading her thoughts, changing into full-human form and no longer blue. I'm Harold. I'm here to explain what you just experienced. Your case is extraordinary. I've never gotten to meet an accidental time traveler. I never get to actually be seen by any of my charges. I'm what's called a *guide*. My normal function is to stay invisible and give you inspiration in the form of signs, etc., to help you fulfill your life purpose."

"A guide? Invisible? What are you talking about? And please stop reading my thoughts."

"Yeah...like, have you ever had the urge to suddenly have Chinese food when you were going to pick up a hamburger? Then, when you're waiting for your take-out order, you meet someone, and they somehow become important in your life?"

"Not exactly that, but I get your drift."

"That's me. You needed to meet that person, so I put you back on track. Of course, you have free will, so you could have continued on to your hamburger, but I do my part to keep you on your path," he grinned widely, like a small child.

"Free will? That crap again?" Emma spat out disgustedly.

"Whoa. No need to get huffy. It's just how it works, whether you like it or not."

"Sorry. Sorry. I'm confused, as you might have guessed. Where am I, and what am I doing here? Am I dead?"

"Oh gosh, no. We just needed to do a little reset. You're different because of the way you got here, so you have one foot in the magical and one foot on the earth. The rules apply differently to you. It's rather chaotic on our side of things because you did this. Kind of like there are rules, but none of them apply to you."

"Did what? I came here, now I'm trying to live my life—have a family, write a book, you know, the usual. Well, the usual again but different, you might say."

Emma got up and tried to walk around but couldn't move her legs.

"Um, there's really no place for you to go at the moment," Harold explained. "This is an in-between place. Think of it as a waiting area at an airport. You stay here until you are ready to board your flight."

Emma rubbed her temples hard with her fingertips. She was developing the biggest headache.

"So, why am I here? Can I leave now and go home? Adam is about to have a stroke."

"Here's what happened," Harold began quietly. "For whatever reason, we don't know why you have been losing your recent memories. We expected your old life memories would fade with time, but not the most recent ones. So, when we realized they were not coming back, we popped you over here to give you a review of what you'd forgotten. Once that's done, I can send you home."

Emma suddenly felt like someone slapped her in the face. The memory of her doctor again telling her she wasn't pregnant affected her physically and emotionally. She started to cry.

"I'm so sorry, Emma," Harold said gently. "It was three months ago. And I'm further sorry because I have to rush you here. I need to get you back home. You can't stay here any longer."

"Will I remember any of this...being here, I mean?" Emma asked.

"I doubt it, but who knows? I can't say anything for certain."

"But, what about..."

The room went black.

Chapter 16

Slowly, the sound of Adam's voice infiltrated her consciousness. She was lying on a hospital bed, and Adam was at her side, holding her hand.

"Emma, please, wake up. I'm here. I'm right here,"

When she opened her eyes, she immediately became aware of the IV needle in her arm. A medicine bag hung on a tall pole, delivering its elixir into her arm. She felt hot and went to push off the blanket covering her.

"Emma. Thank God. You're awake. Honey, don't do that," Adam said, stopping her from removing her blanket. "You need that. The doctors said you were hypo...hypo...something. You were really cold. They need to get your temperature up."

Emma didn't speak. She kept looking around at the sterile room, with machines in the corner at the ready, for what she wasn't sure and really didn't want to know. The nurse's station was right outside her room. One woman glanced up and came running when she saw Emma was awake.

"Well, welcome back," she said with a smile, patting Emma's arm and checking on the IV. "Let me get the doctor. You gave us a real scare."

Emma furrowed her brow and looked at Adam with fear in her eyes.

"You fainted, hon," he said softly.

"How long?" she hoarsely asked, her voice not quite there.

"You've been out for two days," Adam answered.

Emma closed her eyes for a second, feeling extremely weak and helpless.

The doctor walked in with a big smile and stood at the side of the bed.

"Do you know where you are?"

"Hospital," she answered weakly.

"What's your name?"

"Emma Armstrong."

"What year is it?"

"1983."

"Good. Good. We need a couple more tests to check on a couple of things, but it looks like you'll be fine. Your blood count was a little low, which could have been caused by a number of things, too much exercise while not eating properly, dieting, or perhaps an intestinal virus. Everything else looks good, though, so you'll stay here a couple of days until all your numbers are back in the normal range; then, you'll be free to go home and resume your novel. Your husband tells me you're writing a book."

"Yes. Yes," Emma said, her voice sounding a little stronger. "A murder mystery."

"Let me know when it comes out. I love murder mysteries." He turned, patted Adam on the shoulder caringly, and left.

Adam was overjoyed that she was awake and going to be fine, but all she could think about was that crazy life review. She remembered it all—the green mist, Harold, and what she'd learned. She was becoming angry. Nothing, absolutely nothing, was turning out right. She still wasn't pregnant. Her book wasn't done. She was living the life of an ordinary housewife. Just the word left a bad taste in her mouth.

"Honey? You okay?" Adam broke into her thoughts.

"What? Oh sure. This is a lot to take in...fainting, being unconscious for two days..."

"I know. I've already told my boss, and he's letting me off work until you're home and on your feet."

"Adam...no. We can't afford that. The doctor said I'm going to be fine. You don't need to hover." There was an edge to her voice, a blanketed anger trying to push its way out.

"Okay. Okay. Don't be angry. I'm just worried about you, that's all."

"I'm not angry," Emma snapped. I'm sick, I'm frustrated, I'm not pregnant...everything is wrong."

Adam leaned over and gently took her into his arms. "I understand. Don't worry. I'm going to make everything right, you'll see."

Emma immediately felt ashamed at her outburst. He was being so nice. It wasn't his fault she'd traveled back in time and caused chaos for everyone—not his responsibility that she was screwing up everything.

"I'm sorry. You didn't deserve that. We'll be fine. I'll be fine."

Just then, Andrea came through the door with a bouquet of flowers. She smiled widely when she saw Emma was awake. She fairly flung the flowers at Adam and hugged Emma tightly.

"Girl... don't you ever do anything like this again. Can you imagine me on this planet without you? You scared me to death."

Emma smiled at her dear friend. At least Andrea's life had not been altered by Emma's return. She was finishing her education and soon would meet Kyle Carter, the love of her life.

The three spoke for a bit, which raised Emma's spirit some. Then Adam stood, raising the water glass he'd snatched from Emma's bedside table in the air.

"I have an announcement to make. I believe this is as good a time as any. I've been holding this in for days."

"Oh...this must be the good news you were talking about when we were having dinner, and I so rudely interrupted you by fainting," Emma laughed.

"One in the same," Adam nodded. "You are now looking upon the face of a man who will be starting an internship at one of the biggest architecture firms in the city."

"What? How did that happen?" Emma and Andrea threw questions at him simultaneously.

"Magic, and your dad...well, mostly your dad. When he brought in his car the other day for service we got to talking. I don't know what compelled me, but I started telling him about how I wanted to be an architect but didn't think that was in the cards for me, etc. You know, school loans, and how would I earn a living while I went to school...that sort of thing."

"That's perfect that you told him," Emma exclaimed. "My dad can solve any problem. So what did he say, and how did you end up with an internship before you even went to school?"

"Well, first, he gave me all the reasons why I *shouldn't* want to be an architect, years of school, it's a highly competitive career, yada, yada, yada."

"To which you said..." Andrea asked.

"I said, 'Okay, never mind,' and walked out the door," Adam laughed. "Seriously, what he said scared me. I never realized what skills you have to possess to do that job. It's not just drawing a few lines on a set of plans."

A nurse walked in, took Emma's blood pressure, and checked on her IV, interrupting his tale. All were silent until she left the room.

"Go on, go on," Emma urged.

"Even so, afraid or not, I still wanted to do it and told him so. I think he was just testing me cuz as soon as I made it clear I really wanted to do it, he seemed to get excited. He asked for some paper and started scribbling down notes. He made these little boxes with arrows pointing to each other. I had no idea what he was doing."

"He does that when he is trying to figure stuff out. It helps him to make a visual picture of what should be done, when it should be done, and how it should be done. It tells him what the outcome will be."

"Still looked like he was writing in Greek to me." They all laughed. "Then he told me how he started his restaurants, where he failed, and how he finally ended up with three of them and is so successful now."

Andrea clapped her hands together a couple of times loudly, ending Adam's monologue. "Okay...okay...you and your father-in-law got all warm and fuzzy. Please just get to the part about how you're an intern already," she said in that always direct and to the point way of hers.

"He made a phone call."

"That's it? A phone call?" Emma asked

"That's it. He has a very close friend who has a medium-sized firm. He made a phone call...the guy agreed to put me on part-time and teach me everything he knows." Adam beamed.

"But what about school?" Emma asked.

"Oh, I have to do that too. Your dad is going to help me fill out all the papers, and when I get accepted, help me get the school loans."

"But, not to be nosy or anything," Andrea began. "How will you live? If you're a part-time intern, that cuts down your income. Then going to school... you'll have to study. Sooo..."

"I figured that one out. I'll intern in the morning and schedule my classes for the afternoon. I already talked my boss into letting me work at the garage at night. It'll be tough but doable."

"And when will you study...and, for that matter, sleep?" Emma asked.

"In between all the other stuff," Adam said quietly, obviously not having thought it completely through.

"No. You'll quit your job completely. I'll go to work at one of my dad's restaurants during the day. I'll make good money with tips and all. Then at night, I'll write while you study. It'll be perfect."

"Absolutely not." Adam raised his voice. "You're my wife; you're not going to work. I can provide for us."

As the argument escalated, Andrea quietly slipped out the door.

Adam was reverting to type—trying to be the *man* of the house. Emma was having none of it. Finally, she slammed her hand down on the over-bed tray beside her bed. Her eyes flashed with anger.

"No, Adam, this is what we're going to do!" At that moment, there was a flash of bright light.

Adam didn't see it but backed up a step, stunned by Emma's ferocity. "Okay. Okay. We'll do it your way."

Emma looked around the room as the brilliance of the light flash faded. She gulped. The only thought she had was, '*Oh, crap. I did it again.*'

Chapter 17

The day after her release from the hospital, Emma took a long walk to clear her head. She would call her father later and arrange for him to give her a job to help put Adam through school, but for now, she needed some *me-time*. Absolutely nothing was happening the way she wanted it to. Everyone else was excited about their possibilities, but all she saw was more of the same dullness.

Her dilemma was that she truly loved Adam now. He'd become the sweetest, most supportive husband. She didn't want to return to her dull existence and leave him behind, but she didn't want to continue if this was all it was. What was the point?

As she came upon the park where she'd met Florence, she glanced over at the bench, but it was empty. Had she seen her, she might have turned around. There was no more time for mystic riddles that she didn't understand. A decision needed to be made.

"Looking for me?" a voice came, first in her head, then from behind her.

Emma wheeled around quickly to see Florence walking behind her. Her eyes widened, then became tiny slits of anger. She ran.

"No...no...not today," she shouted as she took off.

"Yes, today," Florence answered as she suddenly appeared in front of the fleeing Emma.

Emma stopped dead in her tracks. It was no use. She stared at the woman, then got a sick feeling in her stomach. She couldn't see Florence's aura. In fact, all the auras had disappeared everywhere. The world was as everyone else saw it. No magical bursts of light anywhere.

Florence guided her to the bench. Emma sat down, defeated and sad.

"You are no longer a seer," Florence stated flatly. "To put it more bluntly, you are simply lost in time and space."

Tears began to run down Emma's cheeks. She buried her head in her hands and cried for a long time. All her frustration with her non-accomplishments and mistakes gushed out, riding on each individual drop of water. Florence put her arm around her and let her sob until there were no more tears to shed.

"I'm sorry, Florence," Emma sniffled. "I can't figure out what's wrong with me. I'm all over the place in my emotions. I'm angry one minute, totally depressed in the next, and yelling at everyone. I'm changing, and I don't like it."

"That's because you don't know where the treasures lie," Florence said softly.

"Please, please, no more riddles. I don't get them. I'm *that* stupid. I need help. I need direction. Just tell me when I'll get pregnant and when my book will sell. If I knew that, I'd be the best little time traveler you ever saw. As long as I know when it's coming, I can relax."

"As would every other person on this planet," Florence chuckled. "I'm not a fortune-teller, Emma. I am a guide, a soul-protector. In your case, particularly, there are no rules. Your accidental drop into this timeline created quite a ripple in the field. Like a rock wall being hit by lightning and breaking apart, the rebuilding of it will involve rocks being placed in different places from their original station. No one can predict exactly where they will go."

Emma understood, but she didn't want to. It meant that nothing was certain; everything was up in the air, and possibly, the rocks she wanted, meaning her book and Brian, might not make it back into the new wall at all.

"A householder's life," Florence said simply.

"What's that?"

"A householder's life is a phrase used by many Masters and sages. It is to live the ordinary, from which the miraculous can sprout. The life of one who can be happy in the mundane, working, paying bills, giving of themselves for other's benefit, opens the door to the greatest riches of the heart."

"So, if I live the *ordinary*, as you call it, then I get what I want?" Emma asked, hopeful.

"Emma, darling. There is no card catalog that contains *all the possible lives of Emma Armstrong*. You can't just pick one and suddenly have the existence you desire. We've talked about free will, possibilities, and choices. All life is lived in the moment, and change can happen in an instant. As Willow said, 'With the blink of the eye and the snap of a finger,' your direction can be altered." Florence sat quietly, waiting for Emma to absorb her words.

Suddenly, Emma jumped up, angrier than she'd ever been. "I'm sick of listening to your incoherent enigmas," she shouted. "The *'if,' 'wait for it,' 'maybe it can happen,'* and *'I can't tell you what it will be,'* stuff is old and boring. I have a brain. I'll figure it out myself. The way I see it, I've done some good stuff since I've been here. Adam doesn't hit, his family is kinder, and my mom and I get along, so I'm doing just fine, thank you very much. What the hell do I need you for?"

"I'm sure you don't," Florence smiled gently.

The statement took Emma by surprise. She was expecting an argument, a lecture, or at the very least, some push-back. Was she trying to trick her, being all nice to make her want to live this *householder life* thing?

"Well...well... you're right. I don't," Emma said, her conviction waning.

"Then our time is over," Florence answered gently. Kissing Emma on the cheek, she looked into her eyes. "I know you're worried about not seeing the auras anymore. They were removed as you didn't use them. Their presence didn't help you. Now you can, as you put it, 'figure it out on your own.' And lovely one, always remember where your true power lies."

As was now so common to Emma, the older woman took a couple of steps and then disappeared in a light gush of warm air.

Emma stood in that same spot, staring at the emptiness. Her stomach churned. A slow fear crept over her. *What have I done?*

Chapter 18

The morning after her talk with Florence, Emma awoke to Adam hollering at her from the other room. She'd fallen asleep at her desk, only now there was no typewriter in front of her. Instead, a computer screen stared back at her. On the screen was her novel, halted mid-sentence, obviously where she'd put her head down and dozed off.

"Come on, jailbait, I'm pretty sure Andrea can't get married without her matron of honor."

Emma jumped out of the chair. It had happened again. She'd lost time. *What year is it? Oh, my God, oh my God!* She looked around the room. The whole room was different. The bed had a different comforter, and the nightstand was new. She grabbed the newspaper on top of it.

When she leapt up to retrieve the newspaper lying on the bed, she looked down and realized she was pregnant. She was staring at her belly when Adam came running in. He looked so handsome in his light grey suit and navy blue tie.

"I'm pregnant," she said excitedly, looking at Adam.

"Better you than the bride," he chuckled. "Come on. Do you need some help getting into your dress?"

"Um...yeah...probably. Thanks."

How far along am I? From the size of my stomach, maybe six months or maybe more? I don't know. There's no way I'll be able to fake these lost years. She looked at the newspaper. It was June 15th, 1990. *Seven years?! I've lost seven years. I'm twenty-six frikken years old. If I'm twenty-six, then Adam must have already graduated. Oh man, I missed it. And, apparently, I missed morning sickness, so maybe it's not all bad.*

After Adam helped her dress and they walked into the living room, she was stunned. They lived in an entirely different house. There was a new, soft-looking powder blue sofa with white end tables and matching silver lamps with white and blue shades. The room had an open construction leading into the dining area and kitchen. It was beautiful. She fought the urge to ogle, ooh, and ah. Glancing out the massive front window, she saw a well-manicured lawn. The houses up and down the street were lovely middle-class homes trimmed and well kept up. Some had children's bikes or other toys on the lawns.

Turning towards the mantle over the fireplace, she saw pictures of her and Adam. There was a photo of both their families surrounding Adam, who was holding up his diploma, grinning from ear to ear. As she looked at the array, she couldn't step into the photos like before when Harold had presented her with her missed-year life review. It made her extremely sad. She had no memory of all these beautiful moments.

Adam grabbed her purse and helped her down the outside steps to the car, which was no longer the old Chevy they'd had before. This was a much newer Toyota Corolla. The other vehicle in the driveway was a VW. Not the one from when she graduated, but a new model. She assumed that was her car.

As they made their way to the church where Andrea was getting married, Emma had the urge to tell him who she was. She wanted to blurt out about the time travel, their past life, and how they now had this new one. It would feel so good to be honest about it all. Then, if she ever had another brain dysfunction where she forgot everything, he could fill her in. It would be so nice not to hide it all. But would he believe her? Probably not. If someone had come up to her when she was in her old life and told her they'd traveled back in time to participate in a do-over of their life, she'd have called the cops and an ambulance for them.

Maybe Andrea, Emma thought. *She might believe me. I mean, I have to tell somebody. What's the point of going back in time to change things, but then not remember the things that you've changed?* "I mean, really, what *is* the point of that?" she said aloud.

"Point of what, hon?"

"Um...the point of...me...me walking down the aisle all pregnant and worried what people will think. I'm not the bride, right? I'm a happily married pregnant lady, right? I am happily married, aren't I?"

"That's a weird question. I certainly think we're happily married, don't you? Are you mad at me for something I don't know about?"

"No, no, no... don't be silly. Oh, oh, oh..." she cried out in a panic, grabbing her neck, searching for her dolphin. "My necklace. My dolphin necklace. I forgot it. We have to go back. I can't go anywhere without it."

"I put it in your purse. You've been so forgetful lately, so I just put it in there cuz I didn't know if you wanted to wear it with your bridesmaid dress."

Emma leaned over and gave him a big, fat kiss on the cheek. "How did I ever get so lucky?" she cooed.

"And don't you forget it," Adam teased, kissing her hand.

The church was decorated beautifully. There were pink bows at the end of every pew. Flowers stands were everywhere, bursting with Andrea's colors of pink, white, red, and yellow, with baby's breath mixed in. The aroma from the buds was enchanting all on its own.

Most everyone was already there, mingling, chatting, finding a good seat. Happiness was palpable in the room. Emma missed the auras. Their vibrancy added that magic touch to all she saw. Florence had said she 'didn't use' them. She had no idea what that meant.

Racing back to where Andrea was dressing, she burst through the door, apologizing all over herself for being late, stopping abruptly when she saw Andrea in her gown in front of the mirror. Andrea's gown was magnificent. It was a white satin dress with fitted, long sleeves and a slight flair at the bottom. She wore a crown veil that extended to her midback. It was so Andrea, simple and elegant.

Emma went to her and gave her a hug.

"You're absolutely gorgeous. Now I'm worried that Kyle might faint when you walk down the aisle. Your beauty will make him absolutely lightheaded and giddy."

"Oh, stop," Andrea tried weakly to protest, but she was so incredibly happy it was hard to argue. She loved her gown and the way she looked in it.

Andrea's mother appeared and gave Emma a hug. She had Andrea lift her dress so they could put on her blue garter.

Emma's breath caught in her throat. She was supposed to give the bride a gift. Adam hadn't given her anything, so what would she do? Quickly, she opened her purse. Inside was a tiny gold box with a pink ribbon around it. *Oh, thank goodness,* she thought.

"For the most beautiful bride there ever was on the beginning of her new adventure," Emma said, handing Andrea the box.

Emma hoped it was something good since she had no idea what it was. It would probably be okay if she had bought it, but if Adam had bought it, who knows, it might be ringside seats for a boxing match. Thankfully, it was a delicate gold chain with two tiny jeweled hearts hanging from it. Emma breathed a sigh of relief.

"Oh my gosh, Em! It's beautiful. It will go perfectly with my gown. Will you put it on me?"

"My pleasure," Emma said, fastening it around her neck. Andrea looked in the mirror and squealed with delight. Everyone laughed.

The bridesmaids filled in the rest of the needed wedding rituals, giving her something old, new, and borrowed. The blue was the ribbon in the garter.

The wedding went off without a hitch. After the applause, the couple walked back down the aisle as Mr. and Mrs. Carter and headed for the reception, which was being held at her father's Beverly Hills Restaurant.

As soon as they walked in, Emma spotted someone—a very odd someone. Adam saw the questioning look on her face. "Are you okay? You're not having any pain or anything, are you?" he'd asked, concerned.

"No. I thought I saw an old friend." Before she could chase down the man, someone grabbed her to say hello, and the man disappeared.

Chapter 19

The reception was huge. At least two hundred people flooded into the restaurant. Emma spent a good deal of her time in the bathroom. Her pregnancy was at the point where she had to pee every few minutes. Many times, she thought she wouldn't make it because there seemed to always be a line. Once, she even had to elbow her way to the front, shouting, "Pregnant lady coming through." The women laughed, many having experienced the same thing, letting her get through.

Emma found two chairs at one of the tables, sat in one, and put her swollen, painful feet on the other. She was already exhausted. Adam brought her a plate of food and some water and went off to schmooze with the other patrons for a bit. She was glad for a few moments alone. The dancing had started, so the floor was filling up. Others stood in groups to the side, just watching and chatting.

The respite gave her time to think. *How am I going to fill in the blanks of the past seven years? What if Adam starts talking about a vacation we took or a special anniversary or something? I won't know how to respond. In fact, what if anyone mentions a memory I don't have? Why does this keep happening to me?*

Suddenly, someone whispered her name. It was like they were standing right next to her, talking into her right ear. She turned around, but no one was there. It happened again and again. Then the voice croaked out one word, 'outside.'

Emma looked around the room. All was normal. No one else seemed to have heard a voice or seen anything unusual. Putting her shoes back on, she quietly slipped out of the room.

Once out the front door, she stood there for a moment.

"Psst...psst...over here," a voice called in a stage whisper.

77

Emma rounded the corner. Over towards the back of the building where the bride and groom's limo was parked stood a man motioning for her to come to him. He looked like he was right out of the 1930s, complete with a dated three-piece suit, not like the double-breasted type the men wore today. His outfit also had a watch on a chain in the vest pocket. As Emma inched closer, she recognized the gentleman. It was Harold, her guide.

Emma started to laugh. "Harold? Is that you?"

"Yes, it's me. I'm here to help you," he said earnestly.

"Help me what—remember how people dressed in the thirties?" Emma giggled.

"I know, I know, I screwed up. I'm never supposed to be seen, but I thought it might be fun. Then, when I got to the party, I realized I was dressed all wrong. So, now you're the only one who can see me. If someone walks by, act like you're tying your shoe or something, unless you want it to look like you've gone round the bend and are talking to invisible people."

Emma continued to giggle. "Well, first of all, pregnant lady here. I'm not wearing shoes that tie. Secondly, why do you want to stay invisible? I think you look charming. Everyone in Southern California is an actor. You could say you came right from the set of a period piece you were filming."

"Oh. Good one. Okay. But why would I be here anyway? I'm not a friend of the bride or groom. They'll know I don't belong and kick me out."

"For heaven's sake, Harold. There are so many people in there you won't even be noticed. You could be a friend of mine that my dad asked to come or something. Stop worrying about it. Can we go back inside? I have to get my feet up; they're killing me. Then you can tell me why you're here, scold me, or whatever you came to do."

"Sure, sure, sure. Sorry. And yay, you're finally pregnant," Harold babbled as they walked.

They took a table in the back corner of the room. Emma sighed happily once her shoes were off and her feet were elevated.

"So, why are you here, Harold? I thought all of you magical beings were through with me," she said a little harsher than she'd intended.

"Like I said, I'm never supposed to be seen, only guide as inspiration like we talked about before, but I couldn't let you lose those seven years with no memory of them. It doesn't seem fair. I mean, a lot happened, not the least of which is the fact that you didn't fall in the pond and didn't get sick. That's a biggy," Harold told her earnestly.

"So, how come no misty room? How come no cartoon genie illusions? Are you just going to explain to me what happened or what? I doubt I would remember all you told me anyway. Last time you had me experience everything which *reinstalled,* for lack of a better word, all I'd missed."

Adam walked up to the table. He smiled at Emma and kissed her on the cheek.

"Hi, I'm Adam, Emma's husband, and you are..." he said, holding out his hand.

"Harold...um and old, old, friend of Em's... Emma's, from way, way back," he said nervously.

"Nice to meet you, Harold," Adam said without blinking an eye.

"Em, sorry to leave you alone for so long, but my boss is suddenly full of ideas about this new client project we just started. If things work out, he's going to turn the whole thing over to me. That will really put me on the map. I'm glad you have Harold here to keep you company. I shouldn't be all that much longer." He kissed her again and left.

"See? Even Adam didn't give you a second look." Emma said. "I'm not sure if I should be relieved or worried. You're a nice-looking man. Couldn't he have been the teeniest bit jealous? I realize I look like a beached whale at the moment, but he should remember what I used to look like."

"Yeah, yeah, yeah," Harold said hurriedly. We don't have much time. They only gave me a couple of hours."

"*They*, who? Willow and Florence?"

"No. they've stepped back, so to speak."

"You mean, dropped me like a hot potato," Emma said sarcastically, her eyes filling with contempt.

"It doesn't work like that." Harold answered in a pleading, frustrated voice."

"How exactly does it work? Florence gave me riddles to solve but never explained how I was supposed to live here and make the life I wanted. Willow basically said 'buh-bye,' and I haven't seen her since."

Harold let out a heavy sigh. "Florence gave you everything you needed to know. You just didn't listen."

"I did listen. She just didn't say anything worth listening to," Emma spat out.

Harold sat back in his chair. "What's happened to you? Why are you acting this way?"

"What way? Standing up for myself? Not whimpering and cowering like I did in my old life? Demanding what I want instead of just going along to get along?"

Harold really didn't like all the attitude she was giving him. He had the slightest desire to leave right then and there, but couldn't do it. He had a job to do...inspire and protect his charges as best as possible while not stepping on their free will.

"Let's just get this over with. Then you can get back to your party and your life," he said, ignoring her outburst. "Take my hand."

Emma hesitated a moment, then did as she was told. His hand was warm. She felt herself being injected with a feeling of peace and comfort. It was coming from him. He told her to close her eyes. Within thirty seconds, seven years of memories flooded into her mind and body. All the emotions and pictures inherent in each event filled her entire being. It was quickly done. He let go of her hand, got up, and walked out the back door without so much as a goodbye.

Chapter 20

The next day, Monday, Emma was still sorting through her memory recovery. She apparently had gotten an agent a month ago, but so far, no book deal. Her new representative was Mabel Stewart, a sixty-year-old, energetic, knowledgeable dynamo who worked at a medium-sized literary agency. She'd walked Emma through the difficulties of the publishing business. Still, she was quick to add that she felt Emma's mystery series would definitely sell. She'd explained that being a first-time author might take a little longer. The best part was that she was enthralled with Emma's writing and vowed to find her a top publisher.

When she'd blinked out, she had been doing the last of her edits on the second in her "Dumb-Ass Criminal Murder Mystery Series," entitled, "How Could I Forget to Put Bullets in the Gun?" She was proud of it. She wanted to have it done and to her agent, before the baby was born. Mabel had told her that having two books ready would be more appealing to a publisher. It would show she was a prolific writer and not just a one-off author. It seemed entirely doable.

It broke her heart that she'd missed Adam's graduation. Well, her body was present, at least. Now, in retrospect, her mind had been filled with the excitement and pride of her husband on that day, but it wasn't the same. These memory recoveries were never as deeply felt as having experienced them in real-time.

Time, Emma laughed to herself. *What the hell is time? I seemed to be nowhere in time. I'm just living, forgetting, going through the motions. It's like a non-lived life. I know I did it, but more like an observer than a full participant. I simply cannot keep having these memory lapses.*

Emma stepped away from her computer and stretched her aching back this way and that, trying to relieve the kinks. She wandered around the house, checking out their new home. It indeed was beautiful. She smiled as she now remembered the day they found it, the day they moved in, and all the painting and fixing up they did to make it perfect. It was the day after they'd hung the last picture, proclaiming the house was finally done, that Emma found out she was pregnant. They were both over the moon and took it to be a sign. She walked into the already set up nursery, gazing at the crib with the mobile already attached, just waiting to entertain its new addition.

Apparently, they'd also talked about names over the past months. Emma was insisting on Brian if it was a boy. She didn't want to consider girl's names. In her heart, it just had to be Brian. She'd waited so long.

Adam wanted the boy's name to be Ryan, and if it was a girl, she would be named Kathleen, Katy for short. After much wrangling, cajoling, and arguing, Adam had finally worn Emma down. She agreed to let the boy be called Ryan. She liked the name, plus it was only one letter off. Add a B to Ryan, and you've got Bryan, so it's the same. It was all good.

She made a glass of decaf iced tea and walked out on the back deck to rest a bit. They lived only a few blocks from the beach, and she could hear the sea lions barking and smell the ocean air. This was her happy place. The problem was, she wasn't—happy, that is. She had this stirring inside her, like a foreboding. Ever since the auras disappeared, it had been there. It waxed and waned but never entirely went away.

The baby kicked really hard, and she rubbed her belly where the sensation had happened. "Not long, little one. Soon we'll be back together." She had also learned that she wasn't six months pregnant, as was her first thought when awakening from her memory lapse; she was eight and a half months pregnant. No wonder she could barely waddle from place to place.

As she was washing her glass in the sink, the phone rang. Lumbering over to it as fast as she could, she was almost out of breath when she got there.

"Hello."

"Emma, it's Mabel. We did it, honey; we got a publisher. And it is Hanson Publishing, the second biggest publisher out there. Congratulations! You're a published author!"

"Oh my God, oh my God, oh my God," Emma shouted into the phone. "I can't believe it! Say it again!"

"You're a published author! You're on your way, honey. And they're just biting at the bit to see the next in the series. How soon can you get that to me and start working on number three? We'll just keep 'em coming, and they'll keep publishing them."

"Soon! Very soon! I'm just doing the final edits on it now," Emma enthused. "So, what's next? When will it come out? Maybe this is an indelicate question, but how much are they paying me?" Emma kept peppering her with questions.

"Whoa, whoa, whoa," Mabel laughed. "Take a breath. They're paying you an advance on sales of $20,000, practically unheard of for a new author. The book will be out next spring. Now, let me get off the phone and review the contract they just faxed. I'll have it messengered to you tomorrow and we can discuss it then. If we don't have any changes we want to make, you can sign it, and we'll get it right back to them. Sound good?"

"Thank you so much, Mabel. Thank you, thank you, thank you," Emma enthused.

"Don't thank me, you did the work. I'll talk to you tomorrow. Now go get off your feet. When is the baby due again?"

"Two weeks."

"Perfect. That'll give you time to absorb all this excitement, have your baby, and then we'll get to work. You'll have a couple of months to snuggle and coo at your little one, after which we'll have to start on the prerelease television appearances to get the excitement going. Once it's out, there'll be more appearances and book signings. You're going to be a busy, busy girl. Talk soon! Bye."

Emma walked around the living room, almost in a daze. She picked up the phone three times to call Adam but decided not to. Instead, she dashed out the door and grabbed the fixings for his favorite meal, some balloons, a large poster board, and a couple of felt-tip pens.

The lasagna had fifteen minutes to go, during which time she made her poster board message. It read: "Congratulations, you're about to become a famous author's husband, with all the perks and extras that entails." She drew hearts in the corners, and at the bottom, she drew a book with an arrow leading to the phrase – "Best Seller."

When Adam walked into the house, he stared at the sign for a minute, then let out a loud "Whoo hoo!" He scooped Emma into his arms and swung her around gently, as he was always very cognizant of her condition.

"Jailbait, we got it all," he laughed happily, giving her a long, tender kiss.

Chapter 21

After dinner, Adam and Emma moved to the couch to watch television and snuggle. However, they didn't do much watching as they talked through much of the shows that came on the screen. The exhilaration of the book deal and the plans for what happens next had them babbling excitedly about the future.

Emma suddenly grabbed at her stomach and bent over a little. "Ow, ow, ow. Okay, little one, calm down. No need to beat mommy up from the inside," she chuckled.

"Big kick, huh?" Adam smiled, touching her belly.

Emma let out what sounded like a little shriek and bent over again. "Wow. That one really, really hurt."

The third time it happened, Emma's face turned fearful. "This isn't right, Adam. I think we need to get to the hospital."

"Okay, let me grab your bag," he said, trying to remain strong and calm for Emma. "It's going to be fine. Maybe the little guy just thinks he's been in there long enough." He grabbed a blanket off the back of the couch and helped her to the car, tucking the blanket around her.

By the time they got to the ER, Emma had started to moan as her pain deepened. Once inside, the nurses took her right in. They called her OB. During the examination, Emma began to bleed lightly. Still, it kept steadily increasing, and her water had already broken. Her contractions came one on top of the other. Adam was there holding her hand.

Her OB arrived within minutes. Everything happened quickly. The doctor determined the baby was coming immediately and was in breach. Hard as he tried, he couldn't maneuver the baby into a better position. Emma began rapidly losing more blood.

"We've gotta do a C-section right now," the doctor shouted.

The attending nurses quickly pressed the foot-pedal brakes on the bed to make it mobile so they could roll her upstairs.

"No time," the doctor hollered. We'll do it right here." he snapped, calling for the anesthesiologist on duty to come and give her a spinal block.

Emma was terrified; Adam was white as a ghost. Everyone was moving very quickly. It was chaos.

"Just save my baby," Emma cried. "Please don't let anything happen to my baby."

"I plan to save both of you," the doctor answered her, still focused on the task at hand.

The anesthesiologist administered the block, and Emma went completely numb from the waist down. They draped her so she couldn't see anything, and a nurse took Adam out and had him dress in a protective gown and mask. Emma was calmer once he was back inside, but her eyes kept rolling up in her head like she was going to pass out. She had a tight grip on the dolphin necklace, which she still had around her neck.

"She's bleeding out," the doctor shouted to a nurse. "Get some blood down here, stat."

Emma was in and out of consciousness, then suddenly opened her eyes widely and smiled. "Harold," she said sweetly. I see them; they're pink and blue and perfect. It'll all be okay now," she whispered before she passed out completely.

After almost forty-five minutes of pure terror for Adam, Ryan Adam Armstrong made his grand entrance, weighing in at seven pounds, eleven ounces. He was perfect from head to toe. The doctor told Adam that Emma would be fine. They got the bleeding stopped and were giving her a transfusion to replace what she'd lost.

"She'll be weak for a few days," the doctor said, shaking Adam's hand, "but she's young and healthy and should bounce back just fine."

"Thank you so much, doctor...so much...thank you, thank you." Adam pumped the physician's hand like he was trying to draw water from a well.

"You're welcome, son. As soon as they get your boy cleaned up, we'll bring him to Emma's room for a meet-and-greet."

Adam smiled from ear to ear. They'd let him peek at his son as soon as he was delivered, but quickly whisked him off to the neonatal unit to run some tests and ensure he was healthy after his ordeal to get into this world.

By the time Adam got to Emma's room, they'd cleaned her up, put on a fresh gown, and brushed her hair. As he walked in, the nurse was placing the necklace on the bedside table, where Emma would see it as soon as she woke up.

"Congratulations, Mr. Armstrong," the nurse smiled. "You've got a beautiful wife and now an equally beautiful son. I wish you two all the happiness."

As the nurse disappeared out the door, he noticed she had long grey hair tied in a ponytail. He hadn't noticed the color of her hair when they'd spoken previously. She had such a youthful face and her voice such a melodic tone. There was something mesmerizing about her. He shook his head at his odd thoughts. That was how Emma talked about the magic out there in the world if we just looked for it—*mesmerizing*. He guessed she was rubbing off on him.

It took a couple of hours for Emma to become fully conscious again. Earlier, they'd brought Ryan up for a visit but ended up taking him back to the nursery, promising to return when Emma was fully awake. They were sure she would want to feed him.

When Emma awoke, she smiled up at Adam. "Is Ryan okay?" she asked.

"Yes, but how did you know it was a boy? You were out cold when he was finally delivered."

"Mother's intuition, I guess," she grinned happily. "My boy is finally here. All is finally right with my world."

At that exact moment, the nurse wheeled Ryan in. She picked him up from his bassinet and handed him to Emma. Tears streamed down her face. "Hello again, little one," she whispered.

"Okay, would you like to try to feed him now? I know he's hungry," the nurse inquired.

"Sure. Bring me a bottle; I'm up to it."

"What? Em, we talked about this. We read about how breastfeeding is better for the baby."

"That was before. I can't do that when I'll be traveling so much for book promotions and appearances. This way, when I'm gone, you can feed him, or my mom, or whoever we decide, can watch him during the day when you're at work, and I'm out of town."

Adam looked up at the nurse. "Could you give us a minute?"

"Em, honey. You'll only be breastfeeding for a few months. Can't the appearances wait for six months or so?"

"No," Emma said flatly. "I've waited too long for this. I can be a mother and an author. We'll work together. You'll see, it'll be fine."

"But, Em..."

"I said no, and that's it."

And with that, the conversation was over.

Chapter 22

As it turned out, Emma was in the hospital for a little over two weeks. She contracted a severe infection from her weakened state and loss of blood. Unfortunately, that meant she could not have contact with Ryan to avoid the risk of him getting sick, too. Adam stepped up. He spent most of his time at the nursery, feeding Ryan, holding him, and talking to him. He took a gazillion pictures with his new instant camera and had the nurses take them to Emma.

In an abundance of caution, the doctor asked that Adam not go in to physically see her, even with a gown and mask on. He was taking no chances. She was very weak, so he placed her in isolation. Adam could see her through the window of her room.

Once a day, Adam would bring Ryan and hold him up to the window so that Emma could see him. A lot of the time, Emma was asleep and missed seeing her son entirely.

The nurses admired Adam's commitment to his son and wife. They taught him how to change a diaper, hold Ryan over his shoulder, and burp him. When Adam announced that Ryan smiled at him, they laughed and told him it was probably reflex gas. "They don't start truly smiling until around six weeks old," they told him. Even so, Adam was convinced his son was a genius and would be ahead of all babies in his development.

On the fifth day of Emma's fight with her illness, she sparked a high fever. She was in and out of consciousness. She'd become delirious and talked to unseen visitors in her room. The doctors were more than concerned.

Both Emma's and Adam's parents came to the hospital to support Adam. They would take turns bringing Adam food and changes of clothes. He refused to leave the hospital until Emma was well again. The staff let him use the shower in the employee's locker room to clean up and shave.

Emma was indeed talking to people, but no one that the other humans could see. She'd been transported to another realm, an alternate reality where only she could hear and witness those talking to her.

The place where she'd found herself was similar to the green mist room of her first memory lapse. The air was alive with bright colors, sparkling as they played hide-and-seek with each other. The colors melded together to form different hues, then separated and dashed apart like delighted children immersed in a favorite game. There was underlying music that kept time with the undulating hues and shades of light.

"Hello?" Emma asked hesitantly. She was standing, which surprised her. There seemed to be no sickness in her body. Every part of her was whole and healthy.

She tried to explore her surroundings, but her legs wouldn't move. Suddenly, a chair appeared behind her, and an unseen hand pushed her into it.

"Okay...what is this? I take it you want to talk to me, so talk, dammit. Yell at me, scold me, then let me return to my life. I have my son now. I have my book now, which, by the way, is going to sell big. I don't need you and your riddles and enigmas. Let me go home."

She was met with silence. The music continued, the colors danced, and she was stuck in the chair.

"Hey! I'm talking to you. I told you I'm done with all this stuff!"

Willow appeared in front of her. She was as she always was, white, ethereal, with glowing flecks of gold dancing happily in her aura.

"Hello, Emma."

"Finally. Okay, Willow, here's the deal. I'm doing good. I'm not hurting anyone. I'm not misbehaving. So, why can't you guys just leave me alone? I've earned this. I've worked hard to get where I am. I'm going to enjoy all the success I know the future will hold."

"It's not too late to turn the tide," Willow uttered. Then she vanished.

"Oh, come on. Really? You brought me here to be more cryptic than usual?"

Next, Florence appeared. A portrait in grace and peace, she stood there looking down at Emma with soft eyes and a gentle smile.

"It's not too late to turn the tide," she whispered.

"Whaaatttt!" Emma screamed at the top of her lungs. What in the world does that mean? What is the point of any of you? Why won't you just go away?"

"Just turn the tide," Florence repeated. "It's not too late." With that, she was gone.

Emma struggled to move, fighting to stand up. She flailed her arms around wildly, fighting the unseen captors who were holding her against her will.

Suddenly, there was a whisper in her ear. It was Harold. "Turn the tide, Emma. It's not too late."

"Let me go, let me outta here. I don't want to be here; I don't want to see any of you. Get out of my way. Let me go, let me go," Emma kept screaming.

"We're only trying to help you, Emma," the nurse reassured her, holding her down while another nurse injected some medication into her IV. Much like walking out of a fog bank, Emma's hospital room slowly came into her view.

"This should make you feel better," the nurse cooed softly. "Your fever has finally broken. That's good news. You've turned a corner."

Emma looked over to see Adam at the window, looking tired, drawn, and overcome with worry. Her heart went out to him. Through it all, he'd been her rock. She loved him deeply.

She reached over and patted the dolphin necklace on the bedside table. It was her strength.

"What tide?" she whispered aloud.

"What was that?" one of the nurses asked.

"Nothing. Nothing," Emma said weakly, then went back to sleep.

Chapter 23

Three weeks to the day of Ryan's delivery, Adam and Emma returned home with their bundle of joy. Adam jumped out and ran around the car to take Ryan, who was sleeping, and helped Emma out of the car. When they got to the door, Adam couldn't seem to open it, the key wasn't working right.

"I'll go around to the back and come through and let you in," he told her.

"That's okay, I'll come with you."

"No. Just wait here. You're still not one hundred percent."

In a few minutes, the front door opened, and when Emma stepped in, a group of people jumped out everywhere with huge smiles on their faces. They all mouthed but didn't speak, 'Surprise.' Adam had faked the door thing to go in through the back and tell them Ryan was sleeping and not to shout.

A giant banner over the fireplace said, "Welcome Home and Congratulations." Below the printed words, in handwriting, it read, "On the baby and the book."

Emma giggled happily. Everyone she knew was in that room: her parents, Adam's parents, his six siblings, and their significant others, and, of course, Kyle and Andrea. But the face she zeroed in on was that of her brother, Don. He was standing in the back, smiling his silly, lopsided grin.

"Donnie," she cried happily. She trotted over to him and hugged him tightly with her free arm, the other being full of baby. "How long are you here for? How is Japan? Do you like it there? Do you have a girlfriend yet?"

"Hey, slow down. I've already forgotten the first question," he laughed.

Emma's dad walked up and took the sleeping baby from her arms. Ryan didn't even fuss. He just snuggled down into his grandpa's arms. Once the Corbells, both grandma and grandpa had their turn, the other set of grandparents got to hold him. Ryan behaved like he knew he was the star of the show. He would peek open his eyes, then fall back asleep, allowing himself to be loved on. He'd squish his little face up so cutely every time another person was holding him. It was quite the performance.

Emma hugged Don again and kept touching him. "I can't believe you're really here. Please tell me you're staying for a while this time. We need to go out, catch up, and spend some time together."

"Unfortunately, Sis, not this visit. I have to go back tonight. I was only here to receive a one-day special detail training, then right back, but I couldn't miss my baby sister's party. You're a mom, you have a baby, *and* you're an author. It's incredible. Congratulations. And Adam is so perfect. You're a lucky woman."

That I am. They only got to chat for less than twenty minutes when Don's driver came to pick him up. They promised to write a lot, and he would make calls when he could.

After he left, Andrea pulled Emma away and hugged her.

"I'm so glad you're okay, Em. You scared me to death. You are okay, right?"

"More than okay. I have my beautiful baby and my book...life doesn't get any better than that."

"And that handsome hunk of a husband of yours. Don't forget him. I don't know if anyone told you or not, but he never left the hospital. He was with Ryan the whole time, then back to you, then back to Ryan. He was a true hero."

"Right, right, of course, Adam. He's my rock," Emma smiled.

Glancing over at the kitchen table, she saw it was full of gifts spilling onto the floor.

"What's all this?" she asked Andrea, walking over to admire the display.

"Well, since you wouldn't let me give you a baby shower..."

"What wouldn't let you? I have no friends other than you. There was no one to invite," Emma laughed wryly.

"We could've asked your sisters-in-law, your mom, your mother-in-law, your agent."

"Nah, that wouldn't have been any fun. I don't know my in-laws really. We hardly ever socialize. I've been so busy with the book, then Adam with school, and now his new job. You know how it goes. The time just gets away. Besides, who needs more friends? I have you. That's enough for me."

"Okay. Sweet and a little weird, but I get it, I think. However, today you will have a baby shower with all your non-friends and love it," Andrea laughed. "All planned by yours truly."

Emma told her guests that she was going to slip away for a quick sec and take a hot shower in her own shower. She was dying to get into some comfortable clothes.

In the shower, as the hot water warmed her form, she closed her eyes and sighed deeply. She was happy. The future was bright. She had it all. She deserved it all.

A whisper started in her ear. She couldn't quite make out the words at first. Then, like the sound of a car from a distance, gaining speed and sounding louder, a voice screamed in her ear, "It's not too late to turn the tide. It's not too late to turn the tide. Hurry."

Emma jumped, grabbed her ear, and almost fell down as she darted out of the shower, trying to run from the assaulting words. They repeated themselves again and again, so loudly that she thought her eardrums would explode. Then, ever so slowly, the cacophony abated. She grabbed two towels and wrapped one around her body and one around her head. Wiping the steam from the mirror, she leaned in and looked closely at her face. The fearful reflection slowly turned into defiance.

"I'm not turning anything," she said firmly to the reflection. "I'm right where I want to be. I want *nothing* to change. I deserve this life. It's mine, and I'm going to keep it."

Once she was calm again, she rejoined the party. However, things had changed. Once again, she saw auras, but not on everyone. Three people, her mother and father, and Andrea's husband, Kyle, were noticeably absent from the aura. She had no idea what that meant, but it unnerved her.

Chapter 24

The next three months flew by. Ryan was a delight, although not quite as attached to Emma as she'd like him to be. His father's presence seemed to be the most calming influence, and his sweet little face would light up when Adam entered the room. When she asked his pediatrician about it, he assured her it was only temporary. He had bonded with Adam in those first few weeks when Emma was so sick, so it might take a bit for him to find the same safety in her. She didn't like it but understood it. As much as she tried not to, she considered Ryan *hers*. In her old life, she'd raised him without a father. This life gave him a dad, but crudely put, he was her possession.

As requested, Emma had gotten the second book to her agent and was now working on book three. She was struggling a bit with it. However, Ryan was taking up most of her time, and splitting her focus between him and her novels was getting more difficult.

Her agent was wonderful and completely understanding about it all. She said there was no rush, as the first book hadn't even come out yet. If that sold well, the next would follow in another six to eight months, so she had more than enough time to work her way through number three. Mabel just asked that she send chapters as she wrote them.

"So, when do we start the pre-release appearances and all that for the first book?" Emma asked.

"Soon. There is a glitch with the publisher. Nothing serious, just some technical stuff that is throwing the release date back a bit," Mable answered cautiously, not to upset her client.

"A bit? How long is a bit?"

"Maybe a couple of months, that's all."

"That's all? So now, instead of next spring, will it be next summer? That's just short of a year from now," Emma whined.

"Honey, that's the business. Nothing happens fast. Don't worry. It will all work out. Look at this this way: you'll have more time with your little cutie before you start traipsing around the country doing interviews and book signings."

"Sure," Emma said disappointedly. "Yeah, that's good...more time with Ryan."

"Believe me, when all this starts, you'll think a hurricane hit you. You'll be so busy, you'll forget your own name."

"Okay, Mabel. Thanks. I'll talk to you later."

Emma walked around the living room, thinking and trying to figure things out. None of this had started as early as she'd wanted. This time around, she'd planned to have Ryan at nineteen like she'd done in her last life and be a best-selling author by the age of twenty-two. The two coinciding this time around was already causing all kinds of problems. If it had gone her way, Ryan would have been three years old by the time her first book came out. They'd have had those years to become really close, and probably, she could have hired a nanny and taken him with her on her trips and appearances. It would have been so cute bringing him on television shows with her.

Now, she was stuck with an infant, a book a year away, and her twenty-seventh birthday in only two months. Maybe she shouldn't have stopped Adam from hitting her. Perhaps if she'd endured those eight months with him, she'd have *Brian,* not *Ryan,* and her plan would have come to fruition like she'd wanted. This baby was not really hers. He liked Adam better.

This streak of selfish thoughts continued for over an hour. She struggled mightily with them. It was as if there were two people inside of her—warriors on totally different sides of good and evil. There was the good Emma, who was kind and giving, and the other Emma, who was self-absorbed and had no care for anyone else. As if donning a robe, the bitter, angry Emma was beginning to cover the very skin of her kinder self.

Her pacing was interrupted by Ryan crying in his bassinet.

Emma looked down the hall towards Ryan's room. "Oh, shut up," Emma hollered, covering her ears. "I don't want to be bothered right now. Just go back to sleep, please."

Emma's voice immediately caught in her throat. "Oh my God, what is wrong with me?" She ran to Ryan's room and scooped him up, hugging him tightly. "Momma didn't mean it. I'm so sorry, little one. Momma is just having a bad day. You're my precious boy. My sunshine," she cooed. Ryan stopped crying and even gave her a little smile.

After feeding him and changing his clothes, Emma carried him around for the rest of the day, never putting him back in his bassinet. She held him while he slept and talked to him while he was awake. She did everything she needed to do with one hand. His beautiful little aura stayed pink the rest of the day. In her personal aura color palette, this color was the color of peace and happiness.

Maybe that was the tide I was supposed to turn. I hope that's what they were talking about. At least I caught myself. I don't know who that horrible woman was, so rigid and selfish, but I'm turning my back on her. "Hear that everybody?" Emma said out loud. "I'm turning it around. I'm back to my kinder self. I won't be selfish or impatient, I promise. It's still a good life, even if it is a little later than I wanted. That's all that counts, right?" Emma listened for a few minutes, hoping that she might hear Harold whisper in her ear that it was all okay. The only sound she heard was the gentle breathing of her beautiful son in her arms.

Chapter 25

Emma's birthday in November was a quiet affair. Adam planned a nice dinner, which he cooked himself. Kyle and Andrea were the only guests.

Five-month-old Ryan was the star of the evening. He cooed and smiled at everyone, charming them with his giggles and facial expressions. It was the perfect night. The only slight drawback to the evening was that Emma still could not see Kyle's aura. Andrea's was pink and happy, and Adam's was his usual blue and white, which was her symbol of strength and a caring soul. Kyle's lack of an aura troubled her, but she only let it do so momentarily. The night was too fantastic to worry and fret.

Adam gave Emma a beautiful gold charm bracelet. He'd added the first two charms—paired hearts representing him and Emma, and a tiny cradle denoting their beautiful baby boy. Andrea and Kyle gave Emma a beautifully expensive pen set. It was for 'all the books she would be signing,' they'd said. The night was perfect.

The next day, Emma continued living her *householder's life*. The one that Florence had explained to her. Doing this, she'd been told, was the basis for all good things that would then come to pass. After her fall down the rabbit hole of selfishness, self-absorption, and how she'd yelled at Ryan, there was a strict regimen to her routine. No way she would visit that horrible twin inside her that could behave that way. She'd even made up a song about it. It went, "I'm living a householder's life, free from tension and strife. I'm keeping on the path, controlling my wrath, and being a good little wife. Before you know it, I'll see all the good things coming to me. Yes, for this happy wife, a householder's life is the best thing that could ever be."

The ease of existence heading into Christmas was a true gift. She wrote, played with Ryan, and had lunches with Andrea at least two times a week. Her dad and mother had even been talking about a possible reconciliation.

Even though they'd been divorced for many years, their friendship remained intact. Initially, it was for Emma and Don. However, they discovered they still liked spending time together once Don was in the military and Emma was married. The best part of the holiday season was that Don would be home for a whole week at Christmas.

Christmas was fun, even though Ryan was much too young to understand the concept of Santa and gifts. He loved the lights, bright paper, and bows. They got him tons of toys for him to grow into and lots of cute outfits.

The three were sitting on the floor next to the tree when Adam got up and retrieved an envelope out of the desk drawer. It had a tiny little bow pasted on the top of it. He handed it to Emma.

"Another present? Adam, it's too much. You already got me so much."

"Okay, I'll take it back," Adam said in mock seriousness, reaching for the envelope.

"Not on your life," Emma giggled, holding up the envelope to the light. "It's small, like a check or maybe a gift certificate for a day at the spa....oooh, that would be nice. Perhaps it's the title to the new car you bought me. Is there a car out in the driveway with a bow on it," she laughed.

"It's better, and something I think you want even more."

Emma ripped the envelope open and read the letter inside. It said her book was back on track and would be released on April 20th, as originally planned. Emma was stunned. She read it over three times to be sure, then jumped up and ran around the room, laughing and squealing happily.

Emma hugged Adam and kissed him all over his face. "I'll take that to mean you're happier with that than a car," he laughed.

"Yes, yes, yes," Emma squealed, scooping up Ryan and dancing with him around the room. "You don't know it, little one, but your mom is about to be famous. Everyone will know who your mother is."

Ryan giggled delightedly as they did their bouncy, happy dance around the room.

"So, why didn't Mabel call me? Did she call you and just want you to relay the message?" Emma said, sitting back down, out of breath from her outburst and happy dance.

"She actually called two days ago. You and Ryan were out to lunch with Andrea. She was leaving for two weeks for the holidays and had just gotten the news. I told her I had the perfect way to let you know. She also wanted me to tell you she would call you right after New Year's. You two have a lot to plan out."

"I'm so excited I can barely breathe," Emma giggled, "but we have to get ready to go to Dad's for dinner. Mom and Don will be there too. This is absolutely the best Christmas ever."

Chapter 26

The new year started out at warp speed. The prerelease promotions began in February. The first of which she got to do from home as they were all on radio shows. She was connected by phone to the listeners, so they were easy to do.

In late February and early March, she began her television interview teases. It was two full weeks of every Good Morning show nationwide. There was Good Morning, America, Good Morning, Seattle, Good Morning, Philadelphia, and down the list. Then, she had some time off until the actual release date, after which she would make the next round of shows. These would include reappearances on the morning shows, plus other journalism news programs, which would take her into May. It was an exhausting schedule.

Emma was treated like a princess. Everywhere she went, she was taken by limousine. Mabel was by her side for every appearance. They did her makeup and told her how great she looked, how wonderful her book was, and how happy they were to meet her. It was pretty heady stuff.

They started the *after-the-book release* tour in her home state of California, then worked their way across the country, with the last stop being New York.

"Hey there, jailbait, I miss you," Adam said when he finally got a call through to her at her hotel.

"Oh, honey, I miss you both so much, too," Emma cooed. "I'm exhausted but happy. How is Ryan? Does he miss his momma?"

"Of course. I show him your picture every day and try to get him to watch you on the television shows. I don't think he quite gets that it's you on the screen. He fidgets and looks away until I turn the cartoons back on."

"Everyone's a critic," Emma laughed. "Hug him big for me. I'm so glad this is my last show of this round. I want to sleep in my own bed next to my husband and hug the cutest little boy in the world."

"So, what time are you getting in tomorrow? When should I pick you up at the airport?"

"Oh, sweetie, you don't have to pick me up; there'll be a limo there for me to take me home."

Adam was silent for a moment. He had the momentary feeling of dread, of being replaced and no longer needed. He shook it off.

"Okay, hon. You're the star, and you deserve the star treatment. Just give me the time you'll be home, and I'll have a nice meal waiting for you and a hot bath with bubbles at the ready. You've been gone almost half the month of May. I may forget what you look like," he chuckled.

"Well, take a lot of pictures of me when I'm there because I'll only be home for a couple of weeks, then off for the round of book signings. An author's life is not their own," she said in a comical wilting flower southern accent.

"And how long will the book signings take?" Adam asked, feeling a little frustrated.

"About two weeks, kinda like this show tour."

"But Ryan's first birthday is June 16th. You'll be home for that, right?"

"I'm sure I will. I'll check with Mabel."

"You'll *check* with Mabel? How about you *tell* Mabel your son's birthday is June 16th, and you have to be home for it. How about that?" Adam barked.

"Honey, don't be mad. I have to do what they say, or I won't be famous. I mean, my book won't do well. I don't want to miss this opportunity. I'm not going to say that I won't be there, but if I can't be, I mean, how awful is that? Not really terrible at all. He'll have other birthdays. When he's older, he won't even remember if I was at his first party or not. Look, I'll probably be there, so we're fighting over nothing. We'll talk more when I get home from this trip. Okay? I love you."

Adam didn't say another word, just slammed down the receiver.

Emma was stunned by his anger. Sure, they'd had fights over the years, as every couple does, but he was always the more level-headed of the two of them. He was the one who made the first move to end the argument and make a compromise. His nature was tender and understanding, and he almost always gave Emma her way. She may have changed his destiny, according to Florence, but it was certainly better than the man he was before she'd done so.

As she dressed for the show, she was worried. He'd never hung up on her or walked out on her or anything of the sort. But, she resigned herself to the fact that she could do nothing about it now. She'd see him tomorrow, and they'd talk it through then.

Mabel picked her up in the limo and they headed out for the final appearance. She never knew what show she'd be on until they arrived. There were so many she couldn't keep them straight in her head.

"Now, this last one is a biggy. This woman started her show several years ago and caught on quickly. Absolutely everyone loved her. She had over three million viewers who tuned into her show every day. An interview on her show is pure gold. Don't screw it up," Mabel joked. "Kidding. Kidding. You've been doing great everywhere. Just relax and have fun."

No one was there when they took her back to get her hair and makeup done. "Wait here," Mabel said. "I'll let them know you're here."

In a few minutes, the young makeup woman came in and turned Emma's chair around to look at her face. "Sorry, I'm late. Let's see...yep. You've got great skin. When I'm done," she smiled confidently, "you'll look like a movie star."

Emma kept looking at her. She seemed so familiar. But, more than likely, she looked like every other makeup person she'd sat in front of recently. They were all young, extremely talented, upbeat, and excellent at what they did.

Just as Emma jumped down from the chair, a woman appeared. She had headphones around her neck and a clipboard in her hand. Another carbon copy of all the other stage managers who'd ushered her to and from the green room and onto the stage.

"Hi, Mrs. Armstrong, I'm Felicia, the stage manager. I'm so excited to meet you. I can't wait to read your book. It just sounds so fabulous. Come on, let's get you to the green room."

Emma's face turned pale. She was sure that this Felicia was the same Felicia from when she was on that show in her other life when she'd saved that dog. She couldn't remember the name of it. Her mind started racing.

What if she recognizes me from that other show? What if she thinks I'm a fraud because I was old when she saw me last? Wait, she knew me as Emma Corbell, not Emma Armstrong. In that life I'd changed back to my maiden name after I divorced the old Adam. So, it's conceivable there could be an Emma Armstrong that strongly resembles a younger Emma Corbell. I mean, lots of people look similar. That's nothing new. Oh geez, this is awful. What am I going to do? What will I say?

Before she could answer her own questions, she was ushered out on stage. As before, Della walked to her, hugged her, and led her to the couch.

"Emma...may I call you Emma?" Della began.

"Of course."

"Emma, I can't tell you how excited I am to have you here. I've read your book, and I absolutely loved it. I just got notice that in the first week of sales you sold over 50,000 books. That's unheard of for a new author." The audience applauded.

"Oh, I didn't even know that. My agent hadn't told me that yet," Emma stammered.

So far, so good. She doesn't seem to recognize me. Breathe, Emma, just breathe.

The rest of the interview went much like the others, with Della asking her about her life, her family, and where she got the idea for her book. They talked about her next in the series as well.

Della read some of her favorite passages from the novel to great audience applause. She also told them the book would be on sale in the lobby. And with that, her fifteen minutes of air time was done. She finally let out a huge sigh when it was over. She could breathe again.

On the flight home, she thought about Adam. Her evil twin was shouting in her ear that he should stop being so selfish. Didn't she take a job to help put him through school? It was his turn to let her shine. Her kinder self argued that he was more generous with her than she'd ever been with him for the most part. Look at how he stayed at the hospital the whole time she was sick after she delivered Ryan. Her alter ego said that's just what he should have done. No heroism there. Her kind side argued it was above and beyond. Not many husbands would have been so devoted.

She looked out the window at the ground far below. Who would win the fight between the twins? She honestly had no idea.

Chapter 27

When Emma walked through the front door, the house was deadly quiet. There was no wonderful aroma of dinner wafting out from the kitchen. Ryan's room was empty. It was dark, so she couldn't imagine them being in the backyard, but she checked anyway. Opening the garage door, she found only her car, not Adam's.

She took her clothes out of her suitcase and threw them in the washing machine, then stepped into the shower. Her frustration rose as the warm pellets of water softly hit her body. How could he do this? What was this? Was it some kind of punishment because she dared to have a successful life? On and on the inner dialogue went. Her kinder thoughts and the apology she would make all became enveloped in the blackness of rising anger.

I'm somebody! He can't treat me like a maid...a housecleaner! Who does he think he is?

By the time she stepped out of the shower, she heard Adam and Ryan come in. Ryan was giggling at Adam making funny faces. He'd started barely walking, and his laughter was causing him to fall back on his bottom, which only made him laugh harder. It was adorable. But not to Emma. Her darker side had completely taken over. She felt slighted and ignored. She wouldn't let that stand.

"I see you guys had a wonderful time," she said, each word dripping with sarcasm.

"We did," Adam smiled, picking up Ryan and walking over to Emma, giving her a kiss on the cheek. "Welcome home. Ryan got a last-minute invitation for a play date, so since we weren't exactly sure when you'd be home, we decided to have a little fun. I'll go start dinner now."

He stood there a minute waiting for Emma to take Ryan from him, but she didn't move, simply glared at him. Without a beat, not wanting to upset

Ryan, he lifted him over his head, causing him to giggle. "Come on, buddy, let's go make Mom dinner. I need your help. With that, the two disappeared into the kitchen.

Emma didn't realize it immediately, but her hands were now tightly coiled into fists. She couldn't move. Her breath came in short gasps. The anger she felt rippled through every muscle in her body. Inside, however, the battle raged on. It was as if she couldn't take control. Couldn't stop the fire inside. She felt like she had multiple personalities, like Sally Field in the movie Sybil. That movie was far away yet in this timeline, but her older self remembered its impact on her when she saw it. Something was happening to her beyond her control.

Calm down, Emma, she scolded herself. Where is all this selfishness and hate coming from? Florence said that our destiny is created in the present through thought and action. So, have I created this monster inside me who will stop at nothing to be famous? Is this horrible person I seem to be evolving into, what my destiny is? Sure, I've been snotty with Willow and Florence, but...but what? Emma, you've been nothing but awful since you got here. Everything revolves around you. You only give to others if it doesn't interfere with what you want. Instead of creating your new life with joy and happiness, it feels like your new life is creating you.

Emma walked to the couch and sat down. She grabbed ahold of the dolphin on her necklace and closed her eyes. Immediately, she was transported to a very dark place. She could barely see anything, like the last vestige of light before sunset. It was infinite, no walls, no form. From a distance, an undulating, large piece of formless matter approached her. It began throwing pieces of itself onto her. The blobs hit her legs and arms. She quickly peeled them off. The assault continued. With each hit, she could feel the angst and anger they held. This was her alternate self trying to take control. She called for Florence. She screamed for Willow. No one appeared. Stamping her foot like a two-year-old child, Emma shouted, "Stop it."

Adam came running from the kitchen? "What happened. Are you okay?"

Emma startled and opened her eyes. "Um...yes, yes...sorry. It was a spider. You know how much I hate spiders. It kept running away, so I stomped on it," Emma stuttered. "Oh, hey...could you use another hand with dinner?" she asked sweetly.

"Sure. The more the merrier," Adam said, heading back into the kitchen. He didn't hug or kiss her on the cheek or do anything remotely tender. She knew he was still angry but would never let it show in front of Ryan. It would seem she not only had to fight her own demons, but she had a big fight coming with Adam.

Chapter 28

After dinner, the two played with Ryan. Emma gave him a bath and then tucked him into bed. He was out in minutes. She kissed his head, and her heart swelled as she stared at his angelic face. *I was a better mother the first time around, wasn't I, little one? I promise you, I'm turning over a new leaf. You and your dad are going to be my first priority.*

Adam had gone to put the dishes into the dishwasher. Emma poured herself a cup of coffee and sat at the kitchen table.

"Can we talk?"

"Sure. Speak," Adam replied, continuing on with his task.

"Not like that. Come one. Please, Adam. Sit down. I'm sorry. I'm confused and torn. You have to help me figure it all out."

Adam closed the dishwasher and turned to look at her. "I can't see anything at all to figure out. You either want to be a mother and be here for him, or you want to be a famous author, simple as that."

"That's not fair," Emma protested. "I've been here. I took care of him when he had colic, and I rocked him when he was teething. I've been a good mother."

"Yes, you did those things right up until you had a published book. Do you realize that out of the last three months, you've been gone for over six weeks of it? If you can't do the math, that's half the time. You can add another two weeks or so to for your next tour. That's not mothering, that's dropping by."

"Adam, be fair. This won't last for much longer. The book is selling like gangbusters, so I won't have to do so much promotion."

"Until the next one comes out. What then? Another birthday missed? Maybe you miss his first day of school? When is it *your* choice to go on these promotional tours? When will Mabel not be making decisions for you?"

"Adam, please. I thought you were supportive of my career?"

"I was and still am. I never said a word about your promotional tours until it looked like you might miss our son's first birthday. There has to be a balance."

Emma knew he was right. She simply didn't know how to do it. The thing was, Mabel had told her on the plane that she, indeed, would miss Ryan's birthday. She'd been invited to appear on the Late Show with David Blake on June 16th. How could she tell him that? It was the biggest late-night show there was, and they never asked first-time authors to appear. The fast rise of her book had created such buzz they begged to have her on the show. She just couldn't tell him that. Not now.

"Honey. I love you so much. I hate it when we fight," Emma said, getting up from the table and taking his hand. "Look, as of right now, I'm due back on June 15th, so I'll be here. I promise," she lied. It wasn't exactly a lie. She knew the show was taped early in the day to be aired that night, so she was going to beg and plead for Mabel to get them to let her tape her segment on the 15th and get her home in time for Ryan's birthday.

Adam looked deep into her eyes, and his heart began to melt. His love for her was infinite and true. He could deny her nothing. Fighting with her always broke his heart. He pulled her to him and gave her a soft, gentle kiss.

"I hate fighting with you as well. I just got so upset when you said you would even *consider* missing his birthday...I don't know, I went sorta nuts. You are a good mom; I know that. You're going to be here, and that's what counts. From now on, if something else comes up I'll wait until we can discuss it before I go all crazy."

"My hero," Emma smiled up at him. "Want some popcorn? I feel like a movie." Emma laughed, digging in the cupboard for a pot to pop it in.

When Emma went to sleep, she snuggled up tightly against Adam. He was her safety, her home. However, she still had plenty of *fixes* to do to make everything right. One was Mabel and the show, but the most important was finding a way to summon Florence. She had to find out why everything was so bonkers in her life. How could she rid herself of this mirror-image evil twin she seemed to be carrying around?

The following day, as soon as Adam left for work, Emma became a woman on a mission. She called Mabel and implored her to get the David

Blake show rescheduled. Mabel was not hopeful but would try. However, she was firm in the fact that if she couldn't change it, Emma would have to appear. It was imperative for her career. It was not a happy thought, but she told Mabel that if anyone could do it, she could.

"Flattery will get you nowhere," Mabel laughed.

"Maybe not with you, but how about Mr. Blake? Tell him how great he is, how fabulous an entertainer he is, and all that. Does he have kids? If he does, he'll understand for sure."

"That's a good question. I actually don't know. I hate to admit it, but I don't watch his show. Too late for me. I'm old and fall asleep early," Mabel laughed.

"You're not old," Emma protested, remembering that Mabel right now was the age she was when she popped into this weird, sometimes enchanted, life she was now living.

"You're mature, wise, and absolutely gorgeous for your age." Emma really meant that. Mabel was thin, walked every day, kept herself in great shape, and had the magical ability to look elegant at all times.

"Okay. Maybe flattery works a little bit," Mabel laughed. "Let me see what I can do."

Emma then grabbed Ryan, put him in his stroller, and headed for the park where she'd first seen Florence. She wasn't there. Emma waited, playing with Ryan and keeping her eyes peeled for any signs of the older woman. After a couple of hours, Ryan was getting fussy. She figured she'd try again tomorrow.

Tomorrow, the next day, and the next day also proved fruitless. The only good news in that entire week was that David Blake had agreed to have her on the show a day early to accommodate her son's birthday. He did, indeed, have children and was more than happy to oblige.

When she told Adam about her upcoming appearance on the David Blake Show and that she would be home for Ryan's birthday, he was elated. He loved the show and couldn't wait to see his wife sitting on the couch beside one of his favorite talk show hosts.

Emma had now beaten down the obstacles in her path but was still fighting herself. Her other self felt it was ridiculous to go to such lengths to appease Adam. Her alter ego had something negative to say about every decision she made or thought she had. The battle was wearing her down. She needed help. She needed Florence. If that didn't happen soon, she felt as if she would literally disappear.

Chapter 29

On the day of the David Blake taping, Emma was tired and anxious to get home. Standing in the wings waiting to be announced, she felt a jolt, almost like someone had slapped her hard on the back. She turned around to see who might have hit her. No one was there. She suddenly felt dizzy, like she was going to faint. The stage manager gave her a little shove, pointing to the stage, indicating that it was time for her to enter. As soon as the lights hit her and the applause started, she straightened up and strode out to the desk, where David greeted her, hugged her, and pointed to the couch.

She looked out to the crowd, which was clapping wildly.

"Well, you're a hit before you even say a word," David said.

"It would seem so," Emma answered.

"I can't tell you how happy I am to have you here."

"You're lucky to have me," Emma said arrogantly. Catching herself, she said, "I mean, I'm lucky to be here. I'm grateful to be here... that's what I mean; I'm grateful to you for having me on."

"Ah. A little nervous, I see. It's okay. We're all friends here. Now, let's talk about your book. You've made quite the impact for a first-time author."

"It's not as unexpected as you make it sound. I'm good, so why wouldn't people want to read my book?" Emma was horrified but couldn't seem to control her tongue. She couldn't say the words *she* wanted to say. She was an observer in her own body.

"Well, yes, you are good," David stammered, already regretting he'd agreed to this interview. "But, as you know, it often takes a new author years to become popular. You must live under a lucky star," he chuckled.

"Perhaps. I guess mine just shines brighter than most," Emma smiled. Inside, Emma was fighting tooth and nail to stop this.

By the end of the interview, Emma was able to regain control.

"I'm so sorry, Mr. Blake. You're right. I'm so nervous. I don't know what I'm saying. Thank you so much for having me, and I want to thank everyone for making my dream come true. Thank you for reading my book, and thank you for your support. Oh, and can I say hi to my son Ryan, who will be one year old tomorrow? I can't wait to get home to him. Hi baby, see you soon."

"Well, we all wish Ryan the happiest of birthdays," David said, relieved that the segment was over. He didn't know who the nut-job was sitting next to him, but he would never have her on his show again.

"Thanks again for coming, Emma. Now everybody get out there and read her book. I guarantee you'll like it. We'll be back after a word from our sponsor."

When they cut away, David shook her hand weakly, thanked her, and walked off the stage.

Mabel didn't speak to her until they got into the limousine.

"You're lucky to have me? What the hell was that?" Mabel spit out angrily.

"I'm so, so sorry, Mabel. I don't know what happened? None of that was what I was trying to say. Except for the end part. I was nervous...I...I... I'm just a mess," Emma said, tears filling her eyes.

Mabel sighed deeply. "Okay. Okay. Stop that. I'll fix it. We've had a pretty busy schedule lately. We won't be doing anything for a while now, so get some rest...please."

When they returned to the hotel, Mabel said she was tired and would have dinner in her room. That had never happened before. On the trips, they'd always had dinner together. She pretty much resigned herself to the fact that Mabel and the publisher would probably drop her, the second book would never get released, and her career was over.

In her hotel room, she couldn't watch the show. It was too humiliating. Now tomorrow, oh goody, she got to fly home for Ryan's birthday and watch everyone look at her sideways after having seen tonight's airing. Probably everyone would say they hadn't seen it to protect her feelings. That would even be worse. Well, at least she'd be home and could stay in her bed for the rest of her life.

She felt nauseous when she exited the limo in front of her house. Her humiliation had not diminished overnight. She took a deep breath and unlocked the front door. Everyone was in the backyard. Some of the neighbors with kids Ryan's age were there, her folks were there, and apparently as a couple...like together, together, and Andrea and Kyle of course. *Hail, hail the gangs all here*, she thought as she walked through the sliding glass door.

"Where's my birthday boy?" she said, slapping a smile on her face. Ryan's eyes lit up when he saw his mother. He did his best to run to her, but he still wasn't steady on his feet as he had just started learning to walk. Adam picked him up and flew him into his mother's arms. She gave him a gazillion birthday kisses and tickled his neck, delighting in his peals of laughter.

Adam hugged her and kissed her hello. It wasn't obvious what he thought about her appearance last night. She walked over to the group, who immediately started applauding. She stood there quizzically, watching their faces. Applause? Really?

"We're so lucky to have you here," Andrea laughed. "Yes, blessed are we."

"It's so great to have someone as *good* as you join us," Emma's dad teased.

"Oh, come on guys, I'm embarrassed enough," Emma said, hanging her head.

"Are you kidding me? That was the best thing I've ever seen. I have never laughed so hard in my life. You were precious."

"That's not exactly the word I would use," Emma chuckled.

"Honey, honey," Adam said, putting his arm around her. "You were exhausted and nervous. I'm sure everybody knew when you said they were so lucky to have you there; you meant you *felt* lucky to be there. After you explained it at the end, I'm sure they all empathized with you. You're young, first book, national spotlight... I'll bet it only made people love you more. If not, then they're idiots."

"Then David Blake must be an idiot. He didn't even say a word to me after the segment ended; he just walked off the stage."

"Then screw him," Andrea announced. "Who needs him? We'll boycott his show. I know people." Everyone laughed.

That was probably the happiest moment Emma had experienced since she'd accidentally fallen into this bad version of the Wizard of Oz. These wonderful people loved her. They would protect her no matter what. Their care and devotion was unconditional. These were her lucky stars. Even as she thought that she could feel the more profound stirring inside her, her tormentor wasn't on board with all this love and emotional stuff. She didn't know how she would do it, but her inner evil twin had to go.

Chapter 30

She had the next day all to herself. Adam was at work, and Grandma and Grandpa Corbell were taking Ryan to the beach for the day. Seeing her parents together again after all these years seemed so odd. They appeared to be happy, and she was pleased for them. She'd asked if they would remarry, but they'd said, 'if they felt the need to,' they might. They still had separate homes, but apparently, her father was spending most of his time at her mom's house—the house they'd bought together, the home she'd grown up in.

Emma had a different idea of how to summon Florence—her dolphin. It had worked with that inner self battle she'd had. It was better than standing in the park and hollering her name.

She lit three candles and placed them on the coffee table. She wrapped a blanket around her and sat cross-legged in the middle of the couch. With both hands, she held on to her dolphin necklace.

"Florrreeence...Florence," she repeated softly in a ghostly-sounding tone. "Florrreence, I need to see you. Please come to me. Pleease show yourself."

"Girl! What the hell are you doing? Open your damned eyes," Florence commanded, standing right in front of her.

Emma jumped up, almost knocking over the candles, which she promptly blew out.

"Oh my God, it worked! You're here."

"What worked? You didn't conjure me from the great beyond. You're a damned fool if you believe that hocus pocus brought me here!" Florence exclaimed loudly.

"Cussing? Yelling? What's wrong with you?" Emma said, a little unsure of exactly who was standing in front of her. This certainly wasn't the serene woman she'd met in the park. A bit unnerved, she scampered around Florence and headed for the kitchen.

"Maybe you'd like some tea, I'll make you some. Perhaps that will make you feel better."

"I feel just fine. I'm just damned frustrated," Florence said, following Emma into the kitchen. Well, okay, tea sounds lovely. You got any ice cream? You know how much I like ice cream." She plopped herself into one of the chairs at the kitchen table.

"Uh...sure, chocolate, okay?" Emma was completely confused by this new version of Florence.

"Good. That's good. Chocolate is good."

Once Emma had poured the tea, she sat down and watched Florence eat. After a few minutes of silence, she couldn't stand it anymore. "So, can you help me or not?"

"Help you what, dear?" Florence said, taking her last bite. "Oh, you mean wave a magic wand and fix everything you've screwed up? Nope. Can't do that."

"Then why did you come?"

"To explain things. You've gotten yourself into quite a pickle. Because of your accidental visit here, you've thrown everything into chaos. Nothing is happening the way it's supposed to happen."

"Then how exactly *should* it happen? You told me there are other time travelers. What makes me so different...and so challenging?"

"I swear, girl, sometimes I think you don't understand the English language. The...way...you...came...in," Florence said slowly, enunciating each word. "It was accidental, not planned, not approved, not sanctioned."

"Not approved?"

"If everyone who wished to come back and play with their past were allowed to, it would be total bedlam. I don't have time to explain the hierarchy of it all; let's just concentrate on your current problem." Florence leaned in close to Emma's face.

"You dropped in and immediately dug your heels in, determined to become a star. You weren't going to make a few minor decisions like most people do. Oh no, you were going to *force* your outcome."

"Yeah...okay, I kinda did that," Emma muttered, a little ashamed.

"Remember when we talked about decisions and the ripple effect of choices made? Well, you never let your ripples play out. You kept interrupting them. It started on day one when you talked Andrea into going to the beach. That's not what you did on that day in your previous life. First ripple interrupted. That would have been okay, but then you wouldn't leave well enough alone."

"Now, wait a minute. Are you saying that just because Andrea and I went to the beach on a different day, this awful, mean, evil side of me got created? That doesn't make any sense," Emma argued.

"The first thing you must understand is that everyone has an evil side. So, you're not two people or whatever it is you have in your brain. The next thing you need to get through your head is the nature of choices. Each choice opens up a path. Each path presents endless possibilities. As you travel down these roads, you zig or zag, which opens more doors. But, when you step on that road created by that intention, all of you has to change to accommodate the new goal. Get it?"

"Now I get it less, but continue."

"Your *evil* twin, as you call her, is simply your vehicle to get you to your desires."

"But I don't want her!" Emma shouted. "I hate her!"

"Well, unfortunately, she came into being the moment you started forcing things, shoving things into place as you needed them to be—barking orders at Adam regarding how his education schedule would be, not breastfeeding because it would be a drag on your appearances. She isn't your *evil twin*; she's you—the evolving you that your choices have created."

"But, I went to work so Adam could go to school. That was a nice thing to do," Emma argued.

"True that, however, the decision made was an edict coming *from you*, not a *discussion*. You were not open to any other solution other than your own. That's why your son took many years to arrive. It's a new life. The ripple was altered. Your personal timeline has been changed. Like a hurricane whipping the ocean into a raging sea, you are changing, becoming this more selfish, greedy person you alone have created. This persona has the capability to bring you the things you seek. But at what cost? She has great power."

"But," Emma protested.

"Look. When I asked for chocolate ice cream, you brought me chocolate ice cream, not chocolate with vanilla ribbons running through it. Chocolate is chocolate. It contains certain ingredients that make it that. It can be no other."

"Wait just a damned minute. I don't need to be all mean and insulting in order to be famous. So why is this other me so hateful and rigid?"

"Apparently, you do. Your book was written when you had your memory lapse. Guess who wrote it? Brash Emma."

Emma gasped loudly.

"Approach and intention are everything," Florence continued. "You set your intentions through your initial approach; now you are riding the train you got on from your first timeline alteration. It's just the way it works."

Emma jumped out of her chair angrily. "Will you *please* stop talking like that? I never understand what you mean. These riddles only confuse me. Can't you just say, "Emma, do this or that, and everything will be okay?""

"Define okay," Florence responded.

"Okay. I mean good...pleasant. I'm famous, have a wonderful son and husband, and I just want to live a good life."

"Ah...I see...you want perfect," Florence chuckled.

"Well, not perfect exactly," Emma stuttered. "Just not missing time, or insulting people, or any of the other weird things that have been happening. I don't want to visit any more mystic places where talking heads speak to me. No more people whispering in my ear, no more color stupidity that I'm supposed to know what to do with. I just want to be a famous author. Is that too much to ask?"

"Not at all. However, all of this is your creation. The reason you are having this struggle is, again, because of the way you came in. Mostly, when people travel back in time, they merge into their new chosen selves and continue on. It's like coffee being poured into a cup where the sugar has already been added—the sugar disappears completely, becoming one with the hot liquid. Would it be easier to understand if I said you were being taken up by the mother ship?" Florence laughed at her own joke.

"Listen, old woman," Emma shouted, slapping her hand on the table. "This isn't a joke! It's my life! You and nobody like you is going to take away my life, my book fame, or anything else from me. Got that?"

"And there she is," Florence responded quietly.

Emma's head was spinning. The sentence, "brash Emma wrote the book," had really galled her. Florence was right. She indeed felt like there were two of her, and the kinder her was losing ground fast.

Emma calmed a little. "If I understand this right, I'm still at a point where I can choose to be the nicer version of myself, right?"

"Correct."

"But this nicer version of me may not be a famous author, right?"

"Also correct. There is no way to tell."

"But, you say *brash Emma* wrote the book. How can I go back and erase those memory-lapse years and write the book myself? I know, I'll just blink and snap and go back a bit and fix that part. Then continue on as nice me and have everything I was hoping for."

"As has been your trait since arriving, you don't listen. We had the discussion about the whole *blink-and-snap* thing. That is not how you got here! The blink and snap that Willow was talking about was, and I'll repeat it verbatim, 'In the blink of an eye and the snap of a finger, you have the power to change anything you want to about your life.' *Your life in that moment,* not your past life!" Florence was all but shouting now.

Emma pushed her chair back a bit, finding herself a bit frightened of Florence at this point. Her anger carried with it a powerful energy shift. She was sure she could knock her off the chair with her eyes if she wanted to. She was afraid to speak or ask any more questions. But she had to know what to do.

"Please, Florence," Emma began softly. "I get it now. I somehow appeared here, and now I've screwed it up by being so selfish, thus creating a bad side, or giving power to *my bad* side, or whatever it was you said. But how do I get rid of it, tame it, or at least stop it from ruining everything?"

Florence inhaled deeply, letting out a long, slow breath, shaking her head. She raised her hand and snapped her fingers, and Emma's book appeared on the table before them. She pointed to it.

"This. Are you willing to give up this?" Florence asked.

Emma recoiled in horror as if she was suddenly seeing zombies in her kitchen.

"No! That's why I came here, or dropped in here, or whatever it was I did. Being an author is my dream. Why can't you understand that I just want to control the meaner side of me? That's it."

"I do understand it...perfectly. It is you who does not understand. We keep telling you to use the colors as they are your guideposts; they can tell you where you are needed. Once you remember where your true power lies, it will all be over."

"What will be over? I'll be over? I go back to my old wrinkled, frightened-of-the-world sixty-year-old self? Thanks, but no thanks."

Emma was getting frantic. She would never go back there. Florence remained silent, simply looking into Emma's eyes sadly. Suddenly, there was a pounding on the front door.

"Emma! Emma!" A panicky-sounding Andrea yelled. "Open the door! Emma!"

Emma raced to open it. As soon as she turned the handle, Andrea flew inside.

"You've got to help me. Kyle and I had a huge fight. I think he's gonna leave me." She stopped momentarily, then started to head for the kitchen. "I need a drink. Got any alcohol?"

Emma chased after her. "Wait...Andrea...wait, as you can see, I have compa..."

"Have what?" Andrea asked as she looked through the cabinets for a glass.

"Uh...nothing," Emma said confused. The room was empty. Florence was gone.

Chapter 31

Emma was less than pleased at the interruption. It was all she could do to be civil to Andrea, and was not entirely successful.

"So, what is it? Did you put the cap on the toothpaste wrong or something?" Emma's words dripped with sarcasm.

"Wow... that's harsh. How often do I come to you with my problems? How often do I even have anything close to a crisis, as compared to you, who seems to have them every day?" Andrea shot back.

"So, you're going to turn this into a fight with me? Is that it?" Emma spit out, her eyes turning dark. She could see Andrea's aura change from the muddy red it was when she entered, indicating her fear, to bright red.

"What the hell, Emma? Who are you right now? If you want a fight, I'll give you one, but you'll lose," Andrea shouted.

Andrea's words stopped Emma in her tracks. Who *was* she right now? She certainly wasn't being the friend Andrea had known all her life. She sat still for a second, desperately wanting to tell her longtime confidante what was happening to her—desperately wanted to tell her she was from the future. Her mind wrestled with the idea, but not knowing the ramifications of revealing such a thing, she was worried it could possibly create some horrible disaster of plague and pestilence in Andrea's life. Her head ached from the fear of it all.

"I'm sorry, Andrea. Please forgive me. I don't know what's happening to me lately. The book stuff and my disaster on that one show... I'm, I'm just a mess. Please, tell me what happened."

Andrea had set two glasses on the table and put a bottle of wine in between. She'd removed the two tea cups still on the table and poured herself a glass. She held the bottle over Emma's glass without putting anything in it. Emma nodded yes, so she filled it up as well.

"Okay. We fought because I told him I didn't want children."

"But, I thought you guys talked about that before you were married."

"We did. Now he says he thought it was just a *phase* I was going through back then and would 'get over it.' Andrea said in disbelief. "Can you imagine that? How in the world could he think that? Having or not having kids is a big deal. Did he think I just, on a lark, said, 'Oh yeah, no kids for me, tra la la,' then 'oops, changed my mind?'"

"Yeah, that is pretty weird," was all Emma said.

"So, now, he's threatening to leave me. He wants kids. What the hell do I do?" Andrea's voice cracked as the tears began to flow. "I can't lose him."

Emma bit her tongue. Unless she'd somehow changed Andrea's destiny, she was indeed going to lose Kyle. She knew from her past life that Andrea would be a widow when she was forty-five. So, unless she'd already tinkered with Andrea's future somehow, Kyle was not going to leave her, at this point at least. She would be there when he passed away.

Emma got up, took both their glasses to the sink, and poured the wine out.

"Hey! I wasn't finished with that." Andrea protested.

"You are now. Rather than sitting here getting plastered, let's take a long walk. We need clear heads to figure this out."

Andrea acquiesced, and the two headed out. Emma's heart started beating wildly in her chest as they reached the park. There on the bench sat Florence.

"Can you wait here a sec? I see a friend that I want to quickly go say hi to?" Emma asked.

Andrea looked around. "Where?"

"Over there." Emma pointed to the bench, but when she looked again, Florence had disappeared. "But where did she... that's odd," she said in disappointment. "Huh...well, guess my eyes are playing tricks on me," she said with a small laugh. "Must be the sun in my eyes. As usual, I forgot my sunglasses." Emma hoped that seeing her, albeit briefly, meant she planned to return when Andrea left. She needed to get this conversation over with quickly.

"Let's just stop here, sit on the grass, figure this out, then you can go home," Emma rattled off quickly.

"Talk about the bum's rush. You got a boyfriend on the side I don't know about that you need to get to?"

"Don't be silly," Emma countered. "I just want you to get back to Kyle as soon as possible so you two can work this out, that's all."

By the time an hour had passed, Emma was fidgety and anxious. She kept changing positions, standing up, sitting down, and looking around, hoping to spot Florence again. During most of Andrea's conversation, she'd barely heard a word. For Andrea's part, she was in tears, alternating between fear and anger, and ultimately couldn't see any solution for this impasse.

Emma couldn't stand it any longer. Disdain for the entire conversation and the silliness of all it, overtook her.

"So, that's it. You don't want kids, he does. There's no coming together on that. I think you just need to start divorce proceedings now and cut the cord before it gets any more painful," Emma blurted out.

Andrea felt like she'd been slapped in the face. She couldn't believe the brutality of that statement. She was at a loss to even reply. Grabbing her purse, she ran out of the park and headed towards Emma's house to get her car.

Emma jumped up but didn't chase after her. "Come on, Andie. You know it's the truth. Don't be that way. There *are* no other answers." She kept shouting as Andrea faded from sight.

Then, like an old, demented woman, Emma hung her head and mumbled to herself as she left the park and headed for home. "People. Sheesh. That's what you get for having friends. Why? Why have them? They'll always disappoint. But, money, fame... that's the ticket. And probably Ryan and Adam. Yeah, maybe keep them."

Chapter 32

The next morning, Saturday, Emma stumbled out of bed after a fitful night's sleep and a slew of bad dreams. She brushed her teeth but didn't hear Ryan awake yet, so she made a quick cup of coffee. Letting Adam sleep in, she sat on the back porch and sipped her brew.

Her thoughts were immediately of her dilemma. *If I'm understanding what Florence said correctly, because of my tunnel vision and my everything-for-me desires, I've created this horribly selfish new version of myself. And, to add insult to injury, that is apparently the side that has made me successful. I still don't understand why I can't just be the nice me and have it all. What is the purpose of this? The way Florence makes it sound, it's inevitable. Well, unless I do the color crap and find my power or whatever all that gibberish is.*

"Dammit!" Emma whispered out loud as she paced around the backyard, trying to find some logic in any of this.

"This is so confusing. Is it because I'm a 60-year-old woman in a thirty-year-old body that I'm apparently only mediocre? Is my brain that wilted and weak? Is that why I can't maintain an equilibrium? There has to be an answer. I have to find Florence again. She said this was different from other time travelers, whatever the heck that means. I've got to force her to give me more answers."

As she headed back towards the house, she picked up one of Ryan's picture books that was lying on the small table just outside the door. "Books! That's it...books! There must be books written by masters and sages that would give me an answer. I'll wait until Adam wakes up and can take care of Ryan; then, I'll spend the day at the library."

This newest answer gave her a lift. At least it was some sort of plan of attack. It gave her hope. Walking back inside and putting her cup in the sink, she headed to Ryan's room.

He's sure sleeping a long time this morning. My parents must have really tuckered him out. Apparently, all day at the beach with grandma and grandpa equals rest for momma when baby conks out.

She gasped when she entered Ryan's room and peeked over the railing of his crib. He wasn't there. The crib was empty; it looked like he'd never been in there. She screamed loudly. On autopilot, she ran to the closet and flung open the door as if there were any possibility he could have left his crib. She dashed to the bathroom, frantically searched the backyard, and darted through the front door, hollering for Adam.

"Adam! Adam!" She screamed at the top of her lungs. He was already up and running towards her, awakened by her initial scream from Ryan's room.

"What? What is it?" he said, stopping her movement so she could focus on him. "Honey, what's wrong?" His heart was beating wildly in his chest. He'd never seen her this way.

"Ryan! Ryan! Ryan!" she screamed over and over again, sobbing hysterically, gasping for air.

"Is he sick? Did your parent call? Is something wrong with him?"

"No, they didn't call!" she answered, confused by the question. Why would they call? How would they know?"

"Emma, you're not making any sense. What's wrong with Ryan?"

"He's gone! Someone took him. Someone came and took him away. It's all my fault! It's all my fault!" Emma began running from room to room again, with Adam right behind her.

"Call the police, Adam! Call the police," Emma ordered.

Adam finally caught up with her and grabbed her, pulling her to him and holding her still.

"Sweetheart, it's okay. Honey, did you forget? You called your parents last night and asked if they could keep him overnight because you weren't feeling well. They were more than happy to do so. They said they'd bring him back today in the late morning or early afternoon. Remember?"

Emma was panting so hard in her hysterical state—hyperventilating. She was finding it hard to stay conscious. She kept looking up at Adam, but his words felt far away and muffled.

"Come on, sit down, let me get you some water," Adam said, guiding her to the couch. He quickly returned and handed her the glass. She drank it slowly and then tried to slow her breathing.

"I don't remember that Adam. I don't remember talking to them. Why, Adam? Why don't I remember?" She was calmer, but the terror of her blackout kept her nerves firing frantically. What did this mean? This wasn't like her other memory lapses that lasted years and were returned to her. This was new. This was short. For a few hours, her other self was in total control. What if, during that time, she'd decided to hurt Ryan? Florence said that the more brash Emma was not as fond of Ryan. Was she disappearing? Would she soon cease to exist, and the only one left would be her awful creation? She began sobbing so hard it made her gag. She ran to the bathroom and threw up.

Like a zombie, she walked back into the living room. She was in shock. Not as Adam assumed, from the trauma of it all, but at the realization that when her stronger personality took over control, all her memories, all her life up to her sixty years of existence, would be gone. It suddenly made perfect sense to her. That was the way it had to be. Survival of the fittest. Like someone who had just put on their glasses and could finally read the blurry words on the page, she was seeing everything clearly now. Her insisted upon selfishness birthed a dark soul to drive the engine. In her mind, she was figuratively dying.

As she sat on the couch, unmoving, she could hear Adam on the phone. He'd called Andrea, hoping she would come over and help to calm Emma.

"She said what to you?" Adam exclaimed, shocked.

He listened as Andrea explained Emma's harsh words from the day before.

"I'm sure she didn't mean it. She's been off lately. I think she's just so tired and upset about her appearance on the David Blake show. She's being pulled in too many different directions. You know, trying to be a mom, a wife, a famous author...you understand. Please, please come over."

Andrea, against her better judgment, decided to put her hurt feelings aside for the moment.

"Do you think you could eat something?" Adam asked Emma when he hung up the phone. "I'll make you some eggs and toast. That should help."

She didn't answer and seemed oblivious to him being present at all.

I'll have myself committed, Emma thought to herself. *If my body is confined, then so too will be this awful, evil woman inside me. No more harm will come to anyone. If there is no one for me to insult and no way to cause mayhem on book tours and such, maybe that side of me will shrink like the wicked witch in The Wizard of Oz when they poured water on her.* That image made Emma smile for a moment.

Suddenly, she heard a loud, booming voice, sounding like an announcer at a football game. "You'll do no such thing!" it said. The room filled with fog, obscuring everything except for a lone bright light in the middle. The light had no form but was pulsating rhythmically and throwing flecks of gold from its center.

"What?" Emma's voice was almost a whisper. She peered into the mist, trying to see who had spoken. "Florence? Is that you? Willow?"

The brilliant white light took form. It was indeed Willow, much to Emma's amazement, standing before her. She smiled and felt great relief. Emma had convinced herself that Willow was so angry with her that she'd rain down locusts and famine on her rather than ever speak to her again.

"Emma. Don't give up. You can turn the tide. You are so close. Use the colors. Don't just name them; engage them, talk to them. Those are your weapons. It's not too late to turn the tide."

Just then, a threatening midnight black fog began swirling around Willow, poking at the white blanket of mist surrounding her. The older woman simply held up her hand. Then, like a baseball player swinging mightily and connecting with the orb in front of them, the black emanation was struck, causing it to disappear completely.

"Once you remember where your true power lies, it will all be over." With that, she was gone, and the room came back into view.

Ha! Emma thought. *One has to 'have' power to locate it. It's already over for me.*

Chapter 33

It took Andrea a couple of hours to show up. Even though she was concerned for her friend, the words Emma had spoken still stung. As soon as Emma opened the door, she fairly knocked Andrea over, hugging her tightly.

"I'm so sorry. I didn't mean any of it. Whatever I said. I don't remember it. Did Adam tell you? Please forgive me." Emma gushed.

"Okay, okay," Andrea said, peeling Emma off her. "I believe you. Now stop. You're choking me."

"Sorry, sorry, sorry, come in. Want some coffee? How about breakfast? Adam can make you breakfast."

"Coffee is good. Now, sit down and stop fawning all over me. Let's just talk, okay? I have no idea what the hell has happened to you, but you've got to get ahold of yourself."

"I know. You're right, you're right, you're right. I'm just overtired. Adam made me see that with all the promotion, jetting around the country, not getting enough sleep, not eating right and all, I'm just run down. So, I know what I have to do. I have no more appearances for months now, so it's a lot of exercise, green food, and sleep. Do you believe me when I say I'm sorry?" Emma's face looked like a two-year-old with her bottom lip quivering, ready to cry.

Adam handed Andrea a cup of coffee, then excused himself to let them talk.

"Hey, Adam," Andrea called after him. "Great coffee. Much better than Emma's."

Emma screwed up her mouth and squinted her eyes comically. "Very funny. My coffee is good."

From there, the conversation took on a more normal flavor. Andrea accepted Emma's explanation and apology. The two women walked out on the back porch and sat down.

Emma took a minute to look at Andrea's aura. It was a minty green. She tried to talk to the color in her head. *What do you mean little green color? Is there something I need to know? Oh, for heaven's sake, now I absolutely sound like I need to be committed. How do you talk to a color or 'engage it', as Willow had said.* Just as she had that thought, the color started to ripple and form a picture. It was of Kyle and Andrea hugging and crying. She had no idea what that meant. Perhaps they talked it over and decided it was okay not to have kids and they were hugging and crying because they were happy. Could that be it?

"So, Andrea. Have you and Kyle had any more conversations about the having kids issue? Is he budging at all?"

"We have, and I don't know. He says he loves me and doesn't want to leave me, but he really, really, really wants kids...at least one."

Emma went quiet, staring at the green bushes that lined the fence of her yard. The colors were so vibrant. She couldn't remember them looking so inviting before. Without a word, she walked out to them and began caressing the branches. They felt warm, soft, and alive, like they could almost speak to her. A picture popped into her head. Excitedly, she ran back to Andrea.

"I've got the answer," she exclaimed excitedly.

"If any of it involves you giving me your old maternity clothes, forget it," Andrea responded flatly.

"No, no, no. Nothing like that. What about the Big Brother Program? You know, the one where a guy becomes a big brother to a kid on the wrong track. They take them places, help them with their homework, and teach them right from wrong. Heck, Kyle is a criminal attorney. I'm sure he's seen lots of kids get into trouble and end up in jail. He'd want to help them, right? It's perfect."

"I don't even want a *foster* kid in my house. No." Andrea rebutted.

"It's not a fostering kind of thing. The kids live in their own houses. Most don't have fathers at all or live in horrible situations. The big brother, Kyle, in this case, would pick up the kid a few times a week and mentor him, be his friend, play ball with him, and do stuff like that. You wouldn't have to be involved at all if you didn't want to."

Andrea listened to Emma's words without responding. Her face registered her thought process. The wheels turned as she digested the idea, weighing the pros and cons. A small smile started to appear.

"It might work," Andrea uttered, still hesitant. "He *has* talked about all the things he would do if he had a son. He gets really excited about the idea of teaching him sports and imparting all his wisdom about dating and girls. So, maybe...maybe."

"Listen, this is meant to be. So many kids are lost and alone. Kyle would be the perfect person to help. I'm sure you can make him see that," Emma urged. "Just try."

Andrea had become excited at the prospect by the time they'd finished their coffee. Emma was so relieved, except for one thing. The day was looking up, but would she have another blackout like the one that had caused all this damage between her and Andrea in the first place? Her fear of her other self's power ran deep. How would she keep that from happening again?

There was little time to dwell on her insecurities as her folks showed up with Ryan. Her entire body reacted in relief, seeing him safe and sound. Scooping him up, she swung him around happily, laughing and telling him how much she'd missed him. It was definitely over the top for those watching her, but for Emma, it wasn't nearly enough. Ryan was the one thing she'd never wavered on in this new life. She'd insisted he be here. As in her old life, she couldn't do without him. He grounded her, was her reason for existing at all. As wonderful as it was that Adam had changed and they had a good marriage, she would give up everything and everyone for Ryan.

Chapter 34

As the months progressed and 1991 eased into 1992, Emma became a voracious reader of any spiritual book she could lay her hands on.

In "Secrets of the Veda," she was told that man is a transitional being. Intention is the machine of the inner spirit. This meant that her thoughts, as Florence had explained, were her intentions, which drove her actions.

She learned that Ascended Masters were once humans who had lived on Earth but had learned their karmic lessons and raised their consciousness to the point where they lived permanently on a higher plane. From this lofty space, they continued to help humanity evolve. Apparently, Willow and Florence were two of these ascended beings. It comforted her to know these kinds of people existed but did nothing to answer her questions. She'd be happier if she could get them to be more forthcoming with information.

For all the lessons she was learning about karma and cause and effect, there were no instructions on defeating one's own destructive self. Or at least nothing that she *understood* from the writings. It seemed to her that once you become *enlightened,* apparently, you become unable to say things clearly. Riddles were their language of choice.

She found herself having times when she wasn't so sure she wanted to change anything at all. It was all too difficult. If she could just stop the insults, that would be enough. She was beginning to appreciate the drive and moxie of her alter ego. In her sixty-year-old life, she'd always been so mealy-mouthed and weak. She truly hated that fearful, cowering woman, so she didn't want that person around her either.

Too many choices. She couldn't seem to drive the boat to where she wanted it to go. There were moments she just wanted to let go and fall backward into the pool of water that was her newly-formed self. There was excitement there—riches, adoration. She could be one of the pretty people.

As those thoughts became more pleasing, it became more challenging to think of anything else. The vision in her mind of success and all that entailed was very seductive.

Continuing to read auras and offer suggestions that popped into her consciousness, she tried to *use them* as Florence had suggested. She assumed that when she helped solve another's problem, she was building up her cache of good karma. At least, that was the logic she'd taken from their conversation. But those were becoming distasteful, not productive in her mind's eye. Why was she wasting time on that nonsense? However, she was troubled by her parents' color pictures. It was of the two of them driving away in a car with a 'just married' sign on the back. For as happy as the image seemed, she always got a foreboding feeling in her gut when the picture came to her. She kept asking if they were going to remarry, but they'd just smile and wink at each other, not commit to any plan. This became her proof that the auras meant nothing, as her parents probably weren't going to tie the knot again.

She was bored, bored, bored. Even Ryan held no pleasure for her. Her *Brian* had been a quieter child, extremely sweet, and loved to be read to. Ryan was more active and into everything.

"Come on, Ryan. Time to calm down. How about a story? Don't you want Mommy to read you a story?"

"No." Ryan protested in that cute little toddler voice of his, flopping on his back in protest, covering his eyes.

"Okay, then. It's nap time for you. You don't get to say no to mommy."

As he kicked and screamed, she carried him to his room and put him to bed. She only felt the tiniest tinge of guilt. No way would she have an out-of-control child. She hated being in the park with other mothers who let their kids talk back to them, ignoring their instructions. Brian was *never* like that, and she vowed that Ryan wouldn't be either. Thank goodness her second book was coming out in a couple of months. It would be right after Ryan's second birthday. Her skin was crawling from the everyday drudge of being a mother and housewife.

Her book came out in June of 1992 and, as before, it topped the charts immediately, this time selling 100,000 copies in the first two weeks.

"What do you mean no book tour?" Emma screamed at Mabel over the phone.

"We'll have you on phone interviews and the like, so they can turn off your microphone if you come up with more of your, shall we say, colorful responses.

"Come on, Mabel. I'm not going to do that. It was my first book. I was nervous, exhausted, and didn't understand anything about the business. I've had almost a whole year to think about my mistakes. I won't do that again. I promise."

There was a long silence before Mabel spoke again. "All right. I'm going to trust you but on one condition. You have Adam come with you. Perhaps having him there will keep you from being so nervous. From the times I've seen you two together, he seems to have a very calming influence on you."

"But, I don't know if he can even get off work. And then there's Ryan. I don't know, Mabel." *She thinks I need a babysitter? This is ridiculous!* Emma screamed in her head.

"Those are the terms. Take it or do phone interviews. We're building a great future for you. I don't want you blowing it when people start hating you because you're too arrogant."

"Fine. Fine," Emma snapped. "Let me talk to Adam."

She was not happy at all. Adam would most likely agree to come if she begged him long enough. He couldn't deny her anything. The reality was that she didn't want him to come. She wanted to be free of this house and all her duties here, but she had no choice.

"Come with me, Adam," Emma implored as she cleared the dinner dishes. "If you're worried about Ryan, we can bring him with us. Of course, he'll be your responsibility because I'll be too busy, but he can come. He's over two now and can travel. Please, please, please."

"Honey, I can't get that much time away from work."

"Take your vacation time. Can't you do that?" she begged.

"I suppose," Adam said hesitantly. "But you have two separate two-week tours. The television tours, then the book signings. I can't go on both of them. I only have two weeks. Plus, I'm not sure two weeks on the road would be good for Ryan. There would be so much commotion and activity happening all the time; it wouldn't be the place for a small child."

Emma thought about that and knew he was right on both counts, bringing Ryan and only being able to get enough time off for one of the two-week tours. Would Mabel let her only do shows when Adam could attend? If that was so, she'd miss out on so many. Maybe if she didn't let herself get too out of hand, Mabel would trust her enough to continue on without him.

"Okay, we'll leave him with my folks. He'll be safe there," Emma offered.

"Safe?"

"I mean, they'll take good care of him. He knows and loves them. We can call him every night. Please," she implored.

"Okay. Actually, it could be fun. Which tour would you like me to accompany you on? The shows or the signings?"

"Definitely the first television appearances. You know how nervous I get on those. Remember what happened on David Blake's show," she added.

She hoped playing the *poor me* card would clinch the deal. She didn't mention Mabel's orders or that she'd wanted him there for all of them. Baby steps. Get him there, then get her agent to let her do the rest without him.

"I really wish you'd forget about that," Adam said, hugging her. "You're much more prepared now. You won't have the nerves you had the first time."

"You're right, I know you are, but I still worry. At least this time, I won't be on the time crunch I was last time, and you and I won't be fighting," she laughed, grabbing a pillow off the couch and playfully hitting him with it. "You were so mean to me, hanging up on me and everything."

The two laughed and play wrestled for a few minutes, ending in a long, passionate kiss.

Chapter 35

The first week of small-town shows went exceedingly well. Emma was high as a kite on the adoration and praise she was receiving and struck by the realization of how much she'd missed hearing the applause. However, she'd been humble and reserved and kept her words positive. She expressed gratitude for her success, thanking her family, friends, and beloved agent for all their support.

"I understand you have a beautiful baby boy," the Good Morning Indiana show host said. Do you happen to have a picture handy?"

"Um...not on me, but my husband does, I'm sure," she said, looking towards the wings.

Someone shoved Adam onto the stage, and everyone applauded wildly. He pulled out his wallet and produced a couple of photos. His face was turning beet red from embarrassment. Still, he stayed calm and waited while the cameraman took a close-up of the picture, to which the entire audience went, "Aww."

"He is absolutely adorable," the host enthused.

"Well, what would you expect from this face?" Emma asked, puffing her chest out a bit pridefully. "I mean from *that* face," Emma said, pointing to Adam.

"Oh, right, right," the host said, obviously a little taken aback by the exchange.

Adam shot Emma a look, brows furrowed. He'd heard these off-the-wall comments before and was at a loss as to where they came from. They were so far from the sweet Emma he knew.

The host thanked them both for coming on, and they left the stage.

"You okay, Em?" Adam asked, concerned.

"Sure, sure, just a slip of the tongue. I fixed it, though, right?"

"I guess," Adam said, still concerned. "I don't get it when you pop off like that, though."

"Me either," Emma answered. "Me either."

Mabel walked up and shook her finger at Emma playfully. "Hey, let's not have any more slip-ups, okay? We need these people. Thankfully, this was the last of this set. Whew."

"I'm so sorry. I think I still get too nervous about these things," she said, trying to act humble and ashamed.

Then, it was two weeks at home before the national shows. Emma had a plan. She would fly back east with Mabel, saying that Adam had to join them later due to some work things he had to tie up. Once there, they couldn't very well cancel the appearances at the last minute. However, best-laid plans and all that. Instead of staying in the limo when she picked Emma up, Mabel came to the door. It was early morning, and Adam was just leaving for work.

"Hi, Adam," Mabel said, a little confused as to why he was in a suit for the plane ride. "What's with the clothes? It's a long ride. Won't you be uncomfortable in your suit?"

"Um, sorry. What was that? Long ride where?"

"To Pennsylvania, the first stop on Emma's eastern tour."

Adam looked utterly lost. "Emma," he hollered. "Mabel is here."

Emma, still in the bedroom finishing her packing, gasped audibly. "Just a second, hon, I'm almost ready." *Now, what am I going to do? Crap.*

By the time she appeared in the living room, Mabel had filled Adam in on the agreement that he be present. Both stood there with their arms crossed.

"Okay. Okay. I know. I screwed up. But, Mabel, I told you that Adam couldn't take that much time off work. I figured you'd let me come alone without him after you saw I was okay on the first round."

"You figured wrong. I believe even more strongly now that his presence keeps you from totally blowing up everything we've worked for."

"You mean you won't let Emma do this tour unless I'm with her?" Adam asked, stunned.

Mabel nodded.

"That's kind of harsh, isn't it? Okay, she had a slip of the tongue on that one show, but it was easily fixed. It certainly wasn't a crisis. She's not a two-year-old that you have to keep hemmed in a playpen. She's a grown woman. Sure, she gets nervous, but that doesn't make her any less of a great writer. I'm sure everyone in that audience understands." Adam reasoned.

Emma stayed silent. Adam was doing a great job at defending her.

"The audience may understand, but the producers and hosts do not. They don't like being blindsided by these little off-the-wall comments Emma makes. It makes them look inept. So, the bottom line is, no you, no interviews."

Adam stood there in shock, angry that Mabel was hijacking him this way. He wanted to say no, push her out the door, and slam it behind her. On the other hand, he didn't want to let Emma down. Easy answer—he couldn't.

"I'll come on one condition. Emma does fine on these next set of interviews, she's free to do any and all publicity appearances without me from then on. If I ever do come again, it will be our decision. Agreed?"

Mabel hesitated but finally agreed.

"Okay, I have to go arrange some things at the office. I'll have to catch a later flight. Can you arrange that for me, Mabel?"

"Absolutely," the agent smiled.

Mabel went out to the limo to make the alternate arrangements for Adam's flight. Emma hung back, jumping up and down.

"Wow. You told her! That was amazing! You are the absolute best," she enthused, leaping into his arms.

"Pretty much that's true," Adam answered in mock seriousness, smiling widely. "Nobody, but nobody, mistreats my wife."

Chapter 36

The first two appearances on the national shows went off without a hitch. Emma did her humble thing, blah, blah, blah. Same questions, same answers, same boring interviews. She hated it. Her loathing of the restricting conversations filtered through her slowly, like a leak entering through the roof, then riding along the beams of a house, finally breaking through and causing a flood below.

That evening, she stood in the bathroom in their hotel room and stared at herself in the mirror. She watched her own face change ever so slightly. The tiniest twinkle came to her eyes. A mischievous grin spread across her face. In her ear, she heard a voice. It sounded excited, like a teenager urging her best friend to sneak out her bedroom window and come to a party with her. "Come on, Emma," the voice said tauntingly. "Let's play." With that, the sixty-year-old Emma fell back, too weak to take control. "No, no," Emma cried just before her voice was silenced completely.

Exiting the bathroom, she grabbed her purse and told Adam she had some quick shopping to do. "I want to pick up some presents for Ryan and a couple of things I promised I'd buy for Andrea here in New York."

"You want me to go with you," Adam mumbled, barely taking his eyes off the game he was watching on television.

"No, sweetheart, thanks. I won't be long." She gave him a peck on the cheek and left.

The next morning, Emma and Adam dashed out of the hotel and into the limousine in the early morning hours. She had no makeup on, as they would do that at the studio. The hotel doorman had held the door for them, and the limo driver had done the same. Adam was having difficulty getting used to all this being waited on hand and foot. It made him understand a little more why Emma got so off-center on these trips. Everyone treated her like a queen. *No wonder she gets so nervous about these things. She must feel like she has to live up to some standard of her new status and act a certain way. I'm overwhelmed, and I'm not even doing anything but sitting here in the background,* he thought.

After her makeup was done, she dashed into the bathroom and stayed there until they called her to go on stage. When she emerged, she was not wearing one of the conservative skirt and jacket outfits she usually wore on these appearances. She had on high-waisted jeans, a crop top, and a denim jacket. Her hair, which she'd previously worn pulled back into a sedate little ponytail, fell free around her shoulders. The stage manager's mouth dropped open when she saw her. Mabel looked like she was going to faint.

"You can't go out there looking like that," Mabel said through gritted teeth, desperately trying to keep from screaming at her at the top of her lungs.

"No time for her to change now," the stage manager said, whisking her away.

Emma strode out on the stage like a runway model strutting her stuff. She looked confident and entirely at home.

"Emma, so good to see you again," the elegantly dressed hostess enthused. She never let the momentary shock of Emma's attire register on her face. As the consummate professional, she simply kept going.

"Your new book is breaking records, although I can't say I'm surprised. I thought your first one was good, but this one...wow, I couldn't put it down."

"Yes, it's pretty brilliant, isn't it?" Emma stated in a sweet, syrupy voice.

The hostess laughed, never letting it show that Emma's comment didn't sound like a joke, but more like a conceited, egotistical brag, which she felt was a completely inappropriate. Offstage, Mabel was turning beet red.

"So, Emma, how do you come up with these ideas? The plots are so complicated, yet you wind it all up so neatly in the end. That takes true talent."

"It does. It takes attention to detail and perseverance, which only a few of us excellent writers have. But, Joyce, I'd like to go off-topic for just a minute if you don't mind. I just can't sit here and not comment on your outfit. A certain flair comes with dressing properly, and honey, I think you could use a little help. You should NEVER wear red, and that short jacket makes you look dumpy. Go for long, clean lines. It will make you look taller and slimmer." It felt like time stood still. No one breathed. You could have heard a pin drop on the stage.

Emma turned around and talked directly to the audience. "Come on, ladies. You know what I'm talking about. Here, we have a beautiful woman who is not showing off her best self. She's obviously smart, well-educated, and thankfully likes my books..." The audience relaxed and laughed. "So, let's give her a little help."

With that, the audience broke out into applause. "You go, Emma," someone shouted. "Love your outfit, Emma," another hollered. The entire room was getting into the action. They loved her.

"Well, I thank you so much for the tips and humiliation," the hostess said with a laugh. "You're not wrong about anything you said, I truly never know what I should wear. Thanks for the *beautiful* comment, but since I had my son and packed on a few pounds, I've just sort of given up."

"Well, we won't let you give up, will we?" Emma said, engaging the audience again. "Tell you what. Let's have the audience write down their tips for some wardrobe changes, and you can collect them after the show. You'll try some out and see what you like. Okay?"

The audience went nuts, clapping and whistling.

"Okay. Deal," the hostess replied with a smile. "Now, could we please talk about your book?"

Emma laughed and said sure. The rest of the interview went well, with Emma appearing somewhat humble but still bragging about herself and her talent.

At the end, she said, "You know, I realize it surprises some people when I talk about how good I think I am. Especially my agent," she chuckled, looking back into the wings where Mabel was standing. "But, I think too many women play down their assets. I believe in my talent. I think I'm good. Saying it out loud may be the wrong thing to do, but it's me." Again, the audience sent her off with wild applause.

As soon as the red light on the camera went out, the hostess walked over to Emma and shook her hand. "You may be a wild card, but you've got something. Don't let anyone take it from you like I did. Don't ever compromise."

When she walked offstage, Adam hugged her, but Mabel glowered at her angrily.

"Emma! We've got to talk. This can't stand. That is no way to behave," Mabel chided her.

"Why not? They loved me. You heard that applause," Emma shot back.

"I don't care. That is not how you will behave! You represent my literary agency and the publishing house that gave you a shot and produced your books. You're being disrespectful by behaving like some bohemian with no manners or decorum."

"Come on, Granny, take off your flannel nighty and step into the present. I'll bet you still use doilies at your house and don't sleep in the same bed as your husband. Wake up, old woman!" Emma spouted.

"Emma!" Adam yelled. "Enough!"

"Are you siding with her?" Emma barked, shooting daggers at him with her eyes.

"I'm not *siding* with either one of you. But this is no way to solve your differences. Insults from you, Emma, or orders from you, Mabel, will never breach this chasm. Let's go back to the hotel and order some dinner and talk this through."

"I think not," Emma stated flatly. "The two of you can discuss me and all my faults. I need a drink. I'll see you in the morning for the last show. Tonight, I want to cut loose a little. I'll get another room for the night. I can do that because, you see, I happen to be a famous author. I have money. Then I'll take a cab to the studio in the morning for the last scheduled show. See you both there. Ta!" Holding her head high, she walked away and disappeared down the hallway.

Adam and Mabel stood there, mouths agape. What just happened?

"Look, Mabel," Adam began. "Don't be so hard on her. She's been different ever since she had Ryan. She almost died, and I think that's where her newest reactionary behavior comes from. She was right about one thing, the audience did love her."

"I don't care if they wanted to adopt her," Mabel spit out. "She will not act that way and stay my client. Is that clear?"

"I'll talk to her," Adam replied quietly.

"And when exactly will this great talk happen? Apparently, your wife is out tying one on and getting a room elsewhere. Neither of us will see her until tomorrow. So, good luck with that."

Adam didn't speak again. He simply slowly walked away.

Chapter 37

Emma's night turned out to be wilder than she could have imagined. At the first bar she went into, she was greeted with smiles of recognition by some who had seen her on television.

"Fred, Fred," an older woman remarked excitedly to her husband. "Look over there at the bar. That's Emma Armstrong, the woman we saw today on the show. "Wow. She's even prettier in person."

Fred smiled at his wife and patted her hand. "Okay, Darlene, I know you want to go over there and ask for an autograph," he chuckled. "How 'bout we go over together and say hello."

Darlene smiled at her sweet mate of over forty years. He knew her so well. He held her chair and helped her out of it. Taking her hand, they ambled over to where Emma was seated.

"Sorry to intrude," Fred began, "but we were at the show you were on today...in the audience. My wife jes thinks you're so great. Me too, ma'am. Me too. If it wouldn't be too much trouble, would you mind giving us an autograph?"

Emma smiled broadly. "Of course." She asked the bartender for some paper to write on. Signing her name, she handed it to Fred.

As they started to walk away, Emma stopped them. "Hey. I'd like to buy dinner for the two of you. Would you join me? I'm on my own tonight and could use the company."

Darlene practically peed her pants she was so excited. Fred just beamed from ear to ear, like he'd just been asked to sup with the President or something.

"That would be mighty fine, ma'am," Fred replied, his voice rising an octave from his own excitement.

The three walked about three blocks and found a nice steakhouse to have their meal. When the waiter asked for their drink order, Emma ordered a martini with extra olives. She'd never had one before. She and Adam often shared a bottle of wine, but hard liquor was not their thing. One sip and she was hooked. She'd downed three before their meal was put in front of them.

Darlene was utterly enthralled, initially, with Emma. She hung on every word.

"That dolphin necklace you have is so beautiful," Darlene enthused.

"Yesh, it is," Emma answered, already beginning to slur her words. "Ish magic. I never take it off. I would simply die without it." She laughed, then kissed the dolphin. "Yeppers, this is mine, and no one can take it from me, no matter how hard they try."

Fred and Darlene looked at each other, puzzled by her intensity. Also, they already didn't like her quickly increasing drunkenness.

Emma found out the couple was originally from the Midwest, but the bank Fred worked for gave him a huge promotion to manage one of their most prominent offices here in the city. So, the entire family picked up roots and moved to New York. That was thirty-five years ago. He was now retired and had a nice pension, and the two spent their days doing simple things they enjoyed. They had three children and four grandchildren. One lived here, but the other two had moved away, one to California and the other to Colorado. So, they were constantly on the go.

"How do you do it?" Emma asked. "How are you so happy just doing nothing?" She kept blinking her eyes and rubbing them. The alcohol was hitting her hard, and she was more than a little drunk by the time they'd finished their meal.

"Um...well, I wouldn't call it nothing," Fred replied, stung by the comment. "We're very involved in our community and with our families. We stay busy."

"Yeah, but, idin it, idin it, isn't it slightly borrrring?" Emma elongated the word. She had now graduated from a little drunk to officially three sheets to the wind.

"Fred, I'm getting a little tired," Darlene said, trying to politely find a way to end the evening.

"Sure honey, me too. Mrs. Armstrong, we only live a few blocks from here, so we're going to walk home. Do you need me to hail a cab for you?" Fred said, ever the gentleman.

"Yeppers. Good idee," Emma slurred. "I'll pay it... I'll give 'em money...you know, the bill thingy. I'll come out there...outside."

A cab was waiting for her when she stumbled out of the restaurant, but Fred and Darlene were long gone.

"To the most expensive hotel in the city," Emma ordered her cab driver. He dropped her off at the Ritz-Carlton.

The following morning, Emma roused herself with great difficulty. Hangover does not adequately describe the pounding in her head and behind her eyes. When she could finally focus on the clock, she jumped out of bed. It was 8:30 a.m., and she was supposed to be at the studio no later than 8:00. There was no time to go by and pick up clean clothes at her other hotel. She was still angry with both Adam and Mabel, so she didn't want to call and ask either of them to bring her anything. She'd just have to wear what she had on.

By the time she reached the studio, she was horribly sick from her previous night's introduction to the martini. *God, how many did I have? What did I say to those people? Did I tell them I'm from the future? I hope not. Why can't I remember anything? Oh...yeah...I think they were angry with me at some point in the evening. Oh man, I'll never do that again.*

By the time she made it to the makeup chair, she felt like she was going to throw up. Adam had brought her some clothes, none of which she wanted to wear. But she couldn't wear the outfit she had on, which was wrinkled from sleeping in it and smelled of alcohol from the sweat oozing from her pores.

Emma saw a woman walk through the makeup room wearing a hot pink jogging outfit.

"Give me those. I want to wear those," she ordered.

The woman didn't want to give them up, but Emma was insistent. The stage manager was losing her mind, sure this would probably be her last day on the job because of this crazy woman. Total chaos ensued. Ultimately, Emma got her way and slinked onto the stage decked out in pink. Every step she took to reach the couch and host was torture. Even the sound of her tennis-shoed footsteps sounded like a loud drum pounding in her head.

Once she sat down, her eyes couldn't focus. She kept blinking and squinting as the bright lights caused her eyes to blur and ache.

"So, Emma," the host began, "here we are again with another best-selling book. How does it feel?"

Emma tried to be nice, but she was just so sick. "It feels like...like good...like a dream..."

"A dream come true?" the host tried to fill in.

"Right, right, a dream come true. Could you sit still, please? Stop moving," Emma whined pitifully.

"Um, okay. I'll be as still as possible," the host replied, watching in horror as Emma turned horribly pale. "Emma, are you okay? You don't look so well."

"Ah...smart...you picked up on that, did ya?" Emma answered in barely a whisper. "I think I need to lie down. I'm sorry. I'm coming down with someth..." She stood up, took one step and passed out.

Immediately, people came running. Someone shouted, "Call 911." Others tried to get Emma off the floor. They managed to move her limp body to the couch and lie her down. She still didn't awaken. The audience was quickly removed while the station switched its programming to a rerun of the show. Adam and Mabel came running from the wings, terrified. By the time they got Emma on a gurney and down to the ambulance, she still had not woken up.

Chapter 38

Emma awakened in a New York City hospital. Mabel was in a chair beside her, while Adam stood just outside the doorway, speaking with a physician.

"Is she going to be okay?" Adam asked, his voice shaking in fear.

"As long as she stays away from alcohol," the doctor replied.

"You mean this is a hangover of some sort? I don't believe that. Emma, at most, has a glass of wine. She's not a drinker by any stretch of the imagination."

"That may be true, but apparently, last night, she did. We can still detect a small amount of alcohol in her blood, and she reeks of it as her body is releasing it through her sweat. Here's the problem, however, she is not metabolizing it well, which means there may be something else physical going on with her," the doctor answered, writing in her chart as he spoke.

"I think there is, Doc," Adam blurted out quickly. "She's been acting very odd lately. She has these times when she just suddenly starts insulting everyone. Often, she doesn't even remember what she said to them. Then, other times, she'll just say she got confused, and the words got jumbled up in her head. Could she have a tumor or something in her brain? This isn't her, Doc. I promise you. She's normally the sweetest person on the planet."

"How long has this been going on?"

"Um, minimally in the first part of our marriage, but after she had Ryan and had all those complications it's become more frequent. Could this be because of that? Sometimes, she forgets things completely...has no memory of phone calls she's made or who she has spoken to. Can you help?" Adam, for all his strength, was shaky and pale. The fear he felt was evident.

"Let me run some tests. I can't speak to her condition right now, other than to say her vitals are good.

"Why is she still unconscious?" Adam asked fearfully.

"She's not unconscious; she's just sleeping it off."

"Oh," Adam said quietly. "How long will all the tests take?"

"We should get the results in a couple of hours."

"Adam?" Emma said weakly. "What happened?" She had yet to notice Mabel was also in the room.

"You passed out, honey. The doctors are going to run some tests."

"It's okay, Emma," Mabel piped up. "If I'd known you were sick, we never would have fought. I'm so sorry."

"Thank you, Mabel," was all Emma said. She didn't feel the need to apologize for her behavior but was too weak to fight.

Emma whimpered and grabbed her head. Adam grabbed her hand and squeezed it tightly.

"It's okay, Em, I'm right here. Don't worry; we'll get through this together, whatever is going on. If you have a problem with alcohol, we'll get you help."

Aww, ain't that touchin', Emma thought. She could see Adam's pain but only minimally felt it. She wouldn't allow old Emma's deeper feelings for Adam to surface. In her mind, he had become simply a useful person in her life, no more, no less.

"Adam, can we talk? It's important. Mabel, could you excuse us for a moment?" Emma asked softly.

"Sure. I'll go get some coffee. It's going to be fine," Mabel answered, heading for the door.

"Close the door," Emma instructed Adam once Mabel had left.

After he did so, he came and sat on the side of the bed and took Emma's hand.

"What is it, hon?"

"We've got a problem. As you may have noticed, I'm not the woman you married." She let the statement hang in the air for a few seconds before she spoke again. "We have to set some ground rules. I'm going places. My success knows no bounds. We have to work something out."

Adam sat there stunned, not understanding where this was going.

"It's time you knew that I'm not from here," she continued. "Well, I'm from here, but not from this time. That's not exactly right either. I'm from this time, but was created by the old me who is actually a sixty-year-old woman who time-traveled back to change her life. So, voila, I was manifested, for lack of a better word."

"Emma, do you know how nuts you sound right now?" Adam almost shouted, frustrated at yet another display of how sick she was. His heart leapt into his throat. His wife was truly losing her mind. A million future thoughts shot through his head in an instant. What about Ryan? She couldn't be with him now. Would he have to put her someplace where she couldn't hurt herself? A second in the mind can produce a million images and questions.

"I know you don't believe me. Heck, I wouldn't believe me if I were you, but can't you see it? Can't you feel it? Did the woman you married have this much strength? Was she ever rude to others to make a point? Did she speak her mind? You and I are, in essence, strangers, linked together only by the fact that I happen to look like her, and we were married before I came into power."

"Power?" Adam asked, aghast at the statement.

"Yes. Once I was able to gain dominion and take over, your Emma left. Along with her, she took all her memories. I have no recollection of the early happy times you had together or how you cuddled and cooed. Of course, I get gut-level intuitions about the old Emma, but nothing concrete. I know she had some nonsense belief in magic, or nice things out there, blah, blah, blah, but I don't know who she knew. I don't see life as she saw it. I'm new. So, you see, your wife, your precious Emma is gone. No more. Finis. A whisper in the wind. Dead. Is that plain enough for you? But, I must say, I've done a remarkable job imitating her. That comes from that intuition thing I was talking about."

Adam had been caressing Emma's hand when she began speaking and was now rubbing it so hard it was beginning to hurt. The more she spoke of being from the future and tried to convince him that it wasn't a crazy idea, the more his pressure increased in lock-step with his rising fear.

"Adam, you're hurting me," Emma cried, pulling away. "I know it sounds nuts, but please, please believe me. We have to find a way to coexist for Ryan's sake. I may be outspoken, but I'm not heartless."

Adam dropped her hand angrily and began pacing around the room. He would pause, poised to say something but not utter a word, and then pace some more.

"Would you stop that? You're making me dizzy. Emma touched her hand to her chest, looking for her dolphin. "Oh, my God. Where's my dolphin?" she cried out, trying to sit up to search for it. The pounding in her head beat tortuously against her temples, causing her to lie back on the pillow. "I can't lose my dolphin," she said, almost in tears.

Adam reached into his pocket, retrieved her necklace, and tossed it to her. "The EMTs took it off when they were attending to you," he said.

"Oh, thank you. Thank you," Emma cried out in relief.

"What's so special about that damned thing anyway? Sometimes I think you love it more than you love me or even Ryan."

"I do," Emma said matter-of-factly. This is everything to me. It's the constant in my life. I need it as much as I need air to breathe. You wouldn't understand."

"If you aren't Emma, then you should have no attachment to the dolphin. It was hers. So, why is it so important to you, this not-the-previous Emma?" Adam grilled her.

"Good question, my man. I don't have an answer. Again, this is the gut feeling I spoke about. It has importance to everything about me in some way. It must be my good luck talisman or something. No matter, I just need it."

Emma looked up at Adam, who had the saddest expression on his face, and, for the briefest moment, felt sorry for him. Her intention was not to hurt him, only to make their relationship more realistic. He was a good man by all standards—not what she would have picked, but good nonetheless. For her rise to fame, she needed him. He could keep track of Ryan and help raise him.

"What about Ryan? Does this new you that I apparently don't know, love her son?"

"In my way," Emma shot back. "He's an innocent in all this. If he'd been Brian like he was supposed to be, more than likely, I'd love him a lot more."

"Brian? Are you trying to tell me that not only are you a different woman, he's a different kid somehow?" Adam shouted, incredulous. "You truly are nuts. And, again, if you don't know anything about Emma, how did you know she wanted to name him Brian?"

Emma simply smiled, not reacting to the comment. The two stared at each other in silence. What she didn't know was that old Emma was listening. She had no power to emerge, but she was listening, wounded deeply by the words new Emma was hurling at Adam.

"We've found the culprit," the doctor announced, walking into the room. Two years ago, when she had her baby and contracted the bacterial infection, the antibiotics took care of it, but not completely. Infections can lay dormant for years before popping up again. That's what's happened here. Her abdominal infection has become active again. And, before you ask the question, yes, bacterial abdominal infections can cause psychological dysfunctions. The disorders of the gut-brain interaction, or DGBI, can be treated. We'll keep her here for a few days to administer the needed medication. Once she's released, there will need to be dietary alterations and lifestyle changes. I would recommend some behavioral therapy along with possibly yoga or meditation." He walked over and patted Emma on the shoulder. "Don't worry, dear, we'll take good care of you."

Adam was more than relieved. He let out a massive sigh of relief.

"See, honey? All this thinking you're a different person is...well, how can I say this kindly without sounding demeaning, all in your head, so to speak. It's been hiding there since Ryan was born. I'm so grateful. You're going to be fine," he ended, hugging her tightly.

Truth be known, Emma was relieved as well. The minute the doctor came up with a physical reason for her personality changes, she'd thought of an alternate plan. Letting him believe it was all a brain/stomach thing would be better. She could, on occasion, act like the old Emma. This would keep him from trying to have her committed or some such nonsense. If she spouted off, she could simply laugh and say, "Oh, there goes my brain/gut thing." It could become a running joke. The more she expanded on the positives in this plan, the more excited she got. The possibilities were infinite. Keep Adam happy, keeps Ryan happy, keeps Emma happy and able to do whatever she wants to. And the best part was, now she had a physical, verified by a doctor, excuse for behaving badly. It couldn't be more perfect.

Chapter 39

When Emma returned home, she told all her loved ones about her gut/brain infection and how it made her say things she didn't mean. If she were to spout off to them, she told them to simply ignore her. The doctor had not given a time or date when this malady would come to an end but said it could be years. He hadn't said that, of course, but she was trying to cover her bases just in case. She had so many plans it made her head spin just to think of them. The only drawback to anything happening at the moment was that she'd begun to feel the old Emma stirring. This made her angry. There was no way that the old woman was going to impede her dreams.

Almost daily, she insulted someone. But since they knew her condition, they'd just laugh it off and tell her to stop letting her gut talk. It became the big joke. She absolutely loved it.

In keeping with her faking the old Emma, she went back to reading auras to keep up the ruse that she was still sweet, little ole Emma trying to be the perfect helper in any situation. It gagged her to do so. But, she felt it necessary.

One afternoon, she was at the park with Ryan. She sat with one of the mothers she knew and chatted as they watched their kids play.

"Boy, Susie is growing so fast. How do you keep up with the cost of buying new clothes every month?" Emma asked.

Susie's mother felt the question was oddly put. It almost sounded like she was saying they were poor and could not care for their child.

"Well, um, we manage," Lynn, Susie's mother, answered. We get a lot of hand-me-downs from my niece. It works out."

"Hand-me-downs, huh? Are you having financial problems? Is that it?" Emma blurted out. The minute it came out of her mouth, she knew it was the wrong thing to say. *How in the world did the old Emma do this?* Emma thought. *I truly don't get the nicey, nice stuff at all.*

Lynn was beginning to collect her stuff and leave in a huff when Emma noticed that Susie had a yellow aura around her. She saw a picture of her falling and cutting her knee.

"Wait," she said, trying to keep Lynn there. "I'm so sorry. I didn't mean it that way. It's just that...well, we're having a few financial problems ourselves," she lied.

"Oh, I didn't know that," Lynn said sympathetically. "It is so hard, isn't it? Kids need so much."

Emma was only waiting for the minute before Susie was going to fall so she could scoop her up, save the day, and be the hero. Then she could get away from this woman. She was no good at this.

Just as expected, in the next two minutes, Susie had climbed up on one of the benches. She started to teeter, and Emma swooped in to save her.

"Oh, Emma. Thank you so much. If you hadn't walked over there when you did to check on Ryan, she could have fallen and gotten badly hurt."

"Right place, right time," Emma said with a smile. "Well, we gotta dash. Adam will be home soon. See ya."

As they headed back to the house, Emma shook her head. Well, it at least gave her something to tell Adam. *Gee honey, see how sweet and helpful I am? Let me tell you how I saved a kid today from getting a boo-boo. Bleh! I need a better plan.*

Thankfully, her third book, which required tours, was released, and she could escape from her family. Mabel had kept her on but was still worried about Emma's lapses into insults. However, it was harder to do as she seemed more beloved than before. The comments about women showing who they were, then the sympathy factor when she passed out on the next show, made her hard to reign in.

"So, what will you do if you pop off with an insult on the air?" Mabel quizzed her.

"I say, gee, please forgive me, I'm nuts and can't control my mouth," Emma answered, laughing like it was a joke.

"Very funny, but yes, you will say some version of that. You will explain your condition, and by the way, the audience will love you for it. People adore being supportive of famous people fighting their way through difficulties. It makes you human."

"They already adore me. Haven't you been reading the papers? But I'll try to tone it down a bit. But, and this is nonnegotiable, I wear what I want."

"Oh, Emma, come on," Mabel groaned, looking at the T-shirt and shorts she had on. "Can't you just wear a dress for the interviews? It simply looks better—more professional. You can take it off the minute you get off stage."

"Nope. My way, or I walk."

Mabel bristled but knew she had to agree to her terms. She had become the agency's biggest client. As long as her books continued to be best sellers, there was nothing she could do.

"Fine. But can you at least ditch the T-shirt? Wear jeans or whatever, but could you please wear a nicer shirt?"

"Yes, mother," Emma said sarcastically. "I actually just bought a couple of new tops I think you'll like. They're beaded, and my favorite is hot pink with spaghetti straps. Very revealing. I think the sparkle will dress up the outfit, don't you?" Emma laughed as Mabel looked like she was going to be sick.

Emma didn't waste any time trying to be subdued on the tour. On the very first show, she strutted out on the stage, did a little twirl for the audience, then plopped down on the couch. The audience applauded wildly.

"So, Fran, how ya been?" Emma asked the hostess immediately.

"Hey, that was my question. Stop reading my prompter," Fran chuckled.

"So, you were going to ask yourself how you are? Don't you know?" Emma retorted. The audience laughed loudly.

Fran laughed with the audience, trying to regain control of the interview.

"Tell us how *you* are," Fran asked when the audience settled down. "Another book, another best seller. Wow."

"Yes. With more to come," Emma looked up at the prompter. She leaned forward and read out loud, "So, Emma, tell me...how do you keep coming up with these stories? They're all so fresh. Each one is different and as engaging as the rest."

"I'll tell you, Fran, it's easy. They pop into my head, and I write them down."

Emma read again from the prompter. "And how is your family and that adorable son of yours?"

"Well, Fran. They're just peachy. Love them both so much."

Emma continued that way for a full five minutes, with great laughter and hoots from the audience.

"Oh, too bad, we're out of questions," Emma said, giving a little pout. "How about we talk about some really important stuff? What do you think...audience...shall we talk about stuff that really matters?"

The people cheered and clapped.

"Sounds great, Emma, but first, we have to cut away for a commercial break. We'll be back in just sixty seconds."

As soon as the cameras panned away, Fran was all over Emma. "What the hell was that?"

"Just having a little fun, Frannie? It livened everything up, don't you think?"

"When we come back on the air, you're going to say that you're sorry, but you just got some troubling news regarding your father or mother or whoever you want to say. Then you're going to get off my stage. You will never be welcome here again."

Emma's eyes flashed with rage. "Wanna bet? And I'm not going anywhere. Just sit down and shut up, and let me make your show great instead of the bore that it is."

Just before the camera's lights flipped red, indicating the show was live again, there was a sudden, unexpected sound, like a firecracker going off. Immediately afterward, a bright flash blinded Emma momentarily, causing her to cover her eyes. When she opened them again, the room was filled with a smoky blue haze. The audience had disappeared from view. She was no longer on the set, but was completely enveloped in the mist surrounding her. A disembodied voice called out. "Emma, Emma, Emma," it repeated over and over again. "Wake up, Emma. Wake up! Remember where your true power lies." As suddenly as it appeared, it disappeared. Emma felt every muscle in her body ripple as she tried to dispel the fear that was encased within.

Fran was sitting in her chair, fuming. Her superiors had told her that Emma could talk about anything she wanted. The phones were lit up with people calling to tell them how much they loved Emma and ask when she could come back.

"We're back. Today, we've been having a lot of fun talking to Emma Armstrong, best-selling author. So, Emma, you said before the break you wanted to talk about something, as you put it, 'that really matters,' so the stage is yours. What's on your mind?"

Emma couldn't move for a minute. She was completely lost in time and space. What had just happened?

"Um, right, right...sorry. I lost my train of thought there for a minute," she said, standing up and facing the audience. "I just wanted to talk to all the women here who don't think they can fulfill their dreams. I want to say that no matter what they are, big or small, important or humble, you can do it. You can have it all. Stand up to your husbands and boyfriends. Stand up to your bosses. Don't let anyone keep you down. If you have to be a bitch to get there, bitch away, honey. Never let anyone stand in your way and tell you what you can and cannot have!" Emma's words grew in intensity. She looked upward like she was talking to God himself. "You hear me? You can't stop me! No one can stop me!" Then, looking back to the audience, "And no one can stop you!"

The audience was on their feet, applauding hysterically, hooting and whistling. It didn't die down for a full ninety seconds. Emma walked back over and sat down on the couch.

She may have elated the crowd, but inside, she felt a terrifying shift. Rage churned in her gut, and fear rode on her nerves. What had just happened, she had no idea, but she vowed never to let it happen again.

Chapter 40

For the next two years, Emma continued her outlandish behavior. Under the guise of the women's movement for equality, she became more popular and sought after. People started driving by her house just to see where she lived. When she was out, she was fawned over like a movie star. She appeared on more and more talk shows for her women's rights issues than she did for her books. It was heady stuff. However, she never forgot her experience that day in the studio. It still had the power to rattle her.

After her fourth book came out, she talked Adam into moving.

"It's for our safety," she told him. "We need to live in a gated community where people just can't keep randomly showing up at our door. With the success of my books and speaking engagements, we're more than rich now. Come on. What's so special about this house anyway? It's a dump."

Adam bit his lip, trying to let the comment pass without responding in kind. Some of what she said had some truth to it. They were experiencing a lot of unwanted attention, at least on his part.

"What about Ryan?" Adam questioned. "He's lived here since he was born. His friends are here. He just started kindergarten."

"He's barely five years old for God's sake. He'll make new friends in a new school. A private school. We can afford that now. He deserves the best."

"I don't know, Em," Adam hesitated. "It's a lot. The house you picked out is way further from my work."

"So, quit your job. We don't need your income. You can be a stay-at-home dad. Ryan would love that. He's always with my folks, with me away so much with book stuff and my women's rights meetings and protests. He would love to have you there all the time."

"Jesus, Emma! Why don't you just divorce me and pay me as a live-in maid and nanny? That would be a lot more honest than trying to pretend that we're in an actual marriage. In fact, that sounds like a great idea. Let's get divorced. I'll take Ryan off your hands, and you can be a star. I'll stay here; you move to the big house with all the gates and security, and we'll both be happy," Adam shouted, storming out of the room.

"Come on, Adam. I don't want that. I don't want to divorce you, honey. I'm sorry. Come on, we can find a compromise," she said softly, trying to sound like the old Emma with a sweeter tone. "I love you, sweetheart. I know I was mean back there. I was having a gut/brain moment. I can't control them. You understand, right? You don't have to quit your job. Actually, the new house would be closer to my folks. That would be good, don't you think?"

Adam just stared right through her. Her gut/brain excuse was getting old. A part of him was beginning to believe she *was* from the future, or whatever that garbage was she'd tried to feed him, or possibly another planet. How did this marriage go so wrong?

"Sit down," Adam ordered. "Now listen to me. You do have some good points. All this attention you've brought to our door is more than annoying. And you're right that Ryan is young enough to not suffer too much from the move."

"See? I knew you'd get it."

"Let me finish," Adam barked. "But, if we do this, and that's still a big *if,* things have got to change around here. First, I have never liked you popping in and out on a whim. Ryan needs his mother. You have to start scheduling things so you have more time with him. Shoving him off on your folks, as much as they say they don't mind, is not good for him. Here's what I'm willing to do. I can work from home two days a week so I can take Ryan to school, pick him up and be with him. Those two days, you can schedule events or protests or whatever. The other three days, you're home with him. Got it?"

Emma had no intention of sticking to that schedule, but would promise him anything to get into the new house. She needed to have a home that was in keeping with her stature.

"Of course. I knew you'd find a good compromise. See? That's why I married you, because you are the brains of this family. Calm, steady, smart."

"Stop it," Adam said, allowing a slight smile to appear. Emma tossed a pillow at him, trying to lighten the mood. He caught it but didn't want to play.

"Oh, come on. Don't be such a fuddy-duddy," Emma teased. "I've agreed to your terms. Let's do this. It'll be fun. We'll get all the new stuff. We could just sell this house completely furnished and save on movers. I love that idea. All new house. All new life."

"So, everything I've provided for us all these years suddenly isn't good enough? Who are you?" Adam said, heading to the kitchen. He grabbed a beer from the fridge and went outside on the porch.

Emma sighed and rolled her eyes. If she had to eat crow one more time to pander to this guy's ego she was going to vomit. But she needed him, and she knew it. Without him, she'd have to spend more time being a mom, and she didn't want to do that. She'd yet to reach the heights that she wanted. Her plan didn't include mommy-and-me time. There were movie parts in her future. Heck, with all this political stuff she was doing, maybe she'd bag it all and become a senator. She was only in her thirties; the world was her oyster, as they say.

Okay, Em. Start the tears now. Go out and beg his forgiveness. Just get this move done.

She did just that. She sobbed convincingly, saying she never, ever wanted to hurt him. He and Ryan were her whole life. She'd give up everything rather than lose him. The only reason she felt confident enough to say she'd give it all up was because he would never ask her to do it. It wasn't in his DNA.

After thirty minutes of tears, wailing, and apologizing for what an awful person she was, Adam gave in. By the time she was done, he was coming up with more reasons why the move was a great idea. He'd do anything to make her smile. They even agreed to donate much of what they owned to Goodwill and buy new stuff.

For the first month in their new home, Emma kept her promise of only doing political things on the two days Adam worked from home. Slowly after that, she inched her way out of it. One day, she just *had* to go because she'd been asked by some councilman to give a big speech. On another day, one of her protestors got hurt, and, *of course*, she had to be there at the hospital.

Before long, the pact was upended entirely. Adam simply resigned himself to the fact that nothing would change. Emma got her house, which is all she'd wanted him for in the first place. Realizing that his wife would always do exactly what *she* wanted, regardless of his wishes, he ultimately decided to work from home four days a week and only go into the office on Fridays.

Adam toyed with the idea of getting a divorce but couldn't go through with it. No matter what, he loved her deeply and wanted Ryan to have his mom, even though her time with him diminished weekly. After her book tours, she treated them both nicer and, for a short time, devoted more time to Ryan upon her return. For the moment, it was enough. He kept thinking that all would die down after a while and life could go back to normal, whatever that was. Nope, divorce just wasn't in the cards.

Chapter 41

Before Emma left for her fifth book tour, she'd started getting massive migraines. She'd never had them before and was at a loss to understand why they were present now. Coinciding with these little stabbing instruments of pain in her head, however, were more aura pictures popping up. One was of Ryan in the emergency room, while a nurse wrapped up his foot. She couldn't shake it.

Why the hell don't these things come with a date on them. How am I supposed to know when Ryan is going to hurt is foot. And, for heaven's sake, it's just his foot. He probably strains it or something. How useless these little peeks into the future, courtesy of old Emma, are. These are probably what's causing my headaches. I've got to get rid of them.

She started to call Andrea to ask her if she had any advice on how to get rid of her migraines, but then remembered they'd had a huge fight last time they'd spoken. Her best friend in the world truly did not like this new Emma. They'd been butting heads for months now on every single issue they talked about. Andrea was a strong personality and not easily bullied or beaten down. Emma had a hard time with strong personalities. She had to put them in their place, and would not abide their trying to convince her of anything—especially when they tried to convince her she was wrong about something.

The limo driver showed up at the door, and Emma put all thoughts of Andrea, Ryan and her migraine out of her head. She'd feel better once she was onstage and surrounded by the people who adored her.

The first show went well. The women applauded, hooted and hollered as usual. Her migraine disappeared and she felt powerful again. She knew this was what was crucial to her very existence. Like air to breathe, she needed to be adored.

As she stepped on stage for the second interview, flashes of Ryan at the hospital again jumped in her head. She shook it off.

"Ladies, good morning," she enthused. "So happy to be here and so happy to see all of you. I've got some really good things to talk about today. I understand now, more than ever, how we can get our point across. And before our gorgeous hostess sitting over there interrupts me and wants to talk about my book, I'll just say, it's a hit. Go buy it. You'll love it." The audience laughed with her.

The hostess was fuming, Emma had power. There was no show now that she could not take over as she pleased. All formatting was thrown out the window. This happened everywhere. However, the ratings dictated, so she was allowed full reign.

"Now, do you want to hear my well-thought-out plan for our next steps?"

"Absolutely. Yes, Keep talkin' Emma, we love you," shouts came from the crowd.

Emma asked for a chair to be brought center stage for her to sit on. Once seated, she smiled and basked in the love she saw on the faces. She paused.

"Okay, my dear ones. Here's our next step. We've let the powers that be know that we want equality, equal pay, equal treatment. But, have we gotten it yet?"

"No!" The audience replied in unison.

"Want to know why? I'll tell you why. Because we're fighting every man out there. The corporations that these men lead are not just going to hand us the keys to the kingdom. They're not going to easily let us through the door. They don't want to give up their money and power, or the perks we provide as we rear their kids, cook their meals and have sex with them. So, we have to take it from them, right?"

"Right," the audience answered.

"How do we do that?" She paused. You could have heard a pin drop. "Each one of us has to put all the men in our lives under our thumbs. We have to crush each and every one of them individually. We have the power to make them hurt. We'll push them so low, they'll be begging to give us what we want." Emma paused. The audience was silent, but the admiration was shifting slightly. Her harsh words were causing a discomfort to grow.

"So, how do we do that? We have to stop doing everything for them—stop being their maids, babysitters, cooks, shoppers and, yes, even their lovers. We have to stop being so nice, agreeable and accommodating. We have negotiation power. Don't just go along, stand your ground, make them lonely, make them ache for conversation and sex. Our bodies are a negotiation tool. Once we control them, we can manipulate them. Once that happens, we win. We take control. We run the corporations. We make the decisions. We let them know what *they* can and cannot do. Are you with me?" Emma shouted, holding up her arms in the air.

The room was deathly silent. No applause. No whistles. No happy shouts. Emma just sat there, stunned. Finally, one woman stood up.

"I have something to say, before I walk out," she said, barely controlling her anger.

"I used to hang on every word you said. I thought you were the one that would lead us to better lives as women, help us move our way into sitting side-by-side with men in the workplace, be appreciated for more than how well we can make a roast. But, ma'am, I'm not a man-hater. Putting men down, or *under our thumbs*, is no better than what they're doing to us. I love men. Most work hard to provide for their families. This life we all live now, their behavior, is what they've been taught for generations. Change is necessary, but takes time. You can't train an animal by beating it, you'll only make it mean. I don't want mean. I want compromise." With that she left.

"Wait," Emma began, terrified by the energy shift she felt in the room. "Maybe I was being too literal...I didn't mean..."

Before Emma could barely finish her sentence, the audience was all but out the door. Every one of them. She just sat there, glued to the spot, staring at the empty seats. From behind her she heard the hostess say, "Let's take a quick commercial break, we'll be right back."

The hostess walked up to Emma and said what she'd been longing to say for a long time. "Please leave the stage and never come back."

When she walked off stage, someone shoved a phone in her hand. It was Mabel screaming at the top of her lungs on the other end. The Boston and Philadelphia shows had already canceled her appearances. For some reason that Mabel could not fathom, their last stop in New York had agreed to still let her appear.

"I'm sure they only want you on so they can rake you over the coals. You fix this or we're done!" Mabel shouted. "No matter the outcome, I'm probably done with you anyway. I can't take it anymore. You've embarrassed us all."

"No, Mabel, please," Emma begged. "I'll fix it. You'll see. Just give me a chance. I promise."

"See that you do!" Mabel said then promptly hung up the phone.

When she exited the studio building, reporters were everywhere, shouting questions at her, surrounding her and not letting her move. Her limo driver wedged between them and dragged her to the car.

Once inside, the car phone rang. The driver lowered the privacy window between them, letting her know her husband was on the phone. She picked up the receiver next to where she was sitting.

"I swear, Adam, if you say one mean thing to me right now, I'll hang up this phone," Emma barked.

"I would, but I have something more important to tell you. I don't know how it happened so fast, or how they even got through the gates, but not ten minutes after the audience had gotten up and left after your speech, or whatever that was, reporters showed up in front of the house. They pounded on the door. Ryan got scared and ran to his bedroom, tripped, fell, and broke his ankle. We're at the hospital right now. They'll be taking him to surgery first thing in the morning. They said the swelling has to go down some first. You need to get home."

"Are you kidding me? I can't come home," Emma lashed out at him. "I need to get to my New York interview. I've got to get them back. Mabel is ready to drop me. I've got to get them back."

"What? Get who back?"

"Them. The people. All those people. They loved me. I've got to get them back."

The phone went dead. Adam hung up.

Emma rested her head on the back of the seat and closed her eyes. *I've got to get them back. I've got to get them back.*

Even though she had two days before she was due at the New York interview, Emma opted to get to the city early. She could use a massage and some time to think. Unfortunately, it didn't turn out that way. By the time she arrived at her hotel in New York, the reporters had been tipped off that she was due. Again, she was surrounded and hounded. The concierge managed to get her inside and up to her room. She tipped the valet, locked the door, and flopped down on the bed and cried herself to sleep.

When she awakened, the room was again covered in the foggy mist like she'd experienced on one of the shows previously. However, this time, she could see that she was still in the room. She closed her eyes tightly hoping that when she opened them, the fog would be gone. It wasn't.

All was quiet. It was unnerving. She could move about, but that was it. She tried turning on the television. That didn't work. Picking up the phone she hit zero for the operator. The phone was dead.

"What do you want?" she screamed at the emptiness. No reply.

"Screw this shit," she said, getting up and grabbing her purse. Thankfully the door opened, but to her surprise, the mist moved with her. She passed people in the hallway. They nodded, so they saw her, but didn't seem to react to the fog that engulfed her.

She opted for the stairs, hoping that it emptied out onto an alleyway where there would be no reporters lying in wait. Her luck held. She was alone. But, where could she go that she wouldn't be recognized, especially since she'd made the news in such a grand fashion.

A kid came riding through the alley. He was wearing a leather jacket, and had on a baseball cap. She stood in his path to make him stop.

"Hey, kid. I'll give you $150 bucks for your coat and cap."

"Sure lady. Toss in an extra fifty bucks and I'll throw in the shoes."

Emma shook her head. "The coat and hat will do fine."

Chapter 42

E mma found a tiny little pub and slinked in, sitting at a small table in the corner at the rear of the bar. She ordered a martini. When the waitress brought it to her, she almost returned it, remembering the outcome of her last martini binge.

What the hell. It doesn't matter how drunk I get. I'm not due on the show for another two days.

She quickly downed the first one, ordered another, and told the waitress to 'keep 'em coming.'

After her second drink, a young man in his mid-thirties approached her table. He was wearing bell bottoms, a long-sleeve T-shirt, and a furry vest that looked like it came out of the Sonny Bono collection from the sixties.

"May I join you?" he asked politely.

Emma looked at him and then started to laugh. "Sure, why not? You just come from a retro party or something?" she asked, pointing to his clothes.

"No," the young man said, obviously embarrassed. "I'm not good at keeping up with the times. I don't get out in public much."

"What's your name?" Emma asked.

"Harold. And you're Emma Armstrong."

"Okay, buddy," Emma said, immediately turning sour. "If you're a reporter, you can take yourself out that door. I've got nothing to say."

"Oh, no, Emma. I'm not a reporter, I assure you."

"Oh, okay then. I see you are empty handed. Let me buy you a drink to put in it."

"No thanks," Harold answered politely. "I can't drink. I mean, I *don't* drink."

"So, what are you doing in a bar then, Harold?"

"I needed to talk to you."

Emma's eyes narrowed. "About what? What could you possibly want to talk to me about?"

"You, of course. Your troubles, your woes."

"My woes," Emma laughed. "You're funny. You talk weird, and you're a man in a bar who doesn't drink. By the way, can you see a blue sort of hazy mist around me?"

"Yes," he answered simply.

Emma was taken aback. "No one else seems to notice it. How come you can see it?"

"That's a story too long to tell. Just know that it is the blue mist that allows me to be here with you right now."

"Oh, brother. I need another drink," Emma sighed, exhaling loudly. She tried to get the waitress's attention, but the young woman was too busy flirting with two handsome hunks at another table. Getting up, she went to the bar and got it herself.

Harold was still there when she returned, sitting up very erect in his chair.

"Okay, Harold, here are my troubles," Emma announced, already beginning to slur her words. "My son is in the hospital with a broken ankle. I can't be there because I fu...excuse me...messed up so badly that I have to stay here and fix everything. I have a husband that I sort of inherited. Don't like him all that much, but he's useful. I have an *older-than-God* agent who wants me to be Miss Prim and Proper all the time, which is totally boring. Oh, what else? Oh yeah. I have a best friend I can't turn to because she barely speaks to me. Oh, oh, oh...one more thing. I get these visions in my head of things that are going to happen. I never understand them. They appear as tiny snapshots in time. I never know the time or where they're going to happen. They just blip into my head with no warning. My conclusion is that I'm either psychic or crazy. So, what can you help me do about any of that?"

"That's truly all very sad. How do you think you might change it? Do you even want to change it?"

"Only the *people that used to love me, now hating me,* part. The rest, I truly don't care all that much," Emma answered, downing the last of her drink.

"My words of wisdom would be. Look deep inside yourself. You might find someone in there that *can* help with everything."

Emma froze. She believed she knew what he was talking about—old Emma. The last time she saw the mist, someone was calling for her. Emma's face turned hard and cold. "That Emma is gone, my friend. She's dust."

She motioned to the waitress, who walked over immediately.

"Can I get you another drink?" she asked sweetly.

"No, but you can have your bouncer or whatever strong man you have on the premises remove this man," Emma spat out through gritted teeth.

"What man, ma'am?"

Emma pointed to the chair, then watched as Harold slowly faded from sight, taking the fog with him. Jumping out of her chair, she grabbed her bag, retrieved some money, threw it on the table, and left without another word.

Dashing back to her hotel, she locked the door and stayed there. She never set foot outside the room again until her interview two days later. Over those days, she tried to reach Adam. He wouldn't answer his cell or the home phone. Mostly, she cried and slept.

Chapter 43

The audience for the New York show was standing-room only. They wanted to see Emma get eviscerated in front of millions of people. John, the host of the New York show, didn't disappoint. He was brutal with her. He didn't pull any punches. No softball questions that could help her redeem herself.

"So, Emma, why don't you tell me how you hate men and how you'd like to put me under your thumb," he began. "You do realize that your little rant basically reduced women from the loved and cherished wives and girlfriends they are to concubines with kitchen privileges."

"I'm so, so, sorry. I don't hate men, and I never meant to be demeaning to women at all. I misspoke. It all came out wrong. I have this condition. It's called DGBI, standing for disorders of gut-brain interaction. It's a real medical condition. You can look it up. When I had my son, I got very sick and got a bacterial infection in my stomach. They cured it momentarily, but the doctors say it can lay dormant and recur. That's what happened to me. It causes the brain to be dysfunctional in a way. I get my words confused sometimes. That's what happened that day. I don't have any control over it."

"In other words, all those words you said about wives not sleeping with their husbands, because it could be used as a negotiation tool, suggesting they stop shopping, making dinner, and all that other stuff you ranted about...that was all from this DGBI thing?"

"That's right. I didn't mean it that way. I meant to say that women need to get men to appreciate what they do for them. How helpful we are. How much of a burden we take off of them. Those traits are beneficial in the workplace as well. Women can be detailed, artistic, devoted, diplomatic, and hard-working. They have stamina and perseverance. These are all assets in the corporate world."

John leaned back in his chair. "I don't buy it, the apology, this sudden medical condition reveal, any of it. I think you said what you truly believe. Now you're trying to backpedal because you got seen for the rude, man-hating woman you are. You don't want to help women. You just want a following. Misery loves company."

"No. No. You've got me all wrong," Emma responded pleadingly. "I love these women. I wanted to help them be alive and truly who they are. I hate that women can't get equal pay or hold high-ranking positions. We're smart. We're tough. We have babies, for Christ's sake. I'd like to see you do that." At that moment, there was a smattering of applause throughout the audience and some light laughter.

"May I," Emma asked, pointing to the front of the stage.

"Be my guest," John answered. "We checked everyone for weapons on the way in," he laughed.

Emma stood in front of the crowd and looked into the eyes of each person there before speaking.

"I want to apologize to you from the bottom of my heart. I really do have a medical condition, and it has gotten me in more than one tight spot, I can tell you that. But please know this...my commitment is real. I wholeheartedly believe that women must be lifted up and allowed to lead. We are natural healers. We are nurturers. We have good brains and big hearts. Just remember that." Emma stopped talking. The audience was silent. Then, one woman raised her hand.

"Yes, ma'am?" Emma said, pointing at her.

"I think that's a great speech, but I'm skeptical. We all, well, I guess I can't speak for everyone, so I'll say *I* was shocked. You broke my trust in you. If you talk so mean and belittling again, are we supposed to assume it's your gut thing? It seems to me that's kinda an easy out. Say bad things, then blame it on your body. It's weird."

Emma ran her hand through her hair, sighing deeply. "Good points. I don't have an answer. But you are so wrong if you don't believe me. You'll be hurting yourselves. You'd be missing out on all I have to give and teach you."

"You know, lady," a woman from the back hollered, "you almost had me. But that, what you just said there, about that lady only hurting herself if she doesn't listen to the great and powerful you...there was no compassion or care there. You basically told her she was stupid for not believing you and your crap. How sick is that? All I heard in all your words and fake apology was someone who got caught showing their true colors and is trying to lie her way out of it."

Emma didn't answer. She simply walked off the stage.

Downstairs outside, the herd of reporters surrounded her again. This time, she stopped.

"So, what are you going to do now, Emma? What are your plans?"

"My plans?" she laughed sarcastically. "You mean, am I down and out? Not by a longshot buddy. I have my books. I plan to do some acting. I have irons in the fire."

"But, do you really think people will buy your books now…after all this?"

"Why wouldn't they? I'm a fabulous writer," she barked at them, standing tall and confident. "Tomorrow you guys will have another story to chase, one that's much more interesting than mine. People still love me. You'll see. Now let me go through. I need to get back to my hotel."

They made a path, and she stepped into her limousine and waved as they drove away.

Back in her room, she tried to call Adam again. No answer. She tried her dad, same result. She tried Andrea. She picked up.

"Don't hang up on me, please, Andie. I need you. I'm sure you saw the show."

"That I did," Andie answered curtly.

"Well, what should I do now?"

"Oh, now you want *my* opinion? Now that everyone else has left you behind, you come running? During all your fame and fortune, you barely had time for a phone call with me, let alone actually meet me for lunch or have a girl's-night-out dinner. Your life was too damned important. Well, Emma, my life is too damned important to let a sorry friend like you back into it."

Emma's face turned beet red with anger. "Bite me," she shouted into the phone, then slammed down the receiver.

"Who needs any of them," she said aloud to the empty room as she paced. "I'm Emma Armstrong. I'm somebody. They'll see. They'll see."

Her sleep was fitful. Her dreams were full of images and colors. Like a slideshow on fast forward, the pictures raced by. The same ones over and over again—her parents driving away in the car and Andrea crying her eyes out. Each time she would awaken, she could barely breathe.

Rather than leave the next morning as planned, she stayed in New York for four more days. She saw no reason to rush home. There was only another fight with Adam waiting for her there. She spent the days getting massages, having her nails done, and getting plastered. It was the only way she could sleep without the awful dreams.

Chapter 44

By the time the limousine pulled up in front of Emma's house, she'd been gone almost a full two weeks. She walked into the deathly silence of an empty home. She wondered if Ryan was still in the hospital. Picking up the phone, she dialed the hospital. She was told that Ryan was no longer there, released four days ago, but she asked if she could speak to the floor nurse anyway.

"I'm so embarrassed. I know he's no longer there, but I was unavoidably detained in New York and, just this second, walked in the door. I realize this is unusual, but could you tell me how he did and is doing? My husband and I are having a bit of a disagreeable time, and he's not home right now, so I can't ask him. Could you give me that information?"

"Um, sure. Ryan is a very brave, sweet boy. He did well with the surgery. He's wearing a cast now that will have to stay on for about six weeks. Once it's removed, there should be no permanent damage or any trouble with his walking or mobility. He's going to be just fine, Mrs. Armstrong."

"Thank you so much," Emma replied.

When she took her suitcases up to the bedroom, she was surprised to see the bed fully made and the room neat as a pin. She opened the closet door to find that all of Adam's clothes were gone. She raced down the hall to Ryan's room. His clothes and toys were gone as well. They'd left her.

"He just leaves me...just like that, and takes Ryan?" Emma raged. "I won't let him get away with this! He'll rue the day he ever crossed me."

She returned downstairs and entered the kitchen, where she found a note on the table. She read it out loud.

"Emma, when you refused to return home to support your son and me, I finally realized the place we held in your life. I've signed over my half of the house to you, (papers are in the other envelope on the table). Your dad and mom have been kind enough to allow us to stay at the beach house until we find something of our own. Both your parents are now residing in your mother's house. They still come to babysit when I need them to, but I'm continuing to work at home as much as possible to keep some stability in Ryan's life. He's very confused right now.

If there is any kindness left in your soul, I pray that you allow me to have full custody of him. You can see him whenever you like, but only when supervised by me or your parents. My attorney believes I will easily win if taken to court. Your disregard for his welfare, both before his accident when you were barely home, and after when you wouldn't fly back when he was injured. Each makes a very strong case against you. I want you in his life. He deserves a mother, but not necessarily the one you are now.

I wish only the best for you. I loved you for a lot of years, jailbait, but you've crushed that love into a million pieces. Please take care.

Emma let out a primal scream and ripped the note to shreds. She grabbed the legal papers and did the same with them.

Grabbing her keys, she went to the garage. Her car wouldn't start. Calling a taxi, she paid them double to get her to the beach house as fast as humanly possible.

Telling the driver to wait, she raced to the front door, pounding wildly, screaming like a madwoman.

"Adam! Adam! Open this door! I want my son! Open this damned door!" she yelled while continuing to kick the door and pound it with her fists.

She sustained this level of assault for a good five minutes. The taxi driver finally exited his cab and came over to her. "Come on, lady, somebody's gonna call the cops on you. Let's get outta here. Obviously, there's nobody home."

Spent and exhausted, she allowed herself to be led back to the car.

Back home, she railed at the Gods and roamed around her house, alternately sobbing for her loss and shouting her revenge.

She tried to call Andrea. To her amazement, Andrea answered.

"I'm so sorry, Andrea, about our last conversation, but I really need you. Adam's left me, and he took Ryan with him," Emma sobbed.

Andrea paused before speaking. She wanted to say something like, "Big surprise. You never spent much time with your kid anyway. Now you suddenly want to be a mom?" But she didn't.

"I'm sorry to hear that, Em," she said, even though her tone was less than sympathetic.

"That's it? Sorry to hear that? You've got to help me get him back. Tell me what to do?"

"I'm not sure I want you two to get back together. I like Adam; he's a good guy. You've treated him horribly. What's in it for him? He should want to return to your insults and absence while you become a *star*? I think not."

"Andie, please," Emma said earnestly. "Can you come over? I have to get everyone back. I can't be alone."

"Who's everyone? Ryan and Adam?"

"Of course, Ryan and Adam, but everyone. All those people who used to love me thought I was smart. They hung on my every word. I was important. I was somebody."

Andrea tried hard to feel sorry for her friend of so many years, but it was almost impossible to do so. Also, she had become used to the pattern. Emma would mess up, hurt everyone around her, feel bad later when she suffered the consequences, and finally apologize. Then, right on cue, she would self-destruct again as soon as all was back to normal.

"I don't hear any remorse for any of your actions, Em. All I hear is a lot of wanting what *you* want and not talking about what you want to give *them*. I just can't do it, Em. I can't get caught up in your drama again. I truly am so, so sorry. If you ever get some help and discover why you have this selfish streak and a desire to fix it, I'm your gal. I'll be there in a heartbeat. I'm going to have to hang up now. Kyle isn't feeling well, so I want to be with him." Andrea quietly hung up.

"What's wrong with me?" Emma raged, throwing the phone across the room. "What's wrong with you, Miss Perfect bitch? I'll figure it out. I will." Slowly, she ascended the stairs and went to bed.

The next day was a carbon copy of her rollercoaster of emotions from the day before. A process server came to the door and handed her divorce papers. Mabel called, saying her presence was requested at a meeting the following week, during which it would be decided whether they would keep her on as a client. She told Emma it was more of a formality as she was sure the odds of them continuing to represent her were next to none.

The only good thing was that Adam called and put Ryan on the phone. She was so happy to hear his voice. He told her how much he loved the beach and his new school that Daddy drove him to every day. Oddly, he never asked if she was coming to see him soon. After she and Ryan were done speaking, Adam got on the phone to say goodbye.

"No, wait. Adam, could you come over and have dinner so we can talk?" She held her breath.

"Maybe in a couple of weeks or so. We're slammed at work. Got this big new job. You know how it goes. I'll call you." With that, he hung up.

She didn't even get angry. She became stoic. "Okay then," she said to the emptiness, "I know what I have to do. Make a list. Decide how I can get back my people. I'll convince Mabel to keep me on. My books are good. That's how all this good stuff started. They started loving me through my books. I just need to go back to the beginning. Adam can rot in hell. He was a drag around my neck anyway. I'll show him. I'll show everybody."

Chapter 45

Ultimately, Emma didn't fight the divorce or the custody agreement. "You're right, Adam. I'm too busy to be a proper mother," she'd said with no snark attached, stating the simple facts.

She'd see Ryan on holidays and birthdays, always supervised, which was enough for her. Her absence didn't seem to negatively affect the boy. He was surrounded by love from his dad, his grandparents, and Andrea and Kyle. They'd become frequent visitors. Ryan loved his Aunt Andrea.

Emma had talked her agents into keeping her on, and in the next two years she produced two more novels in her Dumb Criminal series. However, her sales continued to plummet with each book. She was hardly making enough in royalties to keep up her mortgage payments. Her publisher didn't want to go to the expense of sending her on tours and book signings. In reality, they were afraid to.

She'd tried to be a leader again in the women's movement, but she was persona non grata. Even though she would march with them, no one wanted to hear her speak. Rage turned inward becomes depression. Her days were lackluster. She stopped caring for herself. There was a string of one-night stands, but even the men she met seemed repelled by her after one date.

She had made up with her parents, which was good. However, their relationship wasn't the same as before. They were always just the tiniest bit awkward when they were together, but at least she had some support from them.

There were a couple of small parts in movies, but only a few lines, sometimes a little more. But, on the last one, she was fired for calling the director a jackass because she said he was making her look dumb and stupid. "Oh, my God. Did you not read the script? That's your character! A dumb blond!" So much for acting.

After another year, her agent finally fired her, and the publisher canceled her contract for future novels. As the years ticked by, the cascading failures piled one upon the other. She began needing to sell off furniture and other expensive things she'd bought to keep up her mortgage payments. For the most part, her big life had become very small, consisting of rambling around her house, pretending to write, and watching television. Indeed, it was a lonely existence.

She spent her forty-third birthday alone again. Adam and Ryan didn't even bother calling. Their rift had deepened over the past couple of years when she'd just *forgotten* to visit Ryan, *forgot* his birthday, and even *forgot* Christmas last year. It was no surprise to her. Her love now was the bottle. It was her friend, her constant companion.

On the night of her birthday, she began having the same recurring dream night after night. In each one, only the surroundings and colors were different. She was always in an infinite space with no walls, no buildings, no life of any kind. One night, it would be a green, gloppy, hazy fog that was thick and difficult to define, seeming to go on forever; another night, it would be red, orange, or purple. But despite the expanse, it always felt like a vise enclosing her. Some nights, it would be almost playful and inviting. In most, however, it was dark and foreboding. No matter the color, the voices were the same, repeating the same messages every time. "Stop it from happening." "It's too soon." "Warn them."

This went on for weeks, followed by days on end of the mental pictures. They grew in number. There was one of her parents driving away in their 'just married' car. There was one of Andrea, heartbroken and crying. Added to that was a hospital room filled with flowers and cards, but no one was in it.

From each dream, whether the infinite expanse or the pictures, she would wake up in a cold sweat, screaming at the top of her lungs. Each night after she awakened from the dreams, she would go down and get a bottle of whatever alcohol she had in the house and drink herself to sleep.

They finally stopped as abruptly as they had arrived. She had no idea why but was relieved. She chalked it up to the alcohol, finally flushing them out of her head.

One month later, her father called to let her know that he and her mother were finally going to remarry. The wedding was in two days. He was so excited like it was the first time, not their second, taking place after a long marriage, long divorce, and long, slow reconciliation.

"Can you come, Em?" her father asked enthusiastically. "I know that Ryan would love to see you."

"I doubt that, Dad. Besides, you're only getting married at the courthouse. It's not like it's a big affair or anything. Five minutes, and you're done."

"Five minutes of vows, but a lifetime of love and commitment. It doesn't matter where the I do's are said. It's the what's in the heart that matters. If my memory serves me correctly, didn't you get married at the courthouse? Yep, I definitely think that's a true statement," he chuckled.

"And look how that turned out. No, Dad. I think I'll pass. I don't have anything to wear anyway. I wish you and Mom all the happiness in the world. I promise I'll come by with an expense gift. Now, I gotta dash. Lots of meetings today." She hung up the phone before he could even say goodbye.

She'd not told her folks exactly how bad her fortune reversal had become. They thought she was just taking some time off from writing and living off the millions she had in royalties. She'd kept them from the house in recent weeks, as it was practically devoid of furniture now, save for her bed upstairs, a couple of chairs, and a few paintings. She couldn't face the humiliation.

On the day of the wedding, Emma sat on her bed with a bottle of Vodka that she was drinking right from the bottle. She raised it high in the air. "Here's a toast to my parents. I wish you...I wish you..." Her words drifted off as she jumped off the bed and ran to the closet excitedly. She scanned the few items left hanging there—only three long-sleeved shirts, one skirt, and four pairs of jeans crumpled on the floor.

"Stupid idea, Em," she said, speaking in a British accent. There is absolutely no *wedding attire* in that closet. Oh well, Such is life."

Even though Adam knew Emma wasn't coming to the wedding, he kept checking the door, hoping she'd change her mind. Her parents said they understood, "she's been a bit down in the dumps lately," they'd said, but he knew it broke their hearts. Adam had long ago stopped being angry with Emma. Now, it was mostly sadness and pity. He also had yet to learn exactly how dire her circumstances were.

Many of the Corbell's friends were there, seated on the benches in the small courtroom used for the occasion. Mrs. Corbell wore a powder blue dress, and Mr. Corbell looked dapper in his navy blue suit.

Once outside, the beaming couple was congratulated by all in attendance. They made plans to all meet for brunch at their favorite restaurant, and then the couple was off on their honeymoon.

Mr. Corbell pulled Adam away from the crowd. He handed him an envelope.

"I've deeded the beach house to you and Ryan. We'll be staying in the townhouse," he said with a smile.

"But, you love the beach house. No. This is too much," Adam argued.

"It's not nearly enough," the older man said with a tear in his eye. "You have truly become our son. We're quite happy in the townhouse." He walked back over to join the crowd surrounding his once-again wife without allowing Adam to protest further.

The other couples headed for their cars, and as Mr. and Mrs. Corbell were getting ready to get into their vehicle, Ryan piped up. "I want to ride with Grandma and Grandpa to the restaurant. Okay, Dad?"

Before Adam could answer, an invisible force shoved him backward forcefully, shouting in his ear, "No, he cannot get in the car. Don't let him get in the car!"

Adam reeled back a little bit, and Mr. Corbell reached out to steady him.

"You okay, son?" Mr. Corbell asked, concerned.

"Did you hear that?" Adam stuttered.

"Hear what?"

"Nothing. Nothing." Adam looked around, but there was no one else near them.

"You know, Ryan, I, um, I'm feeling a little bad cuz I forgot to do something. I wanted to pick up this one little surprise for Grandpa and Grandma. I really can't do it without you. Could you help me with that before we go to the restaurant? We can just meet them there."

"Sure, Dad. I'll help," Ryan said happily.

Everybody kissed everybody, and when the car drove off, Adam and Ryan watched for a few moments until they'd turned the corner a couple of blocks up, disappearing from sight.

By the time they'd reached their own car, a loud explosion was heard. Within seconds, police sirens were heard. Adam started the car and sped to the location where the explosion emanated from. His heart was pounding. This was the same street the Corbells had turned up.

All the activity was about four blocks up. He pulled over as soon as he rounded the corner, ordering Ryan to stay in the car. He took off at a dead run. People had already gathered at the scene, gaping at the accident. When he made it to the front of the crowd, he let out a scream, not even realizing he'd made a sound. There, before his eyes, was Mr. and Mrs. Corbell's car in a twisted heap in the middle of the intersection.

Chapter 46

The next couple of weeks were a blur of activity and confusion. Adam tried desperately to reach Emma, but to no avail. He called every hour on the hour, no answer. He went by her house, but she never came to the door. He put off the double funeral as long as he could, hoping he could reach her, but after ten days, they could wait no longer. Poor Ryan was in shock. His grandparents had been his life, his constancy, his safety. They were there almost every day throughout his now tender seventeen years. His grief was immense. He started taking to his bed and sleeping for long hours. He barely ate.

Finally, after a month, they held the reading of the wills. Everything from both parents had been divided between Adam, Ryan, and Emma's brother, Don. Ryan was left with a hefty trust fund. Adam was bequeathed the three restaurants and some money, and Don had been given the remainder of his parents' estates. It was expressly stated that Emma was to receive nothing. Adam was surprised at that. He didn't realize they had any idea how far Emma had fallen. If she managed to turn her life around, the document said, stay sober and get some mental health treatment, she could go to Adam and Don and request a portion of their inheritances be given to her. It was entirely at their discretion. Emma knew none of this, however. She was too busy drinking and feeling sorry for herself.

As Emma's life cascaded downward, the next three months consisted of rummaging through her pants pockets, trying to find any cash she may have, and finding tin cans to sell for more money. Many nights she went bar hopping, getting others to buy her drinks. Her bank accounts had all been closed due to a lack of funds and the overdraft fees from the many checks she had somehow managed to cash without enough money available.

"Twenty, forty, sixty, eighty, one hundred," she said aloud as she counted the twenty-dollar bills. "And two fifties, a five and a ten, two ones, and...um...72 cents in change. Two hundred, seventeen dollars and 72 cents in all," she mumbled sadly. "Okay, okay. It's not all that desperate. I still have soda cans I can collect money on, and um...what else? I still have a few paintings to sell. It'll be okay."

Another round of fog, misty lights, and colors appeared before her eyes. This had begun again in the past week or so. She figured it was because of how little she was eating.

"Just stop it already," she said, waving her arms around wildly like she was trying to swat away a swarm of flies, desperately attempting to dispel the disruption around her. "I'll eat already. Just leave me alone." Suddenly, she heard someone downstairs.

"Hello? Mrs. Armstrong. Los Angeles County Sheriff's Department."

Emma ran down the stairs. A man in uniform stood in the middle of the foyer with two handfuls of mail in his hands.

"What are you doing?" Emma shouted. "You can't come in here! Get out!"

"We're here to see that you leave the premises immediately," the officer answered unsympathetically.

"What do you mean leave? This is my house. I'm not going anywhere!"

"The bank foreclosed on your house two weeks ago."

"That's impossible. No one has notified me. Don't they have to take me to court or something? I know I'm a couple of months late on the mortgage, but I'm a famous writer. I'll be getting a royalty check soon. Then I'll catch up. Now get out of here." Emma stamped her foot angrily.

"You missed more than a couple of months, *and* you missed the hearing. You were notified," the officer said, sorting through the mail and tossing envelope after envelope onto the floor at her feet. "They're all here. The notices of intention to foreclose. The notice to appear. You have to leave the premises immediately."

Emma bent down, picked up the letters, and ripped them up. "I don't care. I'm not going anywhere."

Another officer walked in through the door and stood there, not speaking.

"Well, if you like," he began, speaking like he was talking to a small child, "we can arrest you and take you to jail. From the looks of your empty house, you've got nothing to pack up. You don't look so well either, and you probably haven't had a decent meal in weeks. Perhaps you would like it if we gave you a nice warm cot and some food."

Emma flopped down onto the bottom step. She hung her head. "No, I wouldn't like that. Could you at least allow me time to shower and change clothes?"

"No can do. Gather your things. I'll give you ten minutes."

Emma gave him a dirty look and climbed back up the stairs to the bedroom. Stuffing the money in her holey jeans and putting on some tennis shoes, she grabbed the few pieces of clothing from the closet, put on her dolphin necklace, and tucked it inside her T-shirt.

"Come on, Mrs. Armstrong. Chop, chop," the officer yelled from below.

"I'm coming. Just shut up!"

Her SUV was the only thing that had yet to be sold. It was paid for. She threw her few belongings in the back seat, saluted to the officer, and drove away. When she glanced at the digital instrument panel, she saw the gas needle hugging the 'E.'

"Great! Now I have to spend what little I have to feed this fuel hog."

Before she made it to the station, however, she stopped at the small grouping of shops a few blocks down. There were some clothes shops, a couple of tiny restaurants, and a grocery store that sold alcohol. Her first order of business was to restock.

Inside, she bought a couple of ready-made sandwiches and two six-packs of beer. She truly hated beer, but it was cheap. So as not to be seen sitting in her car, guzzling her booze, she drove around behind the shops, found a little space by one of the dumpsters, and ate her food. She was so very tired.

"So, now what, Emma? "This is another fine mess you've gotten us into," she slurred, imitating the famous Abbott and Costello line. "I have no home," she laughed sickly. "Whadaya think of that? No home." She stared out the window, refusing to cry.

She kept nodding off every few seconds. One time, she woke up choking on a bit of her food. Night was beginning to fall, and the shops were turning over their closed signs, shutting down the lights, and locking up.

"I obviously can't go to Adam. Andrea isn't speaking to me, and my mom and dad, well, I doubt they would roll out the red carpet. Soooo, um...what? What will I do? I'll obviously sleep in my car. And then...and then, tomorrow I'll go see Mabel. I'll tell her about my newest idea for a book. What idea? Well, I'll think of one before I go. Then I'll ask her to lend me some money to keep me going while I write it. On what? I no longer have a computer. Hmm, that could be a problem. It's doable, though. Totally doable. But I'm so tired. I really need to sleep."

She put down the middle seats and crawled into the back of the SUV. She had a couple of towels in the back from the last time she'd gone to the beach. Covering herself with them, she passed out.

A couple of employees exited one of the stores and headed to their car. They saw the SUV tucked away by the dumpster. Walking over, they peeked inside.

"Oh, my God. There's a woman in there," one of the young girls exclaimed. "Do you think she's dead?"

"Let me look," the other said, getting closer to get a better view. Oh, wow. Do you know who that is? That's Emma Armstrong. She's a famous author—or was. I read a couple of her books. They say she went nuts on some television show and turned into a falling-down drunk," she announced sadly.

"Oh, no. Do you think she's all right? Should we knock on the window? Should we call the police?"

"Nah. I can see her breathing. Let's not get involved. Probably better she just sleep it off."

"But what if someone comes and attacks her in the middle of the night or something?"

"She'll be fine. I'll bet when we come in tomorrow, she'll be gone. Let's get outta here."

With that, they walked away, already giggling about their dates for the night and forgetting all about the passed-out former somebody in the car."

The evening stars slowly became invisible, hidden by the clouds, separating them from the view of anyone below. A light rain began to fall, chilling the air. Emma shivered in her sleep, tucking her towels tighter around her body.

Chapter 47

As the sun barely peeked over the horizon the following morning, Emma's body began to shake violently. The reverberation didn't initially wake her. As the intensity grew, like an earthquake gaining momentum as it rose from a 6.0 to an 8.2 disaster, the trembling grew exponentially until suddenly, her eyes popped open wide, filled with terror. She seemed to be in some kind of internal battle. She struggled to open the door but seemed to be fighting with an invisible assailant. Then, like a Phoenix rising from the ashes, she flung open the door, leapt outside, and let out a long guttural sound, not a scream, more of a very deep *aaahhhhhh* sound. She stretched her arms and patted her legs from her hips to her feet like they'd gone to sleep, and she was trying to get rid of the numbness. She inhaled deeply a few times, trying to clear her head.

"I did it!" I'm back, old Emma shouted loudly. She grabbed her head and began massaging her temples. "Good God, woman, how in the world could you consume so much alcohol? If we weren't in the same body, I'd kick your ass. Right now, I've gotta go find Andrea. I hope I'm not too late," she said urgently.

She searched the pants she was wearing and found a little over one hundred dollars and the car keys. Jumping behind the wheel, she turned the key in the ignition. The engine wouldn't even turn over. She looked at the gas gauge. Empty.

"Dammit!" she yelled, pounding on the steering wheel. The dark morning sky was just beginning to accept the morning sun, lighting it up a bit. However, there was still little movement in the area in the form of cars or other activities. "What time is it? Nothing will be open yet."

Stepping out of the car, she walked around the buildings and to the front to see if she could spot a gas station. She could see the lights of an all-night Arco in the distance, about two blocks up. "Great!"

Her first attempts at running looked almost comical, like an arthritic giraffe trying to cover ground quickly. She had no coordination because her body was still recovering from the beating it'd been taking from New Emma's non-care. Finally, she managed to jog and broke out into a dead run.

When she reached the station, she was entirely out of breath. She bent over to try and regulate her breathing a little. Once she got some air back into her lungs, she ran inside.

"Gas. I need some gas," she managed to get out, still trying to catch her breath.

The man sitting in the office with his feet on the desk watching television looked out the window.

"I don't see no car."

"I ran out of gas at the strip mall up the way. I walked here. Do you have a gas can so I can take some gas back to my car? Oh, and could you tell me what the date is today? For that matter, what time is it?" she asked urgently.

The attendant looked at her skeptically. "You don't know what day it is? You on somethin'?"

The old man slowly lifted his overweight body out of the chair. He disappeared into the garage and returned with a small gas can.

"That'll be ten bucks," he said, holding it out to her.

"For that tiny thing? Oh, never mind, that's fine," she said, digging in her pocket and handing him the money. He gave her change for the twenty, then sat back down.

"Aren't you going to put gas in it for me?"

"Nope. I just take the money. You pump the gas," he said, turning his eyes back to the television; then he added, "Oh, it happens to be Valentine's Day...and it's 6:00 a.m."

Emma gave him a disgusted look and ran out the door. Filling the can, she tried to run back to her car, but with the gas can, it was impossible. She never realized a gallon of gas could be so heavy.

I've got time. I've got time. It'll be okay, she kept repeating in her head as she hurried back to her car. *It doesn't happen for a couple of weeks. It's okay. It'll all be okay.*

By the time she'd gotten her car filled up with gas and hopped on the freeway, it was after seven. The sun was bright in the sky, and the traffic was already beginning to slow to the morning-rush crawl. Emma was in motion even though she was sitting, tapping out her frustration on the steering wheel. *Come on, come on, let's go, let's go, let's go.* Taking the next off-ramp, she opted for surface streets. All the way there, she reviewed the awful fights that the new Emma and Andrea had had in the past couple of years. The last one, in which Emma had called Andrea a "stupid bitch" when she wouldn't loan her some money, made her shudder. Would she even open the door? There had to be a way to make her listen.

It was a little after eight when she pulled up in front of Andrea's house. Glancing in the rearview mirror before she exited, she tried to smooth her hair. *Yuck. I look like I put my finger in a light socket.*

Racing to the door, she began pounding on it, screaming Andrea's name. "Andrea! Andrea! Open the door. Come on, Andrea, it's urgent! Andrea"

After what seemed like an eternity, Andrea flung open the door angrily.

"What do you want? Get out of here!" she barked.

"Please, Andrea. I know you hate me, but this is urgent. It's a matter of life and death, Kyle's life and death. You have to listen to what I have to say."

Andrea stood her ground, still blocking the door, not allowing Emma entry. Her eyes turned ice cold.

"You're drunk!"

"I promise you I'm not. I'm... I'm me. I mean, I'm back. I mean, I'm not the other me that's been around for the last few years." Emma tried desperately not to sound like a crazy person but was failing miserably.

"Look at you! You are *absolutely* drunk. You reek of liquor. You look like you've been sleeping in your car. Just when I think you can't sink any lower, you prove me wrong and find a new bottom."

"You're right, I've been disgusting, but I'm not drunk, and I have something to tell you that will save Kyle's life. If you don't listen, he's going to die soon."

Andrea attempted to slam the door in Emma's face, but Emma pushed back, not allowing it to close.

"Listen to me! If you just give me five minutes, just five minutes, I can explain everything. Then, if you still want to kick me out, I'll go quietly."

Andrea was seething, but there was something in Emma's face, something in her tone that sent chills down her spine. She was still more than skeptical, but she let her in anyway.

"Let me get you some coffee," Andrea said curtly, heading towards the kitchen, wondering why she was showing Emma any kindness at all. Emma followed and sat at the kitchen table.

Neither said another word until they were both seated with their coffee in front of them. Andrea had also put a couple of scones on a plate for them to eat.

"You look like you could use some food," Andrea said, shoving the plate over to Emma. "So talk," she said curtly.

Emma took a deep breath. "You've got to get Kyle's heart checked out. He's got an aneurysm. It will rupture in a couple of weeks, and he'll die."

"Oh, for God's sake, Emma. What are you trying to pull here? What is all this garbage?"

"It's not garbage!" Emma protested. "It's the truth."

"And exactly when did you develop your psychic powers," Andrea spit out.

"I'm not psychic...I lived through it with you...I mean...before." Emma was grasping at straws, at a loss to explain herself and how she would know such a thing. She knew how absolutely bonkers she sounded.

Jumping out of the chair, Emma started pacing back and forth, trying to find the right words.

"Look, you won't believe me, but I'm from the future. I know *your* future," Emma said with urgency and fear. "Kyle dies on March third unless you get him to a doctor. I know that he had a physical just four months ago, but they missed it. They told you after he died that this was not an uncommon thing, to have missed it, that is. These things can be hard to spot when they're small...or something like that." Emma was racing through her explanation, making her rant sound more unhinged.

"Shut up!" Andrea shouted. "Just shut up! You're either drunk, or high, or have completely lost touch with reality. I want you to leave. Right now!"

Emma refused to go, continuing her plea. "You've noticed how I've changed. Why do you think that is? It's because I was turning into this new version of myself when I came back here. I got lost in the fame and fortune. I...oh, crap, none of that matters. What's important now is that I'm back. It's me, Andrea, the old Emma." She paused momentarily, unsure how to convince her friend of who she was and how all this craziness came about.

Look, did the Emma you've had contact with in the past years ever, ever, talk about things we did as kids? No. Do you want to know why? Because she didn't have those memories. Remember how when we were in school and had a tough test or something, we'd do this?" Emma walked over to Andrea and tapped her on the forehead, chin, then each cheek as she said, almost like a football cheer, "Today's the day, here we go, we're going to succeed, don't you know." Remember that? Did she ever..."

Andrea interrupted her. "You *are* nuts! Get out!" She headed for the front door and opened it. "Get out."

"Andrea, please, don't ignore me..."

"Ignore you? Ignore you?" Andrea shouted, enraged. "You mean the way you ignored Adam and Ryan after your parents died? And the way you're ignoring Adam now?

"My parents are dead? When? How did that happen? I didn't know." Emma turned pale, tears immediately beginning to flow.

"Oh, for Christ's sake. Everybody tried to call you. We went by your house. Your car was there, but you didn't answer the door—obviously passed out. The attorney sent you letters. And then, when Ryan got sick, the same thing happened. Now, you come here with this fantastical story that you're a different person, trying to absolve yourself of your repulsive behavior for years? It's sickening. Of course, you knew. You just chose to stay away, like you're choosing right now to not visit your dying son. I could kick myself for ever opening the door."

Emma felt like someone had just punched her in the stomach. Her parents were dead? Her son was dying? She began to wail loudly. "I didn't know," she said in between sobs. "I swear I didn't know any of this. Where is Ryan? I have to get to him. What happened? What hospital is he in?"

"Half of me doesn't want to tell you. You were a horrible mother to him. He deserves to die in peace without your toxic presence there."

"Please, Andrea. If you don't believe anything else I've said today, please believe I love my son more than life itself. I have to see him. Please."

"He's at Seaside Hospital," Andrea's words were not said in kindness or from any belief that Emma had changed. It was for Ryan. For all her absence from his life, he loved his mother. She should be there to say goodbye.

"What's wrong with him? Why is he dying?" Emma cried out.

"He's got leukemia. They couldn't find a donor for a bone marrow transplant. They were hoping you would be a match. You never showed up. It's too late now, even if you could be a donor. He has declined so much he wouldn't live through the surgery.

Emma dropped to her knees and sobbed uncontrollably. Andrea bent down, lifted her up, and held her. This was the first moment since all the turmoil had begun with Emma that she'd felt sorry for her. For that instant, she saw her old friend, her bestie, her confidant, and was witness to her deep and all-encompassing pain.

"Go, sweetie," Andrea said softly. "They'll be time for tears later. You need to be with him."

Emma gathered herself, squared her shoulders, and ran out the door.

Chapter 48

Emma ran through the hospital doors to the front desk. Pounding on the counter, she yelled, "Ryan Armstrong...my son...Ryan Armstrong. What room is he in? Hurry. Where is he?"

The woman looked at Emma, the disheveled state of her clothes and hair, the reek of stale alcohol wafting off of her, and decided to check her out more before giving her the information. She looked like she was homeless.

"Please, ma'am, have a seat over there. I need to finish one thing, then I'll look up your son's information."

Emma walked away, but didn't sit down. She paced back and forth a few feet away. The woman was on the phone, her back turned, whispering into the receiver.

"We may have a situation here," the woman said in a hushed tone. "There's a homeless woman here who says she's the mother of one of the patients. She's quite agitated. How do you want me to handle it? Just a sec." She clicked a few keys on her computer. "He's in the ICU."

Emma had walked back up to the counter at the exact moment the woman had said ICU. She spun around and took off running. As she ran down the hallway, she saw a sign indicating that the intensive care unit was on the second floor. Flinging open the door to the stairwell, she bounded up two steps at a time. As she reached the next floor, she could hear the door below open again and footsteps running up behind her.

"Ma'am. Ma'am." A male voice shouted. "Ma'am. Stop."

Emma didn't slow up. She burst through the second-floor door and raced down the hall until she found the ICU. There were six glassed-in rooms with a large circular desk in the center. Heart monitors and other blipping screens occupied one entire side of the desk. Nurses could see every patient clearly from their centralized location.

Emma paused briefly, looking at the glass enclosures. She spotted Adam in the second room to the right of her. He was sitting in a chair, head in his hands. Her heart leapt into her throat. Not even realizing her feet had begun moving, she was suddenly at Ryan's bedside. He was on a ventilator, eyes closed. The whooshing sound of the machine that helped him to breathe sounded like a death knell to her. Leaning over the railing of his bed, she gently kissed his face. She grabbed his hand, holding it tightly, her tears dripping onto his arm and wrist.

Adam jumped out of the chair, shocked by Emma's entrance. At that exact moment, two security guards appeared at the door of the room.

"So sorry, sir. This woman got past us, but we'll get her out of here right now," they said, dragging Emma out of the room.

"It's all right, officer, I know her. I'll handle this," Adam said as quietly as possible so as not to disturb the entire ICU unit. Thank you, though."

Once they left, Adam grabbed Emma by the arm, pulling her close so he could speak directly into her ear and not cause a scene. "Oh no you don't," he spat out through gritted teeth. You don't get to come in here and play the grieving mother. Not after all you've done. Now, you're going to quietly walk to the elevators with me, leave here, and never come back. I never want to see you again," he ordered.

"Adam, please, stop. Listen to me. I didn't know. Not until Andrea told me this morning. I didn't get your messages or anything."

"Of course not, because you were too drunk to answer your phone."

"That was the other Emma. Not me. Can't you tell it's me? Remember when she told you she wasn't the woman you married? Remember that? Well, she wasn't. I am. I know it all sounds like so much gibberish, but it's true. Please, Adam...look at me. Can't you feel it? Can't you sense it?"

"The only thing I feel is ashamed for how long I stayed married to you—how long I didn't see you for the pathetic loser you are. I'm the idiot. I'm the one that never let Ryan see the neglectful, self-centered person that was his mother," Adam continued as quietly as he could, still trying to avoid a scene.

"When your visits became less and less frequent, I told him he should be proud of his famous mother. I made sure he understood that sometimes you had important obligations that kept you from us but that you loved him with all your heart. God! To this very day, he never learned that you were just a sloppy drunk who insulted people on a regular basis and believed they should be honored to have you in their lives." Adam's voice began to choke up. He turned away, speaking softly.

"I kept his hopes up. I let him continue to love you with his whole heart. He read every one of your books and kept them on display, and bragged about you to his friends. I never let him see you for who you really were. That's on me."

When Adam spoke again, his next words were said in a whisper, filled with the overwhelming grief he'd been experiencing for years courtesy of his wife.

"When he got sick, he kept waiting for you to come, asking about you, wondering why you couldn't take a few days off from your busy life to be with him." Adam was crying now. He buried his face in his hands. When Emma tried to put her hand on his shoulder, he shrugged her off. Wiping his eyes, he said in a defeated voice. "Say your goodbyes and leave."

Emma just stared at him blankly. Her voice caught in her throat, and she couldn't speak. There were no more tears to be shed. Her mind and body had become numb. Walking away from Adam, Emma returned to Ryan and combed his hair back from his face, then kissed him on the forehead.

"Goodnight, my sweet, beautiful boy. I love you more than you could ever imagine," she said softly. Without another word, she walked out the door.

Emma sat in the hospital parking lot in her SUV for hours. She was almost in a trance. There was no home to go to, no shopping to be done, no dinner to cook for her family, and no fans waiting patiently for her newest novel. No one awaited her arrival. The even worse joke was that not only was no one waiting for her to appear, but the few who had known her over these last years were certainly hoping she would disappear forever.

Emma kept her eyes on the door of the hospital. There was the tiniest hope that Adam might come running after her. Ridiculous idea, that. He, of course, would never leave Ryan's room for any reason. The sad reality was, as well, that when she did see him walk out the door, it would mean that her son had passed.

Just as she decided it was time to leave, she saw Andrea and Kyle running through the hospital's front doors. She leapt out of her car, racing towards them, and called out.

"Andrea! Andrea!" she shouted into the wind. She was parked so far back from the entrance that they'd already entered and stepped into the elevator by the time she got there. There was no way she could follow.

Adam must have called them. It must be getting close. She thought these things as if she were reading them from a book. There was no emotional involvement in them.

Back in her car, she still didn't move. She wondered when the flood of tears would begin. She couldn't feel anything at all. Time had stood still for her. There was no moving forward, no going back. It was over.

Finally, she started her car and drove away. To where? She had no idea.

Chapter 49

Once she started driving, there was no destination. She turned this way and that way, meandering through the city streets. She finally caught the smell of the ocean. It called to her. Her childhood had been spent there. It was home.

Another few short miles, and she was there. Exiting her car, she walked out to the edge of the sand and sat down. Night had already fallen, and with the full moon high above, the water twinkled and sparkled as the white caps of the waves pushed their way to the shore. She was shivering but didn't really notice. Her mind was only filled with how she was going to end things.

The water looked so inviting. It would be easy to simply walk out and let the rhythm of the waves pull her out to sea. Before she could stand up, as if the ocean had felt her pain and beckoned her to release her own wave of grief, she began to sob. Gut-wrenching pain consumed her entire body.

Images of her past life, the one she'd had before she'd traveled in time, flashed through her mind as if on a runaway train. Every hurt, every fear, every lost dream taunted her. Like she'd just walked through a row of prickly cacti, her skin felt painful, raw, and dry.

The life the other Emma created came in to join the dance. All the hateful words, the only-for-me selfishness, bore down on her soul. She started screaming, covering her ears, trying to block out the sound of her tortured soul's anguish. It had a noise like a pack of rabid animals growling and loudly sniffing the air as they got close to their prey.

"Willow!" Emma shouted. "Willow! Please. Help me. I'm sorry. Don't let my son suffer for my selfishness. Save him, Willow, please save him. He doesn't deserve this. Please, Willow. Please." She continued beseeching her unseen guide to no avail. No clap of thunder or bolt of lightning appeared to herald the acceptance of her plea. No deep voice boomed, "So it shall be."

Nothing. Just waves crashing, immense heart pain, and that awful growling sound in her head.

Finally, having made her decision, she rose. She began walking towards the water when a voice called to her.

"Ma'am. Ma'am. Do you have a minute? I fear I'm lost. Could you help me?" A small-in-stature Asian man beckoned to her. He had the sweetest smile on his face. His eyes twinkled like a small child that had a wonderful secret.

"I'm so sorry to disturb you," he said as he finally reached her side. "I don't know this part of the beach very well, and now that I've walked so far, I'm not sure whether to continue on or go back the way I came. Which would you suggest?"

Emma wiped her eyes. "I'm sure I don't know. If you continue that way, a couple of miles up, you'll find more houses and stairs leading you back up to the highway. I'm sure you know what's behind you since that's the way you came."

"Ah. Very sound thinking," he smiled, his twinkling eyes dancing with delight. "Would you walk with me a bit? I feel I need to go forward. Indeed, that's the direction that is calling to me. I would love a little company along the way."

Emma cocked her head, confused by the strange little man in front of her. He had a softness about him. There was this invisible energy that felt very comforting, almost like a warm blanket or a tender hug.

"What's your name?" she asked.

"I am Master Li, a Buddhist monk, here visiting your beautiful city. And what is your name?"

"I'm Emma." She furrowed her brow and cocked her head. "Beautiful city, huh? I don't see any beauty in this city, or this life for that matter," she blurted out. "My apologies, Master. You probably don't want me to walk with you. I'll only destroy your obvious peace."

The Master laughed heartily. "Then you are exactly the person I should be walking alongside."

"What? That makes no sense,"

The Master took her hand and began rubbing her palm with his thumb. He pressed gently on her fingers and wrist. As he did, a warmth spread through her entire body. She stopped shivering.

"Now that we've put your desperation to sleep, let's walk and talk. My greatest pleasure is meeting new friends."

Emma couldn't speak any of the questions that arose in her head. They came too fast and disappeared in an instant.

"So, Emma, my new friend who can see no beauty, what brings you out here on this night?"

"Why do I feel like I don't need to answer that question—like you already know, she said cautiously."

"That I do, but do you?"

"Of course I do," Emma answered, getting a little huffy. "Everything in my life is gone. I'm homeless; I have no money. I have no friends. My son is dying. There is no future for me. I no longer have a purpose. I've been a waste of a life. So, I think it would be better for everyone if I weren't here." Emma spewed, surprised by her own honesty. She had no idea what compelled her to tell this man her innermost thoughts and feelings. On the other side of that coin, however, she decided it didn't matter. By the time the sun came up, she'd be gone anyway.

"That's quite the burden," was all the Master said.

"You aren't going to tell me I'm wrong, or that I need to get counseling, or, gee, I'm still worth something?"

"Is that what you would like me to tell you?"

Emma started to cry again. "I don't know. Maybe. I don't see any picture in front of me. I see no beauty. I truly don't understand the point of life to begin with when it's so full of pain."

"It is not the life that creates the pain; it is a desire that is the culprit. To desire is to invite disappointment. What you seek can be found inside."

"So, just never *want* anything? That's pretty stupid, don't you think? How in the world would that even work?" Emma felt herself getting frustrated and angry.

"Wanting is fine; setting goals is fine. The *desire* to have these things at all cost creates the pain. It begins a cycle of actions that are counter-productive to one's well-being. That crucial meeting comes at the cost of attending a child's recital. The hours in the office to prove one's worth shove aside the quiet evening with friends and loved ones. Every move becomes about striving; every breath is about future achievement, not how to live today," he smiled, giving his words time to sink in.

"Could you live as happily in a one-room hut as you could in a mansion?" he continued. "Is that quick cellphone conversation better than taking the time to visit a friend in person, listen to their woes, and offer support? It's a matter of attention. Where do you want to place it? Is your attention on attaining, or is your attention on being here in this moment?"

Emma tried to think through his words and understand the logic. The Master laughed heartily again. My dear, you won't find the answers and understanding in your logic. It's inside. Feel for it. You'll find it."

After that, they walked in silence for a bit. The Master finally stopped and pointed to a stairway leading up to the street.

"This is where I get off," the Master smiled, his eyes twinkling. "Thank you for your kindness, dear Emma."

"I didn't do anything," Emma protested.

"You walked with me and kept me company, leading me to my destination. That in itself is what life is all about." He bowed to her and began to ascend the stairs. He stopped at the first one, turned, and smiled at her. "Just remember where your true power lies."

Emma stood there a long time after he left. The warmth she had been feeling left with him, and her tears again began to flow. She tried to hang on to his words; she knew there was hope and wisdom there, but her grief crashed down on her with greater force than it previously had. She started to run after him, but when she got to the stairs he ascended, he had disappeared.

Chapter 50

Emma rambled along the ocean's edge for a couple of more hours. Like walking a tightrope, she stayed between the water and the sand. It was the perfect metaphor for her dilemma: Ocean and die, or sand and live. After speaking to the Master, she wasn't entirely sure which side she would come down on. Her legs began to ache, followed by a whole-body numbness. She was exhausted and felt ripped in two.

Her eyes were suddenly drawn to a woman with a little girl at her side standing by a metal barrel with a fire built inside. She rubbed her hands together to warm them up, then touched them to the face of the little girl. She cooed to the little one and told her not to cry, that everything would be all right soon. The mother was doing her best to comfort her, but the child was obviously in great distress. Emma took a few steps closer. She became captivated by the little girl, touched by the pain in her tiny soul.

"Honey, we only have to sleep here one more night," the mother explained. The lady at the office where they are helping us said that they would probably be able to find us beds tomorrow.

"But, why can't we go back to our old house?" the little girl cried.

"Because, honey, someone else lives there now. When mommy lost her job, we had to give it away to those other nice people. It won't be long, I promise."

The mother looked so beaten down by life. At her feet were a couple of tote bags, with obviously everything they owned in the world: a few clothes and a couple of blankets. On top was a well-worn doll with one eye missing.

When Emma approached them, the woman looked a bit frightened by Emma's appearance.

"I'm so sorry to intrude, but I couldn't help but overhear. I'd like to help if you'd let me. I have an SUV parked a couple of miles back that way. You and your daughter could sleep in it. The backseat folds down. In fact..." Emma said, reaching into her pocket and pulling out her keys and the last of the cash she had. "Here. Take this money, and keep the car for as long as you need to. In fact, just keep the car. I'm meeting a friend here in a bit, and we're going on a long overseas trip. If you come with me right now, we can walk back to it and I'll sign over the registration to you. You could sell it if you want. It's paid for, so it might bring you enough money to get you into a small apartment. You'd actually be doing me a favor. I'll be gone a long time. One less thing for me to worry about."

"But why would you do that? You don't know us." the woman protested. She stepped back a few steps, a little wary of this disheveled woman standing before her.

"But I do. I had a child once and lost him. It would bring me such joy to help you and your daughter out." Emma began to feel very weak. She had to sit down. "If you don't mind, I need to rest for a few minutes."

When she did, the little girl came up and stared at her dolphin necklace.

"That's so pretty." She grabbed for it but Emma pushed her hand away, harder than she'd intended. "Yes, it is. But it's very special to me," she said, holding the dolphin in her hand so the little one couldn't grab it again. She'd planned to take it with her into the ocean. She wanted it to be with her wherever she was going after her death.

"Come on, Patti," the mother said, pulling her away. "That belongs to the nice lady."

Emma watched the child's eyes sadden, with tiny tears beginning to travel down her cheeks. It broke her heart. Her body was starting to feel weaker and weaker. As her breath became more shallow and labored, something warm began to grow throughout her entire being. It felt as if her heart itself was enlarging inside her chest. There was a peacefulness that encompassed her very soul. She felt protected and safe, like when she was a child, and her parents would put her to bed, tuck the blankets tightly around her, kiss her on the cheek, then read to her until she fell asleep. There was a feeling of lightness, of being there but not being there. The sensation was one of complete freedom. She allowed herself to sit with the phenomenon for a few minutes, basking in the magical wonder of experiencing absolutely no pain. Finally, she called to the child.

"Patti," she spoke softly, patting the spot next to her on the sand. "I'm going to tell you a story about this necklace." The girl's eyes widened, and she smiled excitedly.

"This necklace was given to me a long, long time ago. I was told that it had great power. It could grant wishes and make all my dreams come true."

"Did it?" the little girl inquired, already awed by the story.

"You know. It did just that. It brought me here tonight to this beach, and it brought me here to you." Emma held the dolphin to her ear as it was talking to her. "What's that? Well, okay. If you say so."

"What did the dolphin say?" the little girl asked breathlessly.

"It said," she began, taking it off and placing it around the little girl's neck. "It said it wanted to be with you for a while. It said to not forget, though, that you can only use its powers for good. Only the noblest of wishes will be granted. Understand?"

"I do!" Patti exclaimed. "Thank you so much!" she said, throwing her arms around Emma's neck.

Emma smiled weakly, hugged the little girl, then her eyes closed, and she fell backward onto the sand and passed out.

Chapter 51

When Emma awoke, she turned over and stared out the window. Her head was pounding. Dragging herself from her comfy bed, she went into the bathroom to get some aspirin. Peering at the old wrinkled face in the mirror, she scoffed.

"Honey, if you look this bad at sixty, imagine what seventy will look like."

After downing a couple of pills, she went downstairs and put some coffee on. While it was brewing, she walked out on the patio. It was a perfect fall Oregon day. The puffy white clouds danced across the sky, propelled by the winds aloft. Merging with others, they formed a coalition and began to turn darker as the rain started to fall.

Her cellphone rang; it was Andrea.

"Hey, you're up early," Emma said flatly, hoping the pain in her temples would abate soon.

"I wanted to see if I could bring you some breakfast so you can get started on your book," Andrea said excitedly.

"Oh, Andrea. I told you. I'm not going to write any book. I don't have that ability anymore. I'll call the show, thank Della, and have her tell the publisher, 'Thanks, but no thanks.'"

"You'll do no such thing! This is your chance to fulfill your dream." Andrea ordered. "I'm coming over and not leaving until you put words to page. Got it?"

Before Emma could utter another word, the call disconnected. Andrea's words, 'Fulfill your dream,' hung in the air. She walked back into the kitchen. *Fulfill my dream. Fulfill my dream,* she said to herself.

Sitting at the kitchen table, she sipped her coffee and looked off into the distance. The aspirin was doing its magic, and her head was less painful.

Then, like someone turning on a slide projector, images started flooding through her mind. They were of Mean Emma and the life she had just exited.

She jumped up from the table and ran into the bedroom, searching her end table and her still unpacked suitcases from her trip to New York the previous day to be on the television show. She ran into the bathroom and clawed through the drawers. *It has to be here. It has to be here.*

Running downstairs, she flung open the hall closet and searched the coat she'd had on when she returned home. She looked through her purse, turning it upside down.

She plopped down on the couch. "It's not here. My dolphin necklace is not here," she said aloud to the silence. "It's not here because I gave it to the little girl. It was all real. They sent me back," she said, moved to tears. "I screwed it all up, and this is my punishment, having to come back and live with these memories in my face every day—constant reminders of the disgusting person I became."

Andrea knocked on the door. Emma straightened up and wiped away her tears, but her friend could see something was very wrong.

"Honey, what is it? Are you *that* scared to write the book?"

"I don't have anything to say, Andrea. What have I ever done that's worthwhile? Why should I get a book deal just because I saved that dog? I'm sure plenty of writers out there deserve it more. I'm a lonely old woman who has let the years pass by, hiding in her apartment, not contributing anything to this world."

"That's absolutely not true. You're a good person. You deserve it as much as anyone else does. Sure, you're no daredevil, but you're a good person. You helped all those hospitals build wings and stuff for the disabled kids. You're a great listener. You raised a great kid, and now your first grandchild is on the way. That didn't happen because you're some oaf that just didn't care about anyone or anything. Besides, I thought you were going to write murder mysteries like you did when we were kids. They're fiction. It doesn't matter what good or bad you think you have or haven't done in your life. It's fiction; all you have to do is make stuff up. You have a great imagination," Andrea said, trying to sound encouraging.

"I don't want to write stupid mystery novels!" Emma snapped. "They're nothing but trouble."

"They're nothing but trouble? If that sentence made any sense at all, perhaps I'd have a comeback. How is a fiction book trouble?"

"I don't know," Emma said, getting up and pacing around the room. "I've gotta fix myself. I'm broken."

"Honey, honey, where is all this coming from? You're not broken; you're just cautious. And you're the nicest person I know. You'd have to be, to put up with me," Andrea chuckled.

"You wouldn't understand. You've never done a bad thing in your life. You have morals and great character. You're one of the good guys," Emma countered, sitting back down on the couch.

"So are you,"

"You don't know that. If faced with a huge moral dilemma or choice, I might turn into this selfish, horrible person," Emma whined, feeling the pain of the decisions Mean Emma had made.

"I doubt that, but that gives me an idea. Write about that. Think of what a really awful person would do in some situation, and then redeem her or him. People love stories like that, where somebody changes their evil ways and becomes good. That's the basis for every story out there. Redemption is big. Write that," Andrea said, getting excited about her idea.

"I'll think about it, but right now I just want to lie down, let this headache disappear completely, and get a little sleep. I'll call you tomorrow, okay?" Emma said, standing up, indicating it was time for Andrea to leave.

Andrea laughed. "Oh, we're having a 'here's your hat, what's your hurry' moment, are we? Okay. I'll leave, but if you haven't called by nine tomorrow morning, expect me to be at your doorstep."

"Deal," Emma said, hugging her friend.

Emma took a shower, letting the hot water soothe her troubled soul. Images flashed before her eyes of all the destruction she'd caused as Mean Emma. She closed them tightly, willing them to disappear. It was far too painful.

The reality is, that person, that Mean Emma, was me. I have that inside me, she thought, wiping the steam from the mirror. *How in the world do I redeem that?*

Chapter 52

Later that afternoon, Emma sat in front of her computer, staring at the blank Word document on the screen. She couldn't even come up with a title. "Aaaahhhh," she shouted in frustration. "I keep telling everyone I'm not a writer. I can't do this!" Jumping out of her chair, she walked to the door to leave the room and then turned back.

"Okay, there she is—mean, selfish Emma. Wah, wha, poor little Emma wants to throw a fit because she has to write this book and she doesn't want to. That's exactly how she acted, like a two-year-old throwing a tantrum when she didn't get her way. Stop it, Emma! Oh, my God, what if I start acting that way now that I'm back?" Fear ripped at her insides. "I'll stop it by not letting her win."

Sitting back down, she stared at the screen. She didn't have a title, but began typing anyway. She started the story of a young woman who wanted to be a famous author. Recalling images of the life she'd just left, she set the stage for the story that was to come. Slowly, the difficulties of putting pen to paper and the dedication it takes to throw out huge parts of the book that aren't working, became frustrations for her lead character. The build-up of angst and anxiety changes the woman as she fears her dreams of fame and wealth will never come to fruition. Every sentence was straight from the life she'd ruined. Every sentence felt like being stabbed over and over again. Oddly, there was a part of her that reveled in the pain. It's what she deserved for the lives she'd harmed.

She continued on for the next couple of weeks, showing the woman's selfishness. She changed some of the facts, but pretty much it was almost like a journal of her Mean Emma's existence. Once her character sold her first book and it was a success, the tale got darker. Her self-absorption gave her tunnel vision, which took a wrecking ball to any relationship she tried to have. She decided she didn't want children as they would only get in the way of her success.

Over the next few months, Emma was restless as she refined the story. She realized all she was doing was, again, something that she could do alone, something she could do in her safe place away from anxieties. That was only part of the problem. Her biggest struggle was that she had no idea how to redeem the woman in her tale. In her mind, the woman deserved everything she got.

"I can't do this," she told herself. The more she relived that horrible life on paper, the worse she felt. She wanted to run away. She couldn't find redemption for her character and certainly was not finding it for herself. Her angst took up residence in her very soul. She felt like a street mime trying to escape and unseen glass box.

Weeks went by with no more words added to her book. Most days were spent staring at the television, eating, and doing nothing. When Andrea would call or stop by, she would simply say the story was moving along nicely, but it was slow going. All lies.

Her dreams became horror shows. They were reruns of both her inert sixty-year-old life and Mean Emma's reign of terror. People came to her in her slumber, but she never could remember what they were saying or who exactly they were. It was a tortured existence.

During one of her daily game shows, there was a public service announcement letting the public know that the local hospital was in desperate need of volunteers. It gave a number to call to set up an interview. She didn't know why she was moved to do so, but she immediately grabbed the phone and arranged a meeting with them. She figured perhaps she could work at the information desk or pass out books to the patients or something—anything to get away from the book.

The hospital was grateful to have her. They didn't, however, put her at the front desk or passing out books. Instead, they made her a patient advocate. Her job would be helping patients and their families wade through all the mountainous paperwork thrust upon them when they were admitted. She would help them navigate the insurance forms, and find out what their portion would be. If they had any other questions, like about hospital policy, surgical procedures etc., they would ask her and she would find the answers.

It was perfect. She had to attend classes and pass a test on various insurance policy procedures and privacy laws. Also, she had to understand what she could and couldn't say to whom about a patient. It was pretty in depth, but she aced it.

Emma volunteered three times a week at the hospital, and also took a volunteer job as a dog walker for the local shelter. She loved them both. Her writing stood still, but her mood began to change. Her volunteer work gave her a sense of purpose.

In her hospital work, she would fight with insurance companies when they tried to reject specific claims. She read every word of a patient's policy, ferreting out every avenue available to ensure the companies ponied up. It was an eye-opener. The legalese of the large corporations was designed to ultimately allow them to pay the least amount possible and give the most significant burden to the policyholder. Emma found this abhorrent.

She became known in the hospital as the wizard, as she devised inventive ways and workarounds to force insurance companies to pay a higher rate. Soon, other advocates consulted her for advise on helping their own patients. The patients and their families were always so grateful, and there were always lots of warm hugs of thanks. It was a feeling she'd never experienced, at least not since she was a teenager.

The dog walking was her Zen time. They were such loyal creatures, showing such tender emotions in their eyes. She almost felt like she could read their minds.

The work side of her life was improving her mood, but the dreams were not subsiding. Swirls of colors continued to invade her slumber. Sometimes voices spoke to her, but she could never make out their words. Other times, she'd see a small child beckoning to her. None of it was particularly pleasant.

The book sat alone on the computer as she couldn't face it, and was beginning to believe she never would. As much as she wanted to call the publishers and tell them there would be no book, something kept her from doing it. Plus, the truth was, there was no specific time of completion. It was only being published as a favor courtesy of Della's show. So, no one really cared about when it was done. No editor was calling her asking for her latest chapters. The limbo continued.

Chapter 53

Emma worked extra shifts at the hospital, which had become her *happy place*. At home, the book loomed large, and her dreams kept her in turmoil. At the hospital, she was focused, busy, and productive.

On one of her extra shift days, Georgia from billing approached her and handed her a file filled with rejection letters from a patient's insurance company.

"Everybody here says you're a wizard, and I could definitely use some otherworldly help with this case," she smiled.

"Sure, if I can," Emma answered.

"This young gal doesn't have an advocate yet, which I'm hoping will be you if you aren't otherwise swamped with other patients," Georgia said, handing her the file. "Her parents died six months ago in a car wreck. She was on their insurance, but it was only paid up through last month. So, now she has none. Even if she were to try to get her own insurance this second, she wouldn't be covered for six months because it's a preexisting condition. She has cancer and needs surgery, and...well, it's all in the file. You're so good at finding loopholes; I thought maybe you could dig through and see what you can come up with."

Emma opened the file and flipped through the papers inside. "Sure, be happy to. I'll visit her in a few minutes after I've looked all this over."

"Thanks, Em. You're the best!" Georgia said with a smile.

Emma smiled and nodded, already engrossed in reading the pages before her. She read as she walked. Back in her office, she sat down and started taking notes. A business card for McNamara and Tyler, Attorneys at law, was stapled to the file. She decided to start there.

"Mr. McNamara, thank you so much for taking my call," Emma said once they were connected. "I'm Emma Corbell, the patient advocate for Ms. P.

Violet Green. Would you have some time to go over her situation with me? We're having trouble with her health insurance carrier, and I was hoping you could help me resolve this somehow."

"Happy to help if I can, Ms. Corbell, but unfortunately, Violet is in a difficult situation. I don't know if you're aware, but her family owns all the Green's Spa and Retreat Centers here in Oregon, twenty-five in all."

"Oh, I know of them. I've had massages at the one locally here many times," Emma stated.

"Then you realize how wealthy her family is. However, all their funds have been frozen. After the accident, we were in the middle of probate, but then the drunk driver who hit them decided to sue. He found out who they were and immediately began ranting and raving about how the accident was their fault, obviously looking for a quick buck. His lawyers won a motion to freeze everything until the suit was settled. It's not unusual; it's just that everyone knows the guy has nothing. It was obviously his fault, but I think he's banking on us offering him a settlement. So, even though there is money here that could cover Violet's hospital bills and treatment, we can't touch it at this moment."

"That's awful," Emma exclaimed. "How is she living? Is there an allowance of some sort while all this legal stuff is happening so she can eat and take care of her basic needs?"

"Yes. She lives in the family home and is allowed a stipend to cover household bills, food, and that sort of thing. She has a hefty trust fund, but it won't become available until she's twenty-five. No way we can touch it."

"Well, I'm relieved that she has something, but I'm at a loss to know how we will get her hospital bills paid. Was there any other health insurance or an automatic extension on the one she had that, for some reason, didn't kick in or something?"

"No, nothing. I wish I could be of more help."

"Me too," Emma replied sadly. "I'll just have to see what I can do elsewhere. Thanks so much for your time, Mr. McNamara."

"Feel free to call again with any questions," he said.

Now what? She knew that when the insurance ended that was it. There was no way they would somehow agree to keep paying until the estate got settled. Time to go meet her patient.

When she walked into Violet's room, she was napping. The nineteen-year-old looked so tiny in the bed. She was wearing her own pajamas rather than the standard hospital gown. She was painfully thin and pale but still had a glow about her. Her long brown hair had been combed and tied back in a ponytail. Emma started to tiptoe out of the room.

"It's okay. I'm not really asleep, just resting my eyes," Violet said softly.

Emma smiled and walked over to the bed. "Hi, Violet, I'm Emma Corbell. I'm your patient advocate. First, let me tell you how sorry I am for your loss."

"Thank you," Violet smiled. "I think I like you already. You have very kind eyes."

Emma didn't know what to say to that. No one had ever said that to her before. "Well,...thank you very much. I hope we can become good friends while we try to work out all these issues together."

"It's really okay, Mrs. Corbell. The insurance department has already explained everything. But, I have a feeling that it will turn out all right in the end," she said with a slight twinkle in her eye.

"That's the perfect attitude. I'm going to find a way to get you what you need."

"I know you will," Violet answered, seeming a little stronger the more she spoke.

"That's quite a colorful name, Violet Green. What does the P. stand for? I assume you like your middle name better than your first name?"

"Yes, ma'am. I never liked my first name, and Violet Green has an ethereal quality to it, doesn't it? Sort of magical, don't you think?"

"Yes, I do. I completely agree. So, you believe in magic?" Emma inquired.

"Absolutely. It's everywhere if you just don't turn a blind eye. The most miraculous things can happen in an instant," Violet grinned broadly.

The two spoke for two hours about signs, energy healing, ghosts, and the afterlife. Violet was very frank in her belief in life after death. The young woman had no fear. Emma envied her.

"Well, I need to get going so I can wrestle an insurance company into taking you on and waiving the preexisting condition rule. I'll be by tomorrow. Rest well."

"Thank you, Ms. Corbell. I know you'll do everything you can for me." Almost before she'd finished the sentence, Violet dozed off. Just the act of talking took every bit of energy she had.

When Emma walked out of the room, she felt lighter than she'd felt in weeks. She wouldn't let this beautiful young woman down.

Chapter 54

For the next two weeks, Emma tried everything to get any insurance company to waive the six-month preexisting rule. She called hearings and meetings with various companies. They were staunch in their denial. All doors shut in her face.

She had to fight tooth and nail for the hospital to even allow Violet to remain. They agreed to give her palliative care until Emma had exhausted all avenues. Despite her guarantees that the money would be there once the estate was settled, they wouldn't give an inch.

"That can take years," the administrator told Emma. "We're a business, not a credit union."

"But, you're a health facility. It's your job to heal," Emma retorted. "This girl is only nineteen-years-old. She has her whole life ahead of her. Couldn't you at least do the hepatectomy? You remove the cancerous part of her liver, and she has a chance. The longer you wait, the more likely it is to spread. Doing nothing is almost guaranteeing that she will die. And if you send her home...well, then it's truly over," she said, throwing up her hand in frustration.

"I sympathize, but the board will never go for it. I've been down this road before. The times we have allowed it, we've gotten hung out to dry."

Emma opened her mouth to argue some more, but the look on his face told her it was useless.

Emma went home for lunch, feeling defeated and angry. How could she tell Violet? Lying on the couch, exhausted from her fight, she fell fast asleep. The dreams started immediately, but this time, the words became more clear. A voice kept repeating, "Retrace your steps, Emma. It's not too late to turn the tide."

Emma jolted straight up, wide awake. "Are you freaking kidding me? Turn the tide? That again? And I've retraced my steps a million times. When will this end?"

She dragged herself back to the hospital to tell Violet what had transpired. When she got off the elevator, she couldn't do it. Turning around, she hopped back on and rode it down to the garage. She got in her car and pounded on the steering wheel.

"Dammit! Dammit! Dammit!" she shouted over and over again. Suddenly, she got an idea. Starting her car, she drove to her accountant's office. She was there for almost two hours with both she and her accountant on the phone to different people making arrangements.

"Okay. And again, no one must know where this money came from. It was just from an anonymous donor. Got it?" Emma said to her accountant. "So, how long will it take to get there?" she asked.

"All should be done by end of day," he replied. "But, now we need to discuss what this leaves you with. This withdrawal and the penalties come dangerously close to wiping out your entire savings and pension."

"That's okay. I'll just come back to work here. I'm still young enough to work, aren't I?" she laughed.

"Of course. We'd love to have you back. I'm just sorry that you might have to. You've got enough for a few years if you're frugal. Since your townhouse is paid off, that makes it easier. And in a few years, you can file for social security."

"I'll be fine. Worse comes to worse, I sell my townhouse, and that should give me plenty of money."

"I must say I admire you. I don't know many people; in fact, I don't know *any* people who would do what you're doing."

Emma raced back to the hospital and straight into the administrator's office.

"I found a donor to cover Emma's surgery," she panted, out of breath from excitement. "So, tell the powers that be that they need to schedule her right away."

"I just got word about the donation. I now understand why they call you the wizard. She'll get her surgery, but not immediately. Her condition is such that she is destabilizing. We need to make sure she can withstand the operation. She's young, so I'm sure we can get her on track. Don't worry. Have you told her the good news yet?"

"That's my next stop," Emma enthused. "I can't wait to see her face," she said, already out the door.

Emma stopped by the gift shop and bought some flowers. When she entered Violet's room, she was propped up by pillows and looked weaker than when she'd seen her the previous day. When she saw Emma, however, her face lit up.

"Emma. I'm so glad to see you," she said weakly, eyeing the flowers.

"These are for you," Emma said, setting them on the bedside table. I have some good news."

Violet's eyes lit up. "You got me insurance?"

"Better. I got you an anonymous donor. The money is being transferred today, and as soon as they get your strength up, you'll be on your way. You'll have surgery and be up and around in no time."

"Oh, Emma. That's such good news," she said, holding out her arms for a hug.

Emma went to her and hugged her softly. She was all skin and bones. It broke her heart. It took everything she had not to let Violet see her cry.

At that moment, the room became flooded with nurses. They hung new IV bags and gave her some oral medication. They told her that later, they would insert a feeding tube through her nose to provide her with some nourishment since eating had become so difficult for her. Then they turned to Emma and let her know that Violet would now be in isolation. There would be no visitors, not even in gowns. They were taking no chances.

"Okay then, I guess I won't see you for a while except through the glass. You just sleep and let your body get its strength back up. As soon as the surgery is over, whatever day that is, I'll be the first face you see when you wake up."

"Thank you so much, Emma. I love you," Violet said weakly.

With that, they shooed Emma out the door.

Emma came daily for the next four days and checked in with the nurses to see how Violet was doing. Every time she peeked in the window, Violet was sleeping. She was getting better, but the nurses explained that it looked like at least two more weeks before they'd feel safe doing the surgery.

Emma took a couple of days to herself to decompress from the stress of getting Violet the surgery she needed. She tried working on her book, but it was still in the same place. She could find no redemption for her character. There was no sympathy inside her for the woman who had caused so much pain.

The dreams continued. The voices subsided, but on two consecutive nights, she dreamt about Adam, the man he was in her Mean Emma life. He was holding his head and sobbing. She had no idea what that meant. Remnants of Ryan dying, perhaps?

It troubled her to dream about him. She still felt the crossover from Mean Emma's life back to her old one. Only now, with her hospital job, was she beginning to touch a core in herself that felt good. There was a strength building inside of her. It was small, but it was there. Maybe she had gotten started late in life to make these realizations about who she was and who she could be, but better late than never, right?

Chapter 55

For the next couple of days, she kept thinking about Adam. It was like she could feel his troubled energy. In this, her regular life, she hadn't spoken to him since just before Brian was born. Why was she feeling him so strongly now? Doing her best to keep distracted, she opted to take a week off from the hospital and do some spring cleaning, making the staff promise they would let her know when Violet's surgery had been scheduled.

One morning, as she was vacuuming, she heard a voice so clear in her ear that she spun around, thinking someone had gotten into her house. The voice said, "He can't leave."

"Harold? Oh my gosh, Harold...is that you?" No reply came. "Who can't leave? What does that mean?" she said out loud to the room. She didn't know whether to be angry or cry. The thought that she might still have her guides excited her at first. She and Violet had talked a lot about guides, with the young woman believing deeply that they existed and were here to keep us on the right path.

She shook her head and continued with her chores. Nope. She wasn't going down that rabbit hole again.

The next day, she called Andrea and asked if she wanted to drive to the Oregon coast, do a little shopping, and walk along the beach. It was only an hour and a half drive, so it would be a fun day trip. Andrea was all in.

It was a gorgeous summer day, but still cool by the water. The two women walked along the beach sipping their iced coffees and chatting about her volunteer work, Violet in particular. Emma had yet to tell Andrea she'd given the young girl the money for her surgery. She knew what her reaction would be...that she was crazy to do that, what would she live on, etc., etc. Best to avoid the whole conversation.

"So, how's the book coming? Over your writer's block?" Andrea asked.

"Not really," Emma replied with a smile. "I've created this fabulously evil woman, and now I can't figure out how to redeem her. She's just too awful."

"Hmm...that is a dilemma. But, everyone has some redeeming qualities."

"She doesn't," Emma shot back.

"Of course she does. Maybe she like puppies and ends up saving one's life, and it makes her want to turn good because it feels so good. Heck, I don't know. I'm not a writer."

Emma broke out laughing. "No, that was great. I'll get right on that," she said, laughing harder. "Puppies? Seriously?"

"Okay, wise-ass, at least I had an idea, bad as it was. You couldn't even think of puppies," Andrea giggled.

Their laughter died off slowly, and then the conversation stopped. They fell into that wonderful silence that good friends can enjoy when they don't feel the need to be jabbering every second. Suddenly, Emma stopped dead in her tracks. She looked around, up the beach, and behind her.

"What's wrong, hon?" Andrea asked.

"I don't know, it's just being on this beach. It reminds me of one I used to go to a long time ago," Emma said, her voice sounding concerned and worried.

"And that's troubling because?" Andrea asked.

"Because...because..." Emma said, turning in a circle looking around again. "He can't leave," she said, almost like she was in a trance.

Then, like a bolt of lightning hitting a tree, pictures exploded in Emma's mind. "I know where he is. He never left, unlike me...he never left."

"What in the world are you talking about? Do I need to call a doctor?" Andrea asked worriedly.

"I'm fine. I just need to go find Adam."

"Adam? Your ex-husband? The guy that beat you, Adam? That guy? Why in the world would you do that? And more to the point, do you have any idea where he even is?"

"If my hunch is right, I know exactly where he is," she said, still sounding like she was talking to herself and not Andrea.

Emma took off running down the beach as fast as her little sixty-plus arthritic legs would take her.

"Hurry up," she shouted over her shoulder. "Maybe I can book a red-eye flight. That should give me enough time for us to get back to Hillsboro, for me to pack a bag and make it to the airport. Come on."

All the way back to Hillsboro, Andrea peppered Emma with questions about why she was doing this. Why did she suddenly need to see Adam?

There was no explanation that Emma could give. How could she tell her that she'd lived a whole other life? She just kept saying, "I just know he's in trouble, and he needs me."

Andrea finally accepted her answer and asked if there was any way she could help. Did she want her to come along for protection?

"No, I don't need protection, but I think he does."

"Stop with the cryptic answers already," Andrea scolded.

"I'm sorry. I'm so sorry, but how can I explain a feeling?"

That finally appeased Andrea enough to stop her questions.

"Okay," Andrea finally spoke again. "It'll be faster if I book your flight online while we're driving home. Do you want me to reserve you a car?"

"That'd be great. Thanks so much."

Chapter 56

It was just a short two-hour flight from Portland International to LAX. By the time her plane landed and she'd gotten her rental car, it was 8:00 a.m.

"Oh, great," Emma sighed heavily. "Hello, rush-hour morning traffic. I might as well enjoy the ride because this thirty-minute drive will take me well over an hour at this snail's pace." Emma pulled into a coffee drive-through at the first off-ramp she could. She hadn't slept at all on the plane.

She pulled up in front of Adam's house at 9:30 a.m. At least she hoped it was still Adam's house. It was the beach house her dad had deeded him when she and Adam split in her Mean Emma life. It was the last home that Ryan and he had lived in. The home Ryan never got to come back to. She wasn't sure why, but for some reason, she believed he'd still be there.

It took her a while to get the guts to leave the car. She was shaking all over. A part of her prayed that her suspicions were wrong and that he wasn't here. Maybe she was just imagining everything.

The house had peeling paint, and the lawn was terrifically overgrown. The front porch screen door was off and lying on the porch.

She knocked on the door and held her breath. No answer. She knocked again. Still no answer. She listened to see if she could hear any sound from inside. Walking around to the side, she opened the gate to the back deck. As she rounded the corner of the house, she saw him. He was asleep on one of the lawn chairs on the porch. There was a stack of beer bottles on the table beside him. He was snoring loudly. The reek of alcohol coming from his body hit her long before she reached his side. He was grey, overweight, and extremely pale.

Not wanting to startle him by touching him, she called out from a few steps away.

"Adam. Adam." He didn't budge.

She tried speaking louder. He stirred but didn't awaken. Finding a rake on the ground a few feet away, she grabbed it, stood back, and tapped him lightly on the knee in case her voice startled him, and he woke up swinging. It took a few increasingly harder taps to finally get him to open his eyes. He didn't jump; he just stared at her like he was trying to figure out who she was.

"Adam, it's me, Emma," she said softly.

He sat up, turned to the bottles on the table, shook a few until he found one with some beer still in it, and took a drink.

"Ha!" he said sarcastically. "You're not Emma. She died twenty-five years ago after she killed her son because she was too busy being a star to help him live. So, old lady, whatdaya want?"

He didn't seem all that drunk. He must have slept off most of the previous night's bender. He stood, gathered the bottles, and entered the house, leaving the sliding glass door open. Emma followed him inside. The house was worse than she imagined. It was filthy, with clothes everywhere and dishes piled in the sink, counters, and table. Emma passed through to the living room. It was a little better, but not by much. She walked into Ryan's old bedroom. It was neat as a pin, obviously left just as it was before he died. The bed was made. His clothes were in the closet, and on the floor was a blanket and a pillow. This was obviously where Adam spent most of his nights. The gut-wrenching sight brought her to her knees. She physically ached as the pain in her heart spread throughout her body.

Collecting herself, she went back to the kitchen. Adam ignored her like he didn't know she was there or didn't care. She quietly walked over and began moving dishes and filling the sink so she could wash them. The dishwasher was already full of dirty dishes, so she started those and did the rest by hand. Adam didn't say a word; he just walked into the living room, plopped down in his large recliner, and turned on the television. He moved about like a zombie, not really interacting with his surroundings, almost like he was being remote-controlled. No person lived in the body, just an automaton who could be moved from place to place.

It took Emma an hour to clean all the dishes and wipe the counters and table. While she was performing her task, she rehearsed what she would say next to Adam. She had to pull him out of this reality.

Heading back into the living room, she cleared a seat on the couch, grabbed his remote, and turned off the television before she sat down.

"Adam. I need you to listen to me very carefully. It won't make sense to you, but you must believe it. You have to. If you don't, you'll die here very soon...alone."

"And this bothers you because...?"

"Because it's my fault. I caused all this to happen. It was my selfishness, my need to be loved by millions of people at the expense of my family, that landed you here without your son."

"That's a lovely story, lady, and I would believe it if it were true. But, the woman that caused this was my bitch of an ex-wife who, like I said before, died long ago." His voice retained the same tone with no inflections, like playing a single note on the piano.

"Adam. Look at me and listen. I am Emma, your Emma. We met years ago. You used to call me jailbait, remember? We got married, and I kept you from hitting me. Remember that?"

Adam looked at her, and she could see he was listening, but wasn't sure if it was sparking anything in him.

"Once Ryan was born, things began to change. They went from bad to worse. The more famous I got, the more I mistreated everybody. The more attention and fame I got, the more I craved. Then I lost it all, became a falling-down drunk, lost my house, and became homeless. I didn't know Ryan was sick until the last second. All because I was too drunk to answer my door or my phone. How would I know any of that if I wasn't Emma?"

Adam stared at her for a long time, then she watched as he appeared to be trying to reconcile her story with his belief that his wife was dead.

"The Emma you knew did indeed die on the beach twenty-five years ago. But here's where it gets pretty unbelievable. This life that you're living, these years in your memory, were all created because I came back in time when I was sixty years old to be young again and famous. When your Emma died on the beach that day, they sent me back to my time, my sixty-year-old life, back where I started, until..."

"Until? Until what?" Adam spit out. "What is this garbage you're trying to feed me? Time travel, old Emma, young Emma. Get out of my house! You're nuts!"

"Adam, please. You're living a life that has been erased. I don't know how, but you are. You should be wherever you would have been when you turned this age from our first lifetime together. Yes, you had a son, but he's still alive, and he wasn't Ryan; he *is* Brian."

Even Emma knew how crazy she sounded. All she was doing was infuriating him. She wondered if she could simply get him to stop grieving, get some help, and move on with his life. Perhaps he could at least have some peace for the rest of whatever time he had left. She couldn't understand why he didn't go back like she did.

Adam stood up and loomed over her. The rage in his face terrified her. She knew if he wanted to hit her, there'd be no magical way of stopping him this time. She cowered, turning her face away, holding up her hands.

"What the hell is the matter with you? I'm not going to hit you. I don't do that. Emma taught me that. But, YOU ARE NOT EMMA!" he bellowed. "Stop saying that. I'm glad she's dead and gone. Now leave my house!"

"Wait, wait, wait. Okay, I'm not Emma; I just...um...knew someone who knew her back then. I wanted to check on you. She said she'd stopped by several times, and you didn't answer the door. I want to help you. It's awful losing a child, but you have to find a way to move forward."

"Don't you get it? I've been trying to kill myself since Ryan died. I'm just too big of a coward to buy a gun and get it over with. Look, I'm sure you mean well. It won't be long now. The doctor says my liver is shot, and I've got cirrhosis, so pretty soon, I'll get to join my son. That's what I want. I want to be with Ryan."

"But, Adam..."

"Please. I'm trying to be as nice as I know how. Take your *help* and shove it. I don't want it. I don't need it," he said, taking Emma by the arm and pulling her to her feet. He dragged her to the door, pushed her outside, and slammed it in her face.

Emma thought about pounding on it or kicking it and making him open it again, but she knew there was nothing she could do. She realized that the old Emma had claimed yet another victim.

Chapter 57

Emma drove away slowly. Tears blurred her vision as she began to cry. Her heart ached for him. Every muscle in her body was involved with the pain in her heart. It was excruciating. The only thing she could figure out was that when she changed his destiny in that past timeline, he had to finish it out in that timeline. Why?

Her eyes were drooping; she desperately needed sleep. She was close to the beach, so turned into the parking lot and tried to get her bearings. Things had changed a lot since she'd been here all those years ago. She thought about getting a motel close by where she could get some rest before driving back to the airport for her flight home, but she wasn't sure she could make it any further. With no sleep in over thirty-six hours, maybe a nap in the car was in order.

Turning off her car she sat and stared at the water. The sun was high, and tons of sunbathers were out working on their tans. She suddenly realized she was in the exact spot where she'd parked on the last night of Mean Emma's life.

Stepping out of the car, she began to walk, just as she had done that night. Tears streamed down her face as she realized there would be no gentle little Asian man to keep her from going into the sea. There would be no homeless woman with an adorable little girl to give her dolphin necklace to. The beach felt empty and cold to her. When she came to the spot where she'd passed out, she dropped to her knees as wracking sobs caused her body to heave and tremble.

Closing her eyes, she inhaled deeply. "Willow. I don't know if you can still hear me, but I have a request. Please take care of Adam. Remove his pain. Let him live. Give him someone who will love him as he should be loved. You can take me right now if it would help. A life for a life. It would be a good trade. I don't deserve any of what I've been given. I don't want this book to be a success; not the way it came into being. It's not fair. It's not right that I should have any good in my life after how I acted. Just take me and save Adam. He is the true innocent in all of this. Please, Willow." What she didn't know was that Willow did indeed hear her cries. Her sincere offer was a major step for her future.

She rose slowly. Her body felt heavy. It was an effort to walk at all. Finally returning to the car, she got in and fell asleep.

Once she got home to Hillsboro, she'd experienced every emotion a body can produce. There was gut-wrenching pain, some happiness from the good memories with Adam before Mean Emma took over, and anger at the events she'd created. Fear also found its way deep into her pores. The only thing she didn't possess was the answer to the question, 'why was Adam still there?'

The phone woke her the next morning. It was the hospital. Violet was having her surgery that day. Emma dressed quickly and dashed out the door. She wanted to walk all the way to the surgery suite with her.

She made it just in time. Holding Violet's hand tightly she told her how proud she was of her and how brave she was. When they stopped at the OR doors, she kissed the young woman on the cheek and told her she'd be right there when she woke up.

Once Violet disappeared through the doors, she called Andrea and asked if she wanted to come and have breakfast with her at the hospital. Emma didn't want to leave the building until Violet had woken from the surgery. Andrea, dear friend that she was, didn't give it a second thought, and was there within 30 minutes.

Violet's surgery took almost four hours. She was still asleep when they wheeled her back to her room. Emma helped tuck her in, looking down at that sweet young face. There was such peace there. She already looked less drawn and sallow. Her cheeks seemed pinker and healthier.

It took Violet about an hour to awaken. When she opened her eyes she saw Emma sitting there quietly.

"Emma, you're here," Violet smiled.

"I promised I would be," Emma answered, going to her bedside. Holding Violet's hand tightly she said, "You done good, little one. You done good."

Violet was in and out of consciousness for the next few hours, which allowed Emma time to check up on some other patients and do a little work. When she came back to Violet's room, the doctor was talking to her.

"Emma, Emma, come listen. It's a miracle," Violet exclaimed happily. "I told you magic existed."

Emma's heart began to flutter excitedly. "What? What happened?"

Violet pointed to the doctor, indicating that he should explain.

"Long story short, when we got in there, the cancer had already started receding. Instead of spreading it was actually healing. I can't explain it. It's one of those spontaneous remissions we see once in a while, but it's very, very rare. Therefore, we only needed to take the tiniest bit of her liver, no bigger than the end of my pinkie finger. The lab results are back and show no more cancer cells. So, no chemo or any other treatment for this little gal. She'll need to be on a special diet and take it easy for a while, but she's going to be perfectly fine."

In a very un-Emma-like move, she leapt into the doctor's arms and hugged him. "Thank you, thank you, thank you," she repeated.

"Don't thank me, I didn't do anything. Violet must have a guardian angel somewhere who decided she was too young to suffer this illness."

Turning back to Violet he said, "You'll be here a couple of more weeks. I'm not letting you go until we put a few pounds on you and you regain some of your strength back. So, Jello on the house," he laughed.

After he left, Emma and Violet hugged, cried, and everything in between.

"It was you, Emma," Violet smiled. "You're my guardian angel. I love you so much."

"I love you too, honey. I love you too."

Chapter 58

The following morning found Emma a little groggy. She was sure it was the flight to California, the stress of the weeks of Violet's illness, and the lack of good sleep. However, for the first time in a long time, she'd slept through the night with nary a dream. It was hard to wake up, but the day beckoned. Her work for her other patients was behind since she'd spent so much time with Violet. So, it was time to get back into her life.

After her shower, she passed by her home office, stopped, and stared at her computer. "And what do I do with you?" she asked the inanimate object. "Nothing. I don't have the energy to fight with my empty-of-words-to-finish-my-book-with brain right now. Tomorrow's another day and all that."

The next couple of weeks passed quickly. She was busy, and life took on more ease, which made her happy. Finally came the day that Violet was being released. A friend of hers was coming to drive her home. Emma bought her a card and went to her room. This would be a difficult goodbye for her. She knew they would promise to keep in touch, but she was old enough to understand how those things go. Many patients said they would occasionally come by or take her to coffee once they left the hospital. Still, lives get busy, and those good intentions fade. This would surely be the case here.

When she entered, Violet was sitting on the bed, fully clothed. Her few belongings were in a backpack on the bed next to her. As soon as Emma came in, Violet jumped up to hug her.

"Come here," she said, returning to the bed and sitting back down. Emma sat in the chair. Violet dug into her backpack and pulled out a small velvet box. She held it on her lap.

"I want to give you something as a small token of my appreciation. It's in this box." She handed it to Emma, instructing her to wait to open it until she returned to her office.

Emma took it, thanking Violet for her thoughtfulness, and then handed her the card she'd bought for her. Inside, she wrote about how much she would miss her and what a special person she was. Lastly, she included her phone number, saying that she hoped Violet would call once in a while.

Violet's friend came to get her, and there were lots of hugs and tears before she left. Emma rode in the elevator with them down to the lobby. She kissed her cheek and held her hand. "Have a wonderful life, sweet girl. You richly deserve it." She held her tears until Violet disappeared through the double front doors of the hospital.

Back in her office, she closed the door and opened the tiny box. Emma's eyes flew open in surprise when she saw what it contained: a dolphin necklace.

"What?" Emma exclaimed. "This looks just like mine, but that couldn't be." Inside was a note.

"Dear Emma,

You've been my protector and champion since I was admitted to the hospital. No words could ever express my gratitude for all you've done for me. I'm giving you this very special necklace as it holds great power. You see, when I was four years old, my mother and I became homeless. We were sleeping on the beach. This very sad woman approached us and wanted to help. She was wearing the necklace you hold in your hand. It was very powerful, she told me and said to only use it for good. She said the necklace had told her that it wanted to be with me. Unfortunately, she died that night. What she never got to know was that right after she passed out, the dolphin began to glow. Then, almost as if by divine intervention, a man came walking along the beach and approached us as we were trying to wake her up. He acted quickly, calling the ambulance. After they took her away, he and my mom talked for a long time. That very kind man, Mr. Green, ended up becoming my stepfather. I've had a wonderful life. I was careful with the necklace and only used it for good, as she told me. It protected me and kept me safe. Now, I believe it is time to pass it on. It will help you greatly in all the good deeds you do for people like me. I love you very much. Take care, Violet."

Emma grabbed Violet's file. How can this be true? The young girl she'd given the necklace to was named Patti. Could the P in Violet's name stand for Patti, the name Violet said she didn't like? She had to find out. There was no mention in any of her medical records that denoted what the P stood for. She grabbed the card stapled to Violet's file and called the attorney again. He confirmed it. Her name was Patti Violet Green.

Emma couldn't speak. She held the dolphin tenderly. There were no words to say. She was utterly thrown by the fact that someone from Mean Emma's life made it into this life. Perhaps it was the magic of the dolphin. Maybe the necklace was bigger than time itself.

Emma walked through the rest of the day in a haze. She and Violet had exchanged phone numbers and promised to call, but in her heart, she knew it wouldn't happen.

Lying in her bed that night, she couldn't sleep. She tossed and turned and finally gave up. She made a cup of decaf and went to her computer, sitting in front of her unfinished novel.

Redemption. Redemption. My redemption. Her redemption. Maybe they're one and the same.

Ideas began to fly through Emma's brain. She gave her character a severe illness. Through that, and the kindness of others towards her in her time of need, her character began to rue her previous actions. One nurse in particular touched her character the most. It was a young nineteen-year-old girl with a quick smile and a tender heart.

Emma used all the spiritual lessons learned from her other life, the ones she'd read about before Mean Emma came into existence, and those imparted to her by her guides and various spiritual helpers throughout her journey.

She used the young girl to communicate these ancient spiritual teachings to the woman, including how we are all here to help each other to their destinations. Her character very slowly started to absorb them. It took great effort, but the woman's soul became lighter with each step forward. She felt a weight being lifted off of her with every kind act. By the time she had succumbed to her illness, she had become a beloved figure.

Emma worked through that night and into the next day without a break. It took another month to fully complete her manuscript. Her last act was to type out the title. She decided to call it "Remember Where Your True Power Lies." When it was done, she was pleased.

After emailing it off to the publisher, she did her best to forget about it but couldn't. There was excitement in the pit of her stomach. It would be her first published book, and she felt a sense of pride.

Wow... it's taken me a whole bunch of years to do it, but I'm finally going to have a book published. Better late than never, I guess. Besides, I don't think you can age out of writing. As long as I have a working brain, I can write. That's really a nice thought, isn't it?

It only took five days for her publisher to call her, absolutely raving about the book and asking if she would be willing to write another. He was so convinced this was going to be a best-seller that he was fast-tracking it. It would be on bookshelves in six months. Emma's heart jumped in her throat. She was excited and terrified, but she knew she was ready.

Chapter 59

For the next couple of weeks, Emma couldn't settle. She hadn't told anyone other than Andrea about the finished book that she would soon be a published author. She wasn't sure why she didn't share her good news, but it made her anxious, so she kept her mouth closed.

Oddly, she had not been wearing the dolphin necklace since the day Violet returned it to her. She'd kept it on her nightstand since bringing it home. She was a little bit afraid of it. There was a piece of her that felt its power, or whatever it had, was what brought Mean Emma into existence. Perhaps, it had some dark energy hidden within it. Every day, she would look at it, and every day, she left it alone.

Out of nowhere, the dreams began again—voices calling to her in the night. The most current refrain was, "Emma, you're not done yet. Emma, you're not done." Every morning, she would wake up exhausted and confused.

Feeling depleted from the highs and lows she was experiencing—the high of a new book being released and the low of her troubling dreams—Emma decided to take a month off from her volunteer work. Everyone there was very supportive of her desire to take a break. She'd worked hard for them, and they understood, but they insisted that she promise to return, which she did.

The dreams continued and intensified until one night, she dreamed that she was walking on the beach with Master Li.

"What does it mean that I'm not finished?" Emma asked the Master.

"Not finished means not done, not through," the Master laughed at his own joke.

"I know what it means, but I don't know what it *means* in relation to me. What am I not finished with?"

"We are all masters of our own fates, our own destinies. You are not done with yours. Write your destiny, Emma, or it will be done for you; you're not done."

"I thought that's what I had been doing since you guys put me back here. I've been creating my own destiny. I've become a better person and tried to help others. Isn't that creating a better destiny?"

"I didn't say create. I said write. Two very different things," the Master answered.

"So, I should write down what I want? Like a journal or something?"

"A journal simply records the day's events. You need to write your destiny. If you want to eliminate the old Emma, you must write your destiny. If you don't, all will be lost," the Master said before turning into a shimmering ball of light and disappearing.

Emma awoke with a start. The dream was clear and did not fade.

Write my own destiny? Get rid of old Emma? I'm totally screwed. I have no idea what he means by that.

The dreams continued for the next few days, but only with the voices. They kept repeating, "You're not done, Emma over and over, but then a new phrase was added, "Start at the beginning. You're not done."

She suffered for days in the confusion of it all. She took long walks, always thinking of what it could mean. About a week later, she walked to the old downtown Hillsboro district one afternoon. She loved that area. The shops were small and quaint, with clerks and owners who were friendly and kind. Grabbing a cup of coffee at Starbucks, she sat on the bench at the window and watched people walk by.

There was a couple at a small nearby table having an argument.

"I didn't say anything like that," the woman said, obviously frustrated.

"Yes, you did. You said exactly that. You said, and I quote, 'I'm not sure I love you anymore.' Admit it," her companion shot back.

"It's amazing how you can rewrite history. What I said was, and I was joking, by the way, that I wasn't sure how I ever *managed* to fall in love with you. You were giving me a hard time about my shoe-spending habits. You were giving me grief about everything that day, so I said I wondered how I fell in love with you in the first place. Not that I *didn't* love you. Obviously,

I do, but I don't love your nitpicking." The woman sat back and crossed her arms, indicating the ball had been tossed back to him.

Emma chuckled at the fight, tossed her cup in the trash, and walked out. She was about half of the way home when something struck her. That woman said it was amazing how that guy could *rewrite history*. Maybe that was it! Perhaps Master Li meant she should write the story of her return to her past, only write it as if she made the choices that she, nicer Emma, would have made. Perhaps the rewrite would erase the images and taunts from bad Emma's life. Could that be it? It was worth a shot. It would be worth it if it would get rid of her images of Mean Emma. It was all she could think of. It was worth a shot, she figured.

Chapter 60

Emma raced home and sat down at her computer. She already had the title. "My Life as it Should Have Been Lived."

She began the book when she was 17-years-old, the year she started her journey. In this iteration, however, she never lost her dolphin necklace. It was her teenage pride and joy, which she believed had magical powers and would always protect her.

She met Adam and fell in love with him, but had no idea that he could be violent towards women. When they got engaged, he took her to meet his parents. They could hear the argument escalating inside as they walked through the door. By the time they entered, Adam's mother and father were hitting each other. Adam ran over and separated them. His face was a combination of fear, anger, and embarrassment. When his parents saw her, their shame was evident as well.

The next couple of hours were civil enough. His folks did their best to make her feel welcome. But, at that point, she wasn't sure she wanted to be a part of their family. What if Adam was like that? What if he was inclined to hit a woman? She'd not seen it in the time they'd been together, but what if it was there?

That night, they talked for hours about the event. She asked him if he'd ever hit a woman. He told her no, but had come close. He was very honest, however, about his fights with men.

"This may not work," she told him. "I can't live in fear of you."

Adam was beside himself. He'd never met anyone like her before. She had a sweetness and gentleness that so many of his prior girlfriends lacked. They'd been from troubled homes as well, and had developed hard exteriors because of it.

"Please, Emma," Adam implored. "I don't want to lose you. I'll do anything. I won't hit you, I promise."

She agreed to stay with him, but there would be no wedding until she was convinced there would be no violence in their marriage.

Over the months, they talked about how marriage was a partnership. She was not his possession, nor was he hers. Adam seemed eager to learn how to quell his inner anger. He told her he'd been his mom's protector as a child and had vowed never to have a relationship like that when he grew up. However, his own rage simmered deep inside.

As time went by, they explored what triggered him, and together found ways to release his tension. Adam read every self-help book he could find and practiced what they taught.

By the time they wed a year later, Adam was, of his own choosing, well on his way to becoming the man he wanted to be.

In this story version, Emma decided that Brian would be born later in their marriage. She wanted to write and have a few years with just the two of them before introducing a baby into the mix. Her first book was a success, and she started on the rounds of public appearances and television shows. Only in this version, Emma decided that with each book she produced she would give half of her royalties to charity. "It'll keep me humble, she told Adam."

Adam completed architectural school and started earning a good income. By the time Brian was born, they were doing quite well.

She included fights the couple had, and even added one time she almost left him because their arguments had become so bad. It wasn't a perfect life; it was simply a normal life with two people who grew at different times and found other interests, that often caused space between them.

She continued her charity gifts with the sale of each novel that she wrote, ten in all.

There were detailed birthday parties and anniversary celebrations. There were arguments between parents and son as they worked through the trials and tribulations of a young boy growing into a man. She included the first time Brian got drunk, and the time he broke his knee playing football. Also, were the heart-to-heart talks between mother and son, and father and son.

She added detail after detail of what life would have been like without magical beings or Mean Emma. Every page was brutally honest about how humans can get stuck in their own point of view. The unwillingness to compromise can create rifts that can last for years.

Through it all, there was a spiritual overtone. Even as self-help books became the rage, Emma leaned more towards those written by the great Masters. She loved the idea of finding peace and power within. The notion of manifesting our own destiny and creating our own life sung to her. Adam, as well, began listening to the wisdom these books imparted.

When it came to the end of the book, she wasn't sure exactly how to end it. She included the book she'd just written as her stopping place. To her, it was an homage to the Mean Emma for the awakening she'd unknowingly caused in this Emma's soul.

The final chapter was a cliffhanger of sorts. She, Adam, and Brian were on their way to the airport to be on the 'Morning Coffee with Della' television show to talk about her newest book, "Remember Where Your True Power Lies." In this ending, she was sixty, and Adam was sixty-four. Even though she was a little older than sixty now, she liked making herself a teensy bit younger.

Once she was pretty happy with the book, she printed it out to read over. At night she'd sit up in bed and make tiny changes to the copy.

After being satisfied with all of it, she put the pages back in order and held it up in front of her. "That's it," she said with satisfaction. "The end," she declared, drawing a happy face on the title page.

She laid the novel on her nightstand, plopped the dolphin necklace on top of it, shut off the light, and immediately fell into a deep sleep.

Sometime in the darkness of the night, a glow appeared in her bedroom. A translucent Willow emerged, and smiled. Her presence there did not awaken Emma.

"Sweet dreams, dear one," Willow said. Then, placing her hand on top of the manuscript, she uttered quietly, "And the timeline is reset. So shall it be."

With that, Willow, the book, and the dolphin necklace all disappeared.

Chapter 61

"Come on, Emma. Brian is already in the limo," Adam shouted from the living room into the bedroom. "We're going to miss our flight."

"I'm coming. I'm coming," Emma answered, affixing an earring to her earlobe. I should have colored my hair. Lots of sixty-year-olds color their hair, right? This grey makes me look so old, Emma fretted.

"You're the youngest-looking sixty-year-old I know. Now, let's go. No one is going to be looking at your hair. It's your book they care about. So, are you ready? Oh, do you want the dolphin?"

"No. It should stay here and protect the house while we're gone," Emma smiled.

"That and the alarm system," Adam chuckled, shaking his head.

Adam held Emma's hand during the flight, trying to keep her calm. She couldn't stop trembling.

"What has got you so nervous about this interview?" Adam asked.

"I don't know. This book is so different. What if everyone hates it? They're used to my mysteries."

"Honey, it's already hit the best seller's list in this first week. They love it. Besides, you love going on Della's show. She was the first interview you ever did when your first book came out. She loves you, and so do millions of people."

"I guess so," Emma said absentmindedly.

Emma was much calmer the next morning when the limo picked them up from the hotel to head to the studio. She was excited to see Della and talk about her book, which she'd taken almost two years off to write. It was fun to get on the promotion junket again.

Della brought Emma, Adam, and Brian onto the stage. The audience went nuts. They had missed Emma and her books. They were glad to see her.

239

"We decided to make this a family affair today by having Emma's husband, Adam, and their son, Brian, join us. She's told me many times that she couldn't have been the success that she is without these two. So, Adam, what was it like when Emma was writing this book? Did she ask for your opinion, or have you read chapters as she wrote?"

"Oh, no. Emma's very insular when she's creating. Brian and I both know not to peek at her computer until she's finished. She doesn't even want to talk about it or how it's going. Then she gives it to both of us to read."

"So, Brian, do you give her suggestions on what she's written or tell her you don't like something?"

"Gosh, no. Oh, I didn't mean that like it sounded," Brian chuckled. "I mean, I love everything she writes, and pretty much never have anything I think she should change. Every book is so creative and original. For example, when I was little, she would write bedtime stories for me. When other kids got Jack and the Beanstalk, I got, 'The Monkey Had Muscles and Drove Race Cars.' It was great."

"Well, Emma, you certainly have a very supportive family. I'm so glad they were able to join us today. But let's get on to the book. This is such a departure for you. What made you decide to write it. Did you know the woman in the story very well?"

"Not extremely well. She was someone on the periphery of my life, so to speak. Other close friends filled in the blanks for me. I found her life intriguing, and her story gave me hope."

"Hope?"

"Yes. It says to me that everyone has a piece of themselves, no matter how well hidden, that is reachable...redeemable. The Masters tell us that we must live from our hearts, not our heads. The heart wants to include everyone. The head excludes all except what serves the ego. I think that's beautiful," Emma smiled.

"But this woman was so mean and selfish, almost evil."

Emma looked down, considering carefully what she was about to say. "She wasn't really evil in any true sense of the word. She was misguided. We all suffer from the fear that we're not quite good enough, not pretty enough, not rich enough, not smart enough. The list goes on and on. Her reaction to those fears was extreme. She sought fame and fortune to fill the void and quiet the anxieties, hoping that would heal the deep hole inside her. The more it didn't, the more angry she became. She lashed out and hurt other people with her words and behavior. It wasn't until she had lost everything that she found herself and discovered where her true power lay. I won't tell you exactly how, because I don't want to give away the ending."

"Can you at least explain what that means...where our true power lies?"

Emma smiled broadly. "I'll do my best. Our true power lies in our hearts. It's as simple and complicated as that. Someone once told me a story of a very wise old man who asked a woman to walk with him for a bit. When they reached his destination, he thanked the woman for her kindness. She was surprised, insisting that she'd done nothing. He turned to her and said, 'You walked with me and kept me company, leading me to my destination. That in itself is what life is all about. We're all here not to be *better than* or to *compete* with others. We're here to help each other find our way. In other words, to reach our personal destinations.'"

The audience applauded wildly.

"Well, I know I loved it. I couldn't put it down. Are you working on something currently? Is there perhaps another mystery or another heartfelt tale about another lost soul?"

"There's nothing on my computer at the moment, but a lot in my head," Emma laughed. "There'll be more, but I'm slowing down a bit. Take time to smell the roses, you might say."

"We have to cut away for a brief break, but don't go anywhere. We have a surprise for Emma when we return."

Emma looked over at Adam with a quizzical expression on her face. He just gave an 'I have no idea what she's talking about' shrug.

Chapter 62

"Welcome back, everyone. Now, as I promised, we have a surprise for Emma. We asked Adam and Brian here for another reason other than to rave about Emma. Adam, you have the floor," she smiled, pointing to Adam.

Adam turned to Emma and took both her hands in his. "I'm a little nervous," he chuckled. "Della and I plotted this together once I told her what I wanted to do. She was the one who decided it would be fun for me to do it today on this show."

Emma squinted her eyes and cocked her head. "Oh, yeah?' she smiled, looking over at Della. "What have you two cooked up?"

Adam cleared his throat. "Emma, from the day I met you, I've been in love with you. You married me when I had nothing. I had a dead-end job; we never had enough money, but you kept us to a budget and stuck with me. Then you took a job so I could go to school to become an architect. You fit your writing in and around my schedule. As we became comfortable monetarily, I often looked at that ring on your finger—that simple, plain, inexpensive gold band you've worn all these years. You clean it with as much care as if it were covered in jewels." Adam got down on one knee. The audience gasped, knowing what was coming next.

"Emma, my beautiful wife, you deserve diamonds and so much more," he said, producing a ring box from his pocket. "Will you marry me...*again*?" He opened it up to reveal a beautiful diamond engagement ring with a gorgeous wedding band beside it.

Emma's hands flew to her mouth as her eyes filled with tears. She cried and laughed.

"Yes, yes, a million times yes," she answered happily.

"Right now?" Adam asked.

"Right now," Emma questioned. "You mean right here, this minute?"

The audience chanted, "Yes. Yes. Yes. Yes."

"Come on, jailbait, make this old grey-haired geezer the happiest man alive and marry me again."

Emma simply nodded because she was too choked up to speak. The minute she did, the backstage workers brought out a beautiful white arch with flowers intertwined in the lattice and placed a small podium beneath it. They brought two sizeable decorative floor-stand vases filled with flowers and put them on each side. One of the makeup girls brought Adam's ring on a pillow and handed it to Brian. The other brought Emma's bouquet and a white rose for Adam's lapel.

"Shall we?" he asked, offering Emma his arm.

"Not so fast," Della interrupted. "You can't get married in those clothes. Backstage, we have the proper wedding attire for you both. We will take a slightly longer commercial break than usual for you to change. Your attendants will be ready when you return, and then we can begin."

Adam and Emma looked at each other and giggled like teenagers. They glanced over at Della and then literally ran off the stage.

When they returned, Della stood up for the bride, and Brian stood up for his father.

Emma was luminous in her long crème-colored gown and small veil. Her dress had a delicately laced bodice with long sleeves and a long satin floor-length skirt. Adam was dressed in a blue suit. Brian pinned the white rose on his lapel.

The room was silent as the officiant walked onto the stage. It was Willow, in human form, dressed in a pale pink suit and white pearls. She smiled at Adam and Emma.

Emma had no recognition of Willow. In her current life, she'd never had contact with her or any other magical beings. Her Mean Emma life and original past life had been erased from the timeline. All had been reset.

This was no easy task after the accidental way she'd traveled back in time. Total chaos had ensued, and all rules of time travel ceased to apply. Even though they had managed to return Emma to her original life, the Mean Emma timeline had remained active. That's why Adam was still there, and it was where Violet grew up. It was why, initially, Emma still had memories of her time there.

The only way to reconcile the two and save Emma from disappearing completely was to have her rewrite her own life as she would have liked to have lived it. They couldn't send her back for a do-over. All was dependent on whether she could unravel the clues given to her. Her good deeds, like giving away her necklace, paying for Violet's surgery, her volunteer work, and offering her life in exchange for Adam's, began to give her power. She had finally learned to live from the heart, where her true power lies.

Once she wrote her personal destiny piece, her Mean Emma life and her original sixty-year-old life were erased, and the rift in time was healed. She and everyone associated with her had only ever lived the life she'd created on paper.

Once she and Adam joined hands at the altar, the dolphin lying on the mantle back in their house emanated a mystic glow. Although she didn't know it, Willow would always be at Emma's side. Who knows, there may come a time when Willow may again elect to reveal herself to the soul she protected. But, for now, she took joy in her happiness and the life well-lived.

"We're gathered here today to witness the union of Adam and Emma...again. Their love has withstood the tests of time. For years, they have honored their vows of 'for better or worse, for richer or poorer, in sickness and health.' Their strength and love for each other have only grown with time. Adam and Emma, from this point forward, your lives will begin anew; it's a new chapter with new adventures and new puzzles to solve. You will keep the best of the old and revel in the fresh experiences, and the lessons life still has to teach you. The rings you exchange today symbolize all the goodness to come. It is my great honor to help you renew your commitment to each other today.

The rings were exchanged, and then Willow smiled lovingly at them both. "With the power vested in me, I now pronounce you husband and wife again. You may kiss your bride."

The audience applauded loudly, stood up, and cheered. There wasn't a dry eye in the house.

When the raucous noise quieted, Della grabbed Adam and Emma and walked them to the center of the stage.

"Congratulations, you two. I'll tell you. I think this has been my favorite show of all time," Della said, wiping away tears of her own. "Everyone, please run, don't walk, and get out there and buy 'Remember Where Your True Power Lies.' You won't regret it. Emma, we need to have you back very soon so we can talk more about your book. In the meantime, give us one line that you feel encapsulates the theme of your novel."

"That's easy. It is a quote from my favorite children's book, 'The Little Prince.' 'It is only with the heart that one can see rightly. That which is essential is invisible to the eye.'

Photograph by John Wise

ABOUT THE AUTHOR

This book is Michale's initial foray into the world of fantasy book writing. She continues to write her cozy mystery book series, The Heartfelt Murder Mystery series, with books one and two currently on sale. They are Third Time's the Charm, and Focused Hocus Pocus.

Michale calls herself a dreamer. She had always dreamed of being an author. Her writing career had a very unusual start. She began having debilitating panic attacks, so severe she didn't leave her home for almost two years. During this time she started writing in earnest. Her characters were brave, courageous, and able to face any situation. As she wrote how they bravely moved around in the world, she began teaching herself how she could do the same. As she puts it, "I wrote myself out of my house." After fleeing her home she did some regional theater, had some small roles on television and continued to write.

Michale now lives in the suburbs outside of Portland, Oregon. She has a son, and an adorable grandson. She enjoys time with family and friends, long walks, and every 48 Hours-type show there is. Her life is simple according to her. She calls it a heartfelt life. After being locked behind her fears for so long, she more than appreciates the simpler things life has to offer. As she puts it, "Joy is found in the heart, not in the trappings of the size of the activity."

www.ingramcontent.com/pod-product-compliance
Ingram Content Group UK Ltd.
Pitfield, Milton Keynes, MK11 3LW, UK
UKHW021122110325
455992UK00012B/588